MW00874888

OTHER WORKS

*T**wisted Worlds*

Within the Darkening Woods
Above the Ashen Clouds (2024)

The Twice-Cursed Serpent

The Twice-Cursed Serpent
The Shattered Star
The Burning Hand
The Twisted Sword: A Twice-Cursed Serpent Collection

<u>As S.D. Vine</u>
Devoured Gods
Eyes of Stone (TBD)

Map by Scarlett D. Vine

Interior Art by Scarlett D. Vine

Cover by @BookishAveril

Copyright © 2024 by Scarlett D. Vine

This is a work of fiction. All the names, characters, businesses, places, events, and incidents in this book are either the product of the author's imagination or used in a fictitious manner. Any resemblance to actual persons, living or dead, or actual events is purely coincidental.

All rights reserved.

No portion of this book may be reproduced in any form without written permission from the publisher or author, except as permitted by U.S. copyright law.

WITHIN THE DARKENING WOODS

A TWISTED WORLDS NOVEL

SCARLETT D. VINE

PARKER & WILSON PRESS, LLC

For the readers who would rather go to
Middle Earth than Minnesota.

Author's
Content
Note

Within the Darkening Woods is an adult novel meant for those over the age of eighteen. This is a romance with the mandatory HEA ending, and while it is a stand-alone, it takes place in a larger universe. Thus, while our couple's tale will be completely told within this book, and can be enjoyed on its own, there are additional threads about the world that will be left unanswered until later books in the *Twisted Worlds* series.

As a fantasy romance, this book has subject matter in line with the genre, including violence, gore, harsh language, and consensual explicit sexual content. There is a reference off-page animal cruelty involving a horse. And the MMC has a skeleton hand. Readers of *The Twice-Cursed Serpent* who have followed me here will find this a relatively mild experience, as far as violence and language are concerned. However, the sexual content is more prominent and explicit, especially in the second half of the book. There is also impromptu kidnapping, and also rather large and unsettling spiders.

GREAT GLEN

RED GROVE

GOLD GLEN

TO MINNEAPOLIS

THE DARKENING WOODS

Prologue

I never liked fairytales. I liked them even less once they came true.

Around five years ago—at 1:14 am on June 22nd, to be precise—our world collided with another, remaking itself. As a result, so many places and people were lost forever. Familiar landmarks and homes were suddenly gone, replaced with lands and creatures that absolutely did not belong here.

Take Saint Cloud, Minnesota, for example. That city and its suburbs were once home to around eighty thousand people. All gone. Instead, the area became the home of some sort of dark elf enclave. Instead of a land of lifted trucks, dilapidated strip malls, and corn, it turned into an impenetrable bubble that grew only rumors.

An improvement, as far as I was concerned. Saint Cloud was an acquired tasted, and I never managed to acquire it.

Though it did have some hamburgers that will be sorely missed.

Unfortunately, Minnesota was not the only place in the country impacted by the worlds shifting. Some sort of magic swamp settled itself around Phoenix—oh, the irony of that much untouchable water appearing in the Sonoran Desert. And New Jersey acquired angels. Yes, real angels. And no, they weren't the cute and cuddly kind.

This is merely a small list of what turned our world upside down—the whole world—and ruined millions of lives in the process.

See, entire counties disappearing and then reappearing with new residents had the effects one might imagine. Panic. Concern over the missing people. Ruptured families. And grief. So much grief. Disruption of utilities and other necessary services was another result. It was downright apocalyptic, for around a year.

And then the media—traditional and social—came along, and everyone slowly accepted that this was the new normal, and that there was money to be made. To my eternal consternation, that was how we ended up with things like Leprechaun Lives on social media and Nights Out with Night Elves streaming specials, and a bunch of other reality shows, podcasts, and even "magical influencers." *Why be natural when you can be* super*natural?* While some people considered the fantasy beings' arrival as the end of the world, others latched onto them as the best thing to happen to their hum-drum lives.

As for the new creatures themselves, the ones who ventured off the lands that had transported them, some of them tried to blend in with humanity, accepting that returning home was unlikely. Some of them were transported on pieces of land no bigger than a SUV, and thus had nothing to cling to, literally or metaphorically. Many fae seem to be able to blend in with us, as well as nymphs and other more humanoid creatures. There was even a satyr at Princeton University, prominently featured in their press releases.

And other creatures kept to themselves, hidden behind their magical borders, and studied mankind from a distance. Some humans guessed that these recluses refused to try to assimilate, in part, because they were desperately searching for a way home. Others noted that these new creatures, by their own admission, were not exactly friendly with each other, and many of them had to navigate old rivalries while blending in with ours.

As years passed, the idea of searching for a way to send these beings home has seemed more and more pointless. No one knew how or why these new creatures appeared, or how they could return. And if they left, would our original world return in its place? Or would we receive something even more strange in exchange?

As for me, I kept to myself. And I know, *I know*. But before you accuse me of being "not like other girls," consider this—the "other girls" disappeared. Dozens, if not hundreds, of people have disappeared in the years since the new lands' arrival, seeking gorgeous mythological creatures and adventures. Especially young women.

Even as the world around me slowly became obsessed with our new neighbors, even as I watched everyone drift away from their sorrow over what was gone, even as more and more women disappeared, I promised myself one thing—

I would not become one of them.

CHAPTER ONE

AMBER

I was late.

I hated being late. Feeling rushed. Out of control. I blamed the alarm. It was the alarm's fault that it decided to abscond its duty during my afternoon nap, letting the short rest expand into full-on sleep.

Quickly hopping through my room in my one-bedroom apartment, I dug a green knit dress out of my closet, frowning at the wrinkles, but pleased with its clean scent. Oh well, the wrinkles would come out with wear. I threw it on, satisfied that it made me somewhat presentable.

Next was the hair, which was quickly tamed by tugging my red mane into a ponytail. As for makeup, I would have to do with what was already on my face, other than to make sure it hadn't smeared to make me look like a raccoon. A lot had changed since the worlds merged, but raccoons were still generally not considered aspirational. Luckily, I still had on a little makeup from this morning, a layer of nice, human makeup—none of that fae-altered powder that was all over the Internet. In my opinion, it made the skin too shiny, and I wasn't convinced it didn't sap the user's intelligence in the process. Didn't people read their own legends and myths? Fairy magic came with a cost. Why would cosmetics be any different, no matter how much Little Fairy Flavor, the social media starlet, claimed otherwise.

Alright—my appearance would work. It had to. Besides, tonight was just drinks with friends, a couple nightcaps before bed. Sure, my friends would've been fine if I asked for an extra ten minutes to shave my legs, but I didn't need them worrying about me. They already worried enough, as they would no doubt tell me themselves. And the two of them were going nowhere near my legs. Why would they care if they were a little textured?

The bar I was supposed to meet my friends at was only several blocks away from my apartment in northeast Minneapolis, a neighborhood known for its themed bars and specialty restaurants. It was a place where tourists tended not to visit as it wasn't close to the city's more notable landmarks. And even better, the area was just a smidge too inconvenient for a lot of the college students who wanted to drink and walk home. Thus, since it was a Thursday, the area wasn't overly crowded, but it was crowded enough. Parking was a miserable experience—as always—and whatever dubious benefits the new arrivals gave humanity, a solution to parking wasn't one of them. Once I found my vehicle's resting place on a side street in front of some tidy townhouses—free parking for the win—I took a deep breath, preparing for what awaited me. I loved my friends. But they worried. For good reason.

The chosen venue was packed. In order to get in I had to wait in line behind several people dressed in the sort of fantasy attire that used to be kept to Renaissance festivals and Halloween parties before being admitted by a rather intimidating fellow. It was like being in a lineup of the Renaissance's Most Wanted.

All at once the scent of the bar washed over me—stale beer, dust, and male body spray. Music thrummed over the crowd, a deep techno beat that riveted through my body. It took only three steps before a man backed into me, trying to make room for a flock of women attempting to get to the bathroom. What was this? Why were there so many people? It was just a Thursday...

And then a haunting melody carried over the crowd. A non-human melody.

Ah...that explained why this place was so excited—

The entertainment.

A frail woman stood on the worn-down stage, belting out chords that held the audience enrapt, like children staring at a lit Christmas tree. Her pale skin was tinged with violet, made more dramatic by the colored stage lights. Her sharp teeth poked out from behind blood-red lips. She was beautiful, but in an abstract way, like how an insect's exoskeleton carried depths of colors and fine angles. Translucent wings shimmered behind her, fluttering with each sung note. Dust speckled in the air, visible in the brilliant spotlight that shone on her. She was a slender creature, who likely only came up to my bust in height, but only a fool equated size with strength these days. With these creatures, anything could kill.

Well, the audience wasn't going to be distracted from *that* anytime soon. I tried not to frown as I searched for my friends and assumed my Neutral Bitch Face, the friendlier half-sister of my Resting Bitch Face. The bar was dark, but it was easy enough to find them—it was like their gazes bored into me, pulling me closer to their glorious presence.

Or it might have been the fact that my friend Phoebe was the only one bold enough to carry a purse shaped like an eerily realistic stuffed cat. Such things stood out, even in Minneapolis. She pushed her dark hair behind her ears and waved me over like a policeman directing traffic. Her partner, Emily, sat next to her, her dark hair and black t-shirt staid against the majesty that was Phoebe's purse.

I took a seat across from them at the small circular table and winced as my hand made contact with the sticky surface. If this was on top, what lurked underneath this thing? Quickly, I drew it away and let my hands rest on my lap, trying to use the knit fabric to clean my hands.

"We didn't think you'd show," Phoebe said, nudging a very pale beer towards me. Not my favorite, but it would do. I accepted with a smile.

"I keep my plans," I said.

"Too bad you don't have that same attitude about jobs," Emily said, her southern drawl out of place in this bastion of the Midwest. She shrugged when Phoebe glared at her. "What? It's true."

I wanted to be mad at Emily, but I couldn't. I sighed in defeat and swallowed my pain along with the beer. If they started this meeting with my lack of gainful employment, I was in for the lecture of a lifetime. When I was done with my swallow, half of the beer gone already, I interrupted their lighthearted bickering and said, "I know, I *know*, I need to do something else. Which is why I think it's time for me to go back."

That got their attention. "So, you're serious about that?" Phoebe asked, a manicured brow creeping up. "You're insane. What's in Grand Rapids? Cows?"

"Not really...but there's lakes." Grand Rapids was a city, to use the term generously. A city that existed. In northern Minnesota. One that people tended not to go to on purpose.

"Amber," Phoebe said, "look where you are—there's fucking lakes everywhere. There's like twenty in the metro alone."

"Actually," Emily said, "there's twenty-two just in Minneapolis."

Phoebe rolled her eyes. "Lake trivia? Really?"

Emily shrugged. "You're the one who keeps dragging me to trivia nights."

"Is that accurate?" I asked.

"The trivia guy said it is," Emily said.

Phoebe shook her head. "Stop it, she's trying to change the subject. Amber, *why* are you insisting on going back there? You think moving home to that little town is going to magically give you a career?"

"Or a man," Emily muttered. Phoebe glared again.

"I need time," I said. I did. I needed to go home and be with my family. Figure out what I wanted to do with my life. I was twenty-four and, frankly, I had no idea what I was doing. Maybe some time in a smaller town would let me focus on me. Less distractions, of every sort. I liked men, but the selection of available men up there was numerically challenging, so odds were that my plan of geographically-induced celibacy would work.

"Family," Phoebe said. "Is this the same family who made you cosplay as a pioneer girl for some house party?"

"House parade." I rolled my eyes. "It added to the effect."

"This is what happens in rural towns," Emily muttered. "Marching houses." Emily wasn't being fair. It wasn't so much marching houses as it was a self-guided tour through a list of participating homes to admire—that is, judge—the décor.

Phoebe nodded, eyes lit with amusement. "But our point stands—what is there that is better than here?"

"Let's see," Emily said to me, "shall we count the jobs? The ones that were unsuitable for you. You were a caretaker at a plant nursery—didn't like that."

"Too seasonal," I said. I had a degree in landscape design, but what was I supposed to do with *that*? Sure, I learned a lot, but design wasn't exactly transmitted by people reciting it on the street. Unless you were in Dinkytown, the college neighborhood near the University of Minnesota. Odd things happened there. Regardless, jobs were hard to come by. At least, ones I was interested in. Turns out I shouldn't have chosen my major out of a hat.

"You didn't like the library," Emily continued. "Or the auto parts store."

"The store one wasn't my fault. The manager hit on me. Asked me if I needed my 'plugs replaced.'" Phoebe laughed, but it died quickly. I smiled, albeit unwillingly—it was funny, in retrospect.

"Yes, he was a fuckwad," Emily said, "but that brings us to point two—you're as awful with relationships as you are at jobs."

Phoebe reached out a hand to her partner. "Emily—"

"Sorry, Pheebs, but she needs to hear this. If she is planning on running back to Grand Rapids—of all places—she needs to hear that it isn't going to fix things." Emily took a long swig of her gin and tonic. "That's the thing about moving—you bring yourself with you."

"I'm not going to be with someone I'm not happy with."

"Fair," Emily said. "But let's go over some of the reasons you weren't happy, now that the job talk is done. For now. Let's discuss Mark—he didn't like cats?"

"Thus, I didn't like him."

"Alright, that one I can't blame you for. But what about Henri?"

"He thrashed in his sleep."

"...Alright. Greg."

"Called his mother too much."

"Steven."

"Ordered sides with an entrée that came with sides."

"And how is that a bad thing?"

I shrugged. "It means he is never going to be content with what he has."

Emily blinked. Hard. "And now we have the lemon calling the grapefruit bitter."

"Amber," Phoebe said, "we worry about you. You shouldn't be with someone you're not content with, but those are some rather obscure reasons to end a relationship. And...you're not in high school anymore."

I shrugged again. "If they had been adequate in other departments, I may have overlooked some things."

"So," Emily said, looking at the ceiling in seeming contemplation, "in addition to the gentlemen we have just listed, we also have two Adams, a Bryan, and an Andrew who were all inadequate. In bed."

"Hey, I didn't get to *that* point with all of them. Most were just a date or two. That didn't leave the restaurant."

"Still, it wasn't like these were losers, Amber. One had his own business, another was in med school, and wasn't one a new lawyer?"

Two were lawyers. But Emily didn't need to know that.

"So, what do you think I should do?" I asked, slamming the rest of the beer while I waited for them to answer.

"Move in with us," Phoebe said. "We have an extra room. Leave your waitressing job—you're going to anyway—and get something entry level somewhere. Something with health insurance."

"And a 401k," Emily added.

"Sounds fun," I said, not entirely sarcastically. "But I like my job."

"No, you don't," Emily said.

"How could I not? I get to spend my days in a dishwasher's amorous embrace."

Both Phoebe and Emily stared at me, their eyes robotic. Though, that was hardly the strangest thing they've heard me say, so I wasn't sure what the judgment was for.

"This is life, and you're not happy with the one you have," Phoebe finally said, and then frowned. "We're worried about you. Especially since..."

"It was five years ago," I said. "I've dealt with it."

"Kinda hard to deal when a reminder is literally singing behind you," Emily said.

I paused. If only I had another beer. Something—anything—for me to do besides respond. No such luck. "I have the same answer to all of this as always—a fae or elf forest in place of Stearns County is an improvement. Fight me."

Phoebe and Emily nodded, but I could tell they didn't believe me. Because I lied. I'd never get over the fact that my best friend disappeared with the rest of the land when the elf forest arrived. Now, instead of Anna, I had these fairy fuckers. Though it wasn't like I was alone in this—almost everyone knew someone who was now gone. Some had lost everyone.

Phoebe gently shifted the conversation to other topics, namely, our plans for the next weekend—we were going gambling up at Mille Lacs—and let myself enjoy their company. If I ignored who was singing, if I ignored how once in a while some sort of non-human strolled through the bar, then I could pretend that everything was as it should be.

I was about to tell Emily and Phoebe the latest work drama about my coworker who treated her chihuahuas like they were middle-aged roommates when a man caught my attention. He was human—thankfully—and sitting alone at a table against the back wall. There was a bottle of beer on the table that was untouched, his hands resting on the worn wood. He wore black slacks and a black button up and leather gloves that were tucked into his sleeves. Was he some sort of office hipster? Maybe, because he wore a baseball cap, his light hair hidden underneath.

However, it wasn't his questionable attire that caught my attention—it was his even, placid expression, inspecting everyone who passed him by, yet moving little more than his eyes. I took him in—all of him. His finely chiseled features, sharp cheekbones, and defined lips. The way his muscles pressed against his shirt. The way that his posture was both relaxed and commanding. Yes, there was a lot more than his attire that drew me to him.

And then we made eye contact, his brilliant gaze boring into mine. I quickly looked away.

"Nope, you're not doing it," Emily said.

"Doing what?"

"Dating anyone you meet here."

"...You're here. So am I."

"We're women," Phoebe said. "We don't count."

"Don't worry," I said, shifting and turning my full attention back to my friends. "I'm not in the mood to pick up anyone tonight." Even if I wanted to talk to the mysterious-if-dourly dressed man, I didn't have a chance—when I looked back, he was gone.

CHAPTER TWO

ELDRIN

E^{*arlier that day*}

"Why is he sending you?" Siliana asked me, her voice weighed with concern. She stood in the doorway of my bedroom, surrounded by the curved white wood frame, her hands fidgeting with each other, her skeleton hand intertwined with her hand of flesh. Siliana was three decades my senior, and my oldest friend, but we appeared to be the same age. This was typical of all of my people, who were young until it was close to the time that death decided to take us. And it would—death spared no one, especially those who were born from it, those whose lives were tied with the Darkening Woods.

"He needs to send someone," I said, sorting through the varnished chest filled with human clothing that other elves had acquired during earlier adventures beyond our land's boundary. I had the chest sent to my rooms to prepare for this journey, much of its contents spilled across the onyx floors. I needed speed and stealth in order to accomplish my task, and I'd have neither if the humans saw what I was. What I truly was. "And I've done it before," I reminded her. "This isn't my first journey beyond the barrier."

"It's not safe." Siliana's brow furrowed. "I don't like it."

"We'll like it even less if the barrier breaks." I pulled out a black shirt with buttons down the front. It would be tight, but it should fit. "You saw what happened to the Gold Fae," I said. "They're struggling to keep the humans out of their home. Though the humans would leave them alone, if they knew what was good for them," I finished in a whisper.

"We're elves. We know better than to act before watching."

"I don't think the fae had much of a choice." Not everyone's lands arrived with a protective barrier like ours did, but we had protection even in our own world, and it seemed like it had deigned to come with us. We had old enemies that we needed to protect ourselves from, and it seemed we had a similar need here.

"This is ridiculous," Siliana muttered. "It's as if humans cannot understand that we don't want to be here as little as they want us here." My friend had a point. While others tried to make sense of their new circumstances, we elves stayed back. And watched. Some of the other peoples from our home adapted to their new surroundings. Some beings had such a small piece of our home transported that they had no choice but to leave and engage with the humans. But us? We treasured our barrier immediately. We decided to keep to ourselves and hope that, someday, the worlds would right themselves, even if history was not on our side. We had no guarantee that the worlds would ever go back. Unfortunately, in the meantime, our barrier was weakening, and each time someone—*anyone*—passed through it, it weakened further. Soon, it would break. The magics here were...different. Unsuited for our nature. Which made sense, as this wasn't our home.

Siliana and I were in my bedroom in the palace, the wooden branches of the trees that grew within and around the royal residence waving their golden boughs outside my window. The same winds carried the familiar scents of dried leaves and sweet late season flowers. Here, I could pretend that we were home. I could pretend that our lands stretched so far that it would take weeks to cross. But we would never be home. Not in my lifetime.

Siliana watched me burrow through the chest for pants, the ridiculous stiff things that were the fashion for humans. They had marvels of fabrics, and they chose the roughest garments possible to make them. Near the bottom of the chest, I found a pair of leather gloves and tried them on—they would cover my skeleton hand enough, as long as no one touched it.

"Do you think Vanir is right?" she asked. "That a human can fix the barrier."

I sighed. "I cannot know such things. But his logic is sound—and he has many to advise him. It makes sense that we need a willing creature of this realm to make an effective shield against it."

Siliana nodded, her long black hair cascading over her shoulders. "So, they're sending...you."

"What's wrong with that?" I asked, knowing my questions had many answers. Some of which she would never utter out loud.

"We're supposed to be convincing a human man or woman to join us forever, and you're not the most...friendly."

I shook out a pair of black pants, ones of a bearable material. They would suffice. At least they would fit, even though they risked being too short. "I know where to go," I said. "Trust me, there is no shortage of humans willing to come here for the chance to live amongst us. It shouldn't be hard."

My words were circumspect, but I knew better than to let them be otherwise. One could never know who was listening, even in the privacy of my bedroom.

Once, when my father was still king, I would have seen this journey to the human lands as a grand adventure, which was how I treated all my obligations—complete it quickly so that I could spend the rest of my time seeking pleasures. Now, I had no choice but to obey, not if I wanted to live. Vanir was my half-brother. Vanir was now the king. And I was his disgraced older brother, the loser in the battle for the throne. Well, was it really a battle if only one person fought? Regardless, he seized the throne, convinced much of the court to join him, and I would have been dead years ago if not for the worlds merging. Elves tended not to leave competition alive. But after the merge, it was decided that we needed every member of the kingdom possible since our numbers were so low, especially one as "useful" as me. And Vanir did not want to alienate more of his court than he had to, since I *did* still have some friends among the nobles. And thus, I was here, in my room, preparing to be his errand boy.

But this was not the day to dwell on my failures.

"Well, try to choose someone who has new stories, recipes, or something," Siliana said, forcing a small smile. "It's going to get boring eventually with just us. But when you get back, I want to talk to you about something."

"What about?" I held the clothes, waiting for her to leave so that I could change. "Just tell me now."

"Fine, I'll tell you some so that you can think on it—I think you should consider residing in Gold Glen."

"Gold Glen," I echoed. "What do you think our original name for it was?"

"You know as well as I that there is no way for me to answer that." Siliana was right—when we merged with this world, we took on its primary language, rendering our texts an indecipherable mess. If we didn't have the books, those tomes that we could read one day but not the next, we may not have noticed the change in our language at all. "And you're avoiding the topic," Siliana prodded.

I was. The piece of our territory that had shifted from our home was quite large, large enough that Gold Glen was a good day's ride from the palace and its attendant city with a fast horse—if not more.

"Why there? Why do you want me to live in that village?"

"I think it's time you choose a path forward with your life—and you won't be able to do it here with Vanir watching you."

"It's not like I can hide from him, especially now."

"No, but it's better than living under the same roof, so to speak." She worried her mother's garnet ring. "You need to have a life of your own. Find a partner. Have something that isn't...this."

A partner. Even if I was ready to bring someone with me into the hell that was dancing around Vanir's whims, there was no one in the Darkening Woods that called to me in such a manner. Despite what the rumors said, spawned as they were from our lifetime of being close friends, Siliana was committed to another, who was left behind when our world split. All of us left behind people we treasured. Our capital, Great Glen, went with us to the new world, but many of the court were using the holiday from the formal court season to visit estates and family who lived far away. Even the working class used this time to travel, while the demand for their services was less. Thus, Great Glen, which was normally bursting with nobility and their attendants, had been relatively empty when the world split. I still didn't know whether that was a good thing or not.

"I'll think on it," I said. And I would, because Siliana was right. Partner aside, moving far from court would give me an opportunity to live without seeing my brother, which would increase the odds that he'd eventually ignore me. In a place like Gold Glen, I wouldn't be in a position to cause Vanir any trouble—it was not a good place to plan a coup. The village had more cows than elves. But whether I wanted to go to Gold Glen, and whether Vanir would let me, were two very different questions.

CHAPTER THREE

AMBER

I was a responsible woman and valued safety and money over a night's debauchery. Thus, I had only two watery beers the entire three hours we were at the bar, and I spent the remainder of my time enjoying the finer delights of on-tap carbonated water and something that claimed to be a $2 hamburger. No matter—there were few things I wouldn't eat at that price. Emily and Phoebe became outright pleasant once their lecturing was done, and the conversation turned to admiring the wildlife show that was a bar at night. The wildlife show attempted to pull me in a few times with its imitation of a mating ritual, but I wasn't in the mood. However, I *was* in the mood to see what sort of quip would make a man leave me alone the fastest. Apparently, the winner was "Oh, I sell timeshares, we should *totally* connect!" followed by "Yes, my antibiotics are done so I'm ready to mingle!"

Eventually, our night drew to a close and it was time for me to head back to my car. I had work in the morning and the dishwasher deserved to see me at my best. Stabby Tabby in one hand, keys and purse in the other, I strolled along, checking over my shoulder every so often.

The summer night was humid, making the darkness take on a more oppressive feeling than it would otherwise. It really brought out the sewer scent that occasionally tinged the air. Once in a while a car blasting angry music drove by, followed by a fleet of respectable sedans bearing their rideshare stickers. Pedestrians waddled here and there, some inebriated—most not—but none lingered. As a result, the streets were relatively occupied, and this area was well-lit. These streets were about as safe as a woman could expect in a major city at night. But still, one couldn't be too careful in the dark.

A rustling and creaking broke out behind me. I turned, expecting to see a squirrel, or a raccoon. It was not a squirrel, and I wished it was a raccoon.

A dark shape—like a big dog but *leggier*—rushed toward me, knocking me off balance before I could take in what happened.

"Fuck!" I screamed, somehow still standing and slashing and thrusting at the *thing* with the Tabby. The Tabby made sticky contact. The creature hissed and backed off enough so I could see what it was. Or more accurately—what it wasn't.

It wasn't a dog. It was a spider—a dog-sized spider with razor teeth and eerily human red eyes. Lots of human eyes. A black ooze dripped from where I stabbed it, a too-tiny indent in its mass. Then again, Stabby Tabbies weren't designed for mythological creatures, and that's what this was—a creature from one of the new worlds. And apparently someone didn't feel like staying home.

"Help!" I screamed, turning and searching for anyone to save me. I couldn't outrun this thing—I couldn't hope to try. And I was alone. No one was close enough to help. There were some people in the distance, but could they even hear me over the city's noise?

I would have to get away on my own.

Crouching, I faced the creature, trying to stand on wobbly heels. I would get out of its way, and it would hunt something better. Maybe a giant insect. Anything but me.

One step back.

Two steps—

The spider lunged towards me, only this time an unmistakable sensation of fire and then ice broke through the skin on my shoulder. It bit me.

The fucker bit me.

A moment later I collided with the sidewalk, my head somehow mostly avoiding the pavement. My breath knocked out of me, I struggled. I was *not* going to die from some overgrown Halloween prop. My shoulder cried out in pain, a cramping agony that made my arm spasm, even as the fire seared with each movement.

Away. I had to get away. I stabbed at the creature, desperate. Some of my strikes made contact that would have devastated a human. But the spider held on. A full-on hunting dagger would have struggled with something this solid.

Within moments the bite on my arm became numb, a feeling that quickly spread through my arm. I dropped the Tabby. All the feeling in my hand was gone. My arm tingled, asleep and useless. My chest felt as if it were smashed in a vice, smothered as I was by the spider, its bristly body pressed against my face. I struggled to breathe. My mouth filled with its thick, black fur, the creature's dark leathery skin clearly visible through the patchy barbs.

My vision blurred. The spider turned into two and then back into one again as the world melted. My heart raced, the pulse echoing down to even my toes. Each breath was a struggle, a fight against the looming dark. And then...I stopped thinking. About anything.

Maybe it wasn't a bad thing that the spider bit me. This wasn't so bad. Everything felt just fine. I was like a little butterfly singing in a field of cotton candy. Everything was so beautiful and shiny.

Smiling, the last thing I saw was that the spider, mouth open and fangs about to lunge into my neck, was suddenly lifted off me. In its place was a dark figure, with silver eyes so bright I lost myself in them.

CHAPTER FOUR

ELDRIN

Well, this wasn't what I had planned.

I hadn't meant to follow her. I wasn't going to ask her to come back to the Darkening Woods with me. She didn't seem the sort to blindly follow me. That sort were easy to notice since those humans tried to dress like us, in some respects. I had been to the human city before. The first time I was accosted by women wearing long dresses, with pendants dangling over their foreheads. They pointed at my ears, giggling excitedly. That was the last time I left my ears uncovered when leaving the Woods.

The time after that I was followed by a man with his hair tied up, who wore an uncomfortably short tunic over tight leggings. He also smelled like a skunk. For a few minutes he followed me, calling for a "nature child," until I lost him by taking a corner and then hiding in a tree. After that I learned to cover my hair.

But this woman, I had the feeling that she wouldn't have cared about my nature, even if she knew what I was. It did not escape my attention that she ignored every single non-human creature in that establishment. That was a problem. I needed someone who did things like fawn over the singer, maybe at least wear some jewels in their hair. In short, I needed someone who looked like they'd be willing to do anything to see more of the other beings speckled in the crowd. And this one did none of those things.

But I couldn't look away from her, even as I had to move around the bar, distractedly searching for someone else to bring to the Darkening Woods. No matter how much a part of me wished that she showed those like me the slightest attention, gave me some excuse to talk to her. Anything.

As she sat at that table in the bar, her gaze was sharp, intent, her lips curved in a daring smile while she joked with her friends. She was surrounded by curious creatures, denizens both mortal and other, and yet her only concern was for her companions in front of her. Best of all, she made them *laugh*, a true laughter that made one of the friends cough out her drink and the other knock over a purse that I hoped wasn't made of a real feline. It was as if she were a light and everyone else merely insects, pulled to her brilliance.

I wasn't the only one who thought like this—three different men approached and seemed to have left her table disappointed. I couldn't be sure what she told the men, but whatever it was, it made her friends shake their heads afterward.

It should go without saying—it didn't pass my attention that she was beautiful, with hair the color of russet autumn leaves, framing a face as carved and delicate as winter's ice. She wasn't elven. She didn't have our innate grace, or our features designed to complement the splendor of the Darkening Woods. But that was a good thing. Her features made her *her*.

I was only going to follow her to her vehicle, truly. Just to make sure that she could make it home safe. Her steps were steady and her head seemed clear, so once she was inside that vehicle I wouldn't need to fear for her. Then I could commence my hunt in earnest and not think about her again. There were two women who wore tight corsets with braided hair and face paint who kept staring at me at the bar—those two were promising. I still had time to do the task Vanir set for me.

However, the veinwart had other plans.

The name "veinwart" likely sounded better in our original tongue, but humans would probably just refer to the creature as a "giant spider." They were similar to their arachnid cousins, as best as I could tell, except veinwart like to hunt larger, warm-blooded prey.

It wasn't hard for me to get rid of the creature—just two carefully placed stabs with my dagger and it scurried off into the dark, dripping black ichor as it ran. I fatally wounded it, so other humans wouldn't be harmed by it. Those things were a pest in the Darkening Woods and other areas of the old world, though how it got *here* of all places was a puzzle. Our barrier was weak, but not *that* weak—I doubted it came from the Woods. It wouldn't surprise me if some human bought one as a pet from one of the fae and it escaped. Humans had a lot of good qualities—the cuisine, for one—but respect for the dangers of nature didn't seem to be one of them. Not surprising, as they molded their world into such a shape that it was easy to forget that nature existed. The assault on my nose every time a vehicle passed me by reminded me of that.

With the creature gone, I bent over the woman and cursed when I saw the tell-tale dark blue marks on her skin. Gently, I moved back the knit fabric of her dress, showing more of her shoulder. And cursed louder.

She had been bitten, and the creature's fangs had delved far under her skin. It was a bite that had already colored her skin and was spreading by the moment, working its way through her veins.

If I left her here, she would be dead by morning. Humans had their physicians, but it was unlikely they would figure out how to treat this in time, if they could at all. Even in our old world, treating these bites was a skill managed only by a few.

My people had the medicine to counteract the venom, but if I returned to the forest and then brought it back here...it would take too long, not to mention that the barrier would probably snap in the process, its magic gone forever. King Vanir's prime advisor/lackey, a smug man named Ivas, emphasized that this was the last journey the veil could handle. I had to bring back a human—the safety of our people depended on it. Were the two of them overreacting so that I took things seriously? Possibly, though it wasn't necessary, since I was not one to endanger our people. Was he hoping I would fail? Knowing Ivas, most definitely. But I could not take the chance that my retrieving the cure would break the barrier. Not for a human.

Not when we needed one.

For a moment I stared at her as I held her in my arms, her unconscious weight heavy in my grip. Her brilliant red hair fell in waves over her shoulders, cascading towards the ground. Her creamy skin was even and unblemished, her features refined. She was so vibrant, even like this. Much like the warmth from her skin, something about her—something primal—stirred me. Like stepping from the shadows and into the light. Her chest rose and fell, and I could feel every beat of her heart. A beat that would end too soon if I did not act.

That settled it. I was bringing her with me to the Darkening Woods.

And I prayed upon the never-ending Woods that she would forgive me when she realized what I had done.

CHAPTER FIVE

AMBER

I awoke with the world's worst hangover, my vision blurred and head throbbing. It wasn't until I realized that my mouth wasn't stuffed with cotton—it was just dry—that I remembered that I had only two beers. It was impossible that I was hung over. And then a heartbeat later I registered a very sore shoulder and remembered that I had turned into a spider snack and then...

"You're awake," a soft female voice said from next to me.

I turned my head—it felt like it weighed two hundred pounds—and forced my eyes to brave the light, all to take in a beautiful woman. She was dressed in a crimson gown out of a Renaissance festival, with long sleeves hiding her hands. Silver gilt leaves were embroidered on the sleeves' edges, working their way around the cuffs in an elaborate dance. The eyeless faces of little skeletons stared at me from a belt around her waist, likely carved from onyx or another black stone. Her dark hair flowed freely to her waist, and her skin was enviously perfect, almost bright with an innate glow. Her lips were a crimson red, painted with a sort of lipstick, and her eyes were lined with black and highlighted by a dark eyeshadow. She didn't need the cosmetics—she would have been gorgeous regardless—but they took her from beautiful to breathtaking.

Too beautiful. Her pointed ears betrayed what she was—some sort of elf, fairy...thing.

"Where am I?" I asked, my voice breaking. I willed my racing heart to still. If these beings wanted to kill me, they could have just left me with the spider. My memory told me that much. And they also wouldn't have bothered to place me in the world's fluffiest bed, complete with a maroon and gold brocade duvet. And they also wouldn't have bound my shoulder with clean bandages.

Muffled voices told me that there were others in the hall outside the closed door, and the distant chords of mournful violin music worked its way into my ears. I blinked hard, staring out the window, at the tree branches waving their colorful leaves. It was...autumn? How long had I been unconscious? It was summer. It was still summer, right? It had to be. Had to.

The trees were one concern—my room was another. Wherever I was, it was a decoration style I had never seen before. Like Victorian gothic meets Celtic knot chic. The room smelled of crisp fall leaves and a light musk and amber. The white wooden room itself was accented with trim and decorative wood panels that curved gracefully, tips and edges worked into elaborate knots and flourishes. And then there were the skulls, femurs, and skeleton hands that also found their way into various motifs. My own coverlet at first glance appeared to be an elaborately embroidered maroon velvet blanket with little gold designs, until I realized the designs were of skulls. Dark brown stone tiles graced the floors in a whirled pattern, as if there was an elaborate whirlpool on the floor. Alright, this room was nice. Small, but nice. And not a jail cell. And based on the quality of the furnishings, likely not a peasant's home. I've slept at worse places.

Was I some sort of hostage? Such things happened before, like when the orc enclave in Wisconsin had some initial disagreements with their new neighbors. Maybe they were going to patch me up and send me home once they got their seasonings or books or whatever this group wanted.

Ha. Sometimes, I truly amused myself. They weren't going to let me go.

"You are in the Darkening Woods," the woman said, her voice lightly accented with something I could only describe as British, but musical, "in the palace of King Vanir of the Darkening Woods. Home of the elves."

"The what?" I asked. I shifted to sit, noting that I was wearing some fine cotton-like dressing gown—and no bra—but the woman gently pushed me back down. Fighting her would have to wait, as I was going to take a nap as soon as possible. My body told me I had little choice in the matter. "How long have I been here?"

"Around twelve hours," she replied. "You were badly hurt."

Yeah, that I knew. I was there.

"When can I go home?" I yawned, using the arm that wasn't killing me to cover my mouth.

"My name is Siliana," the woman said. "I'm a member of the king's court. And my task is to explain the situation to you. We didn't want to upset you unnecessarily."

"Please, start by telling me when I can go home," I said.

"We brought you here from your city—it wasn't far." Fuck. So, I *was* in the fae/fairy/elf forest where Saint Cloud used to be. It could always be worse, I told myself. It could always be worse.

"That's good to know," I said, "but when can I go back to my city?"

Her jaw clenched. That was my first clue something wasn't right. "You were grievously injured by the veinwart."

"The what?"

"The...spider."

"Oh. That." Veinwart? Sounded like a bad villain from a novel, or some sort of disease.

"If Eldrin had not found you," Siliana continued, "you would've died. There is no human medicine that can treat a bite from one of them. You need to recover your strength, too. The bites are notoriously painful. And tiring."

Wasn't that right. My shoulder still burned where the spider bit, though it had lessened since the initial attack. However, there was still a heaviness to my blood, a weight in my body that I couldn't explain. An exhaustion I had to fight to keep at bay. Couldn't we finish this conversation later? If the elves hadn't killed me by now, surely, they wouldn't while I napped. It wasn't like I was Holofernes, to be killed by an understandably pissed-off woman while I slept. I hoped.

Eldrin. Eldrin…was that the name of the one whose eyes I saw before I passed out? Well, at least I didn't hallucinate eyeballs. There was a literal silver lining. A very thin silver lining.

"You will rest here," Siliana said, "and then we will see about obtaining a proper room for you, if you're not satisfied with this."

"Room?" I coughed. "Like for staying overnight? Why can't I go home? You said you healed me. I won't say anything if that's the point—I figured you were hiding here for a reason. We're in that hidden forest, aren't we, the one that doesn't let anyone in?" Siliana nodded slowly, confirming my guess. "Trust me, I want less to do with you than you do with me."

Siliana's lips pursed and she avoided looking at me. It was oddly reminiscent of the time my mom told me my cat died.

"I'm not allowed to leave, am I?"

Siliana shook her head. "I'm sorry." She did look sorry—I had to give her credit for that. "I'm afraid that if you did leave, it would doom us all. And yourself. You're never going to be allowed to leave here."

"Ever?"

"Not until something drastic changes."

Exhaustion mixed with panic swept over me. I couldn't leave? Well, I didn't want to leave right this minute. I couldn't walk now if I tried. But I was stuck? Here? With...*them*? My fists clenched. This couldn't be happening. This couldn't...

"I'm sorry," Siliana said with more kindness than I expected. "I wish it were otherwise."

"Why?" I asked. "Why can't I go home?"

Siliana took a deep breath. Her face was even, but her brow was slightly furrowed. She hid it well, but I guessed she was severely uncomfortable at having to explain this to me. She wasn't the only one. "Two reasons," she finally said. "The first is that our home and your human world are separated by a barrier, as you noticed—no one and nothing can get in or out without our permission. We decided, when we first realized that our world was swept away, that we would keep the barrier intact and do our best to live as we had before. Our portion of land that came with us isn't small—we can thrive here, until we can figure out a way back. But the barrier is weakening—we need someone from this world to bond with the barrier to keep it intact. The magic is too unstable otherwise. If one more person passes through...I doubt the barrier would survive."

"Bond?" I still didn't understand what this had to do with me staying here forever.

"Magically bond, I mean. It is a simple process. But, it would mean you can never leave," Siliana said. "Not if we want the magic to hold."

Wait, me. She was talking about me. *I* was the human that would be stuck performing elf magic.

Fuck me.

"Ah. So, you want me to be a human anchor. Me."

"...More or less." Siliana paused, her hands clasped on her lap, still hidden under the fabric, the digits moving in a slow rhythm.

"There's something else," I said warily. There was always something else.

"The bond has to be made willingly. No one can force you to join with our magic. And to ensure that you're compliant with the ritual..." Siliana closed her eyes, leaving me lots of opportunity to fill in what she didn't say.

"I'm not all the way healed from that bite, am I?" I asked. Siliana's eyes widened with surprise. "What? I can tell something isn't right with me. This feeling—this heaviness—is too much to be from medicine."

"No, you are not." She took a deep breath. "Your life is no longer in immediate danger, but you only have around one turn of the moon before it will be too late. The spider's venom will ultimately freeze your heart, without the cure from the king. Our people are not affected by the venom to the extent other races are, so we have not had much need for an antidote. He is the only one with access."

"Great." I rubbed my eyes as I sat up, ignoring the wave of dizziness. "Good ol' blackmail. This cannot be happening."

"I'm afraid it is."

"This is worse than Grand Rapids," I said, breaking into a chuckle.

"What?"

"That's where I was supposed to go. Phoebe and Emily and the cat purse said I wasn't going to have a life there, and look—they were right."

"I'm sure this is a shock—"

"Oh, it is. But you know what?" I asked. "This is just the sort of thing to happen to me."

Siliana shifted uneasily. "Well, since you are in shock, as you admitted, I may as well show you the rest."

"What? What could shock me after this? What could possibly be worse?"

Siliana moved her sleeve and revealed her left hand, which was nothing but glistening white bone.

CHAPTER SIX

ELDRIN

"You were supposed to bring a mortal willing to bond with the land and thus secure our barrier," Vanir said, likely peering down his nose. It was a good guess, as that was his favored position.

I kept my head bowed, staring at the intricately etched and polished stone floor. Even in this, his private audience chamber, decadent luxury oozed from every surface. He hadn't changed much of the palace's ornaments since he took our father's throne, but what was there he quickly made even more opulent, to the extent such things were possible. I could see the very tips of his red velvet slippers just at the edge of my vision, embroidered with golden skeleton peacocks with diamonds for eyes. Pretentious bastard. I didn't begrudge him the luxury because I lost the throne—I would have made a poor king—but I begrudged him for that out of all of my brothers, he had to be the one to sit upon it. Unfortunately, my other brothers were with the remainder of the Darkening Woods, where I should have been. And with my mother.

"I did return with a mortal woman, Your Majesty," I said. "And she is now in debt to our kingdom."

"Yes, yes, irksome little spider, wasn't it?" Vanir said. "Though, did you so much as bother to ask this woman's name before you decided to tie our fate to hers?" Vanir sighed dramatically. "Of course not."

My cheeks burned. I was not some young fool to risk everything for a pretty face. Not anymore. That Eldrin was dead. "She needs to complete the ritual in order to save her life, Your Majesty. That is more effective than simply desiring to live with us because we're a curiosity."

"So, you claim. But I can't ignore what my advisors tell me—you were guided by your emotions." Vanir chuckled darkly. "They were ever your downfall. Or was it your laziness?"

My breath caught and I forced my attention to stay focused on the ground, on the little scuffs that marred the floor. I needed to focus on anything but what Vanir had said. How dare he mention this here and now...

"What was it you told me when we were young?" Vanir continued. "Was it that you were 'too busy to learn governing since you were going to be king regardless'? Or was it that learning how our kingdom functioned was 'too boring' for you? And do you remember how you mocked me for attending father's council meetings? Well, unfortunately for you, taking and keeping a throne *is* a part of governing. Something you learned too late."

I stilled, even as Vanir's guard shifted in the corner, allowing me to imagine his hand drifting down to his sword.

Vanir was right—I had said all of those things and worse. I had ignored everything, everything I did not want to indulge in. Not even a decade ago, Father hadn't been so old, and I had time to learn my responsibilities. I had time to enjoy being a prince, hunting and drinking and enjoying what pleasures life offered. Why waste my time boring myself now, when I didn't have to? No matter how much mother and father begged me to turn my attention to more serious pursuits. They knew that while we had some time for me to take to my duties, we didn't live forever. Elves were long lived, but even we had to bow before the rod of time. Even elves were able to be taken by death unawares.

A lesson I did not learn until far too late.

I stilled the argument stirring on my tongue and kept my head bowed.

Vanir wanted this—he wanted a reaction. He wanted an excuse to kill me. Elven kings did not let contenders for their thrones live—one thing we shared with the theatrical, unnatural fae—and I was the greatest threat to his reign. Though that was before our world was torn in two.

"Very well," Vanir said, slapping the arm of his throne. "We are forced to deal with this woman and so we shall. Look at me." Slowly, I raised my gaze to my half-brother.

Vanir's golden hair draped over his shoulders, the silken strands catching on his embroidered green shirt. His brown eyes sparkled with flecks of gold, and he smiled at me, though there was no warmth in it. A golden crown wrought in the shape of leaves rested on his head, and a silver necklace bearing a wooden pendant lay over his shirt. His left hand, his skeletal hand, rested on his lap. His hand that was bare of all flesh. A hand we all had in common, for our domain was the autumn of life, the descent to death and rot.

"She has one month to complete the ritual and save her life," Vanir said, "for if we die, so does she."

"The bond cannot be made unwillingly."

"I will marry her. That should help." Vanir shrugged and grinned, a seemingly friendly gesture. I blinked hard. I had to have misheard. "What?" He asked upon noticing my shock. "I need a wife and she makes enough sense—what human would forego the chance to be an elven queen?"

"I'm just surprised you would turn away from the women of your court." And be with a human, I left unsaid—there would have been less gossip if he decided to marry a pig farmer.

"This is more important," Vanir said, as if he were convincing himself. "The bond is more important. And who cares that she isn't elven? Once she makes the bond she'll live as long as us anyway."

"She will?" I asked, stunned into forgetting who I was speaking to, and forcing away my concerns that his court wouldn't see the matter as simply as him. We weren't immortal, but we easily lived to be three hundred years old, our bond with the Darkening Woods letting us share in the long lives of the trees.

"So I have been told."

"Will the magic take her hand too?" And make it like ours, I meant.

"Probably not. I was told that the Woods never wanted that price from humans before, but regardless, it's not as if her opinion matters."

My bewilderment almost made me overlook how he was speaking this way about *her*. Which was a good thing—if I dwelled too long on the thought of my slimy brother touching her, holding her...I didn't know if I could contain myself. There was no way he would ever love her. Or try. If he saw the spark in her eyes, he would do everything he could to quench it.

"So I'm told," Vanir repeated. "I enquired when we started considering a human to bond with the barrier. Human lives can mirror ours when given the chance. This isn't the first time our realms have blended—though the sheer amount that occurred this time is unusual. Consider cats—do humans really think they are from their world?"

"I never considered cats, Your Majesty." He was right—our original world had humans, and they had to have come from somewhere. There were signs of our worlds' previous mergers that were there, if one knew where to look.

"You're no fun, Eldrin. Even when it would behoove you to be."

Fun? He was just prodding me for being *too fun*. But with Vanir, nothing was ever as simple as the words that came out of his mouth.

I tried to consider the positive side of my brother suggesting that he marry the woman—if she would have him. While my responsibility for the human woman was complete as soon as I brought her to the healers, it relieved me to know that Vanir wasn't intending on keeping her in a dungeon after the fact. I tried to soothe the budding disgust in my heart. If he did marry her, he would be forced to give her a place of honor—even our court, such as it was now, wouldn't tolerate anything less for a queen. She would be safe, more or less. And with time, she could find her own way to be happy. In time, she could hope to gain the acceptance she would need to thrive.

"Now that the human we need is here, is there anything else you require from me, Your Majesty?"

"Oh, Eldrin," Vanir said slyly, sitting up a little straighter, "I'm nowhere near done with you in regard to this matter." My stomach twisted at what was going to come out of his mouth next. "See, I am making the human woman an excellent offer—but *your* task is to ensure that she accepts, and to keep her in one piece until she does. And if she doesn't...well, I don't think you'll be around long enough to worry about the consequences. My throne room could always use another skull..."

I left the audience with my heart thrumming in my chest. Courtiers watched me through wry gazes as I stepped through the halls, but no one approached. Many gave me a wide berth these days. Wise.

Vanir continued to heckle me during the audience, setting out the rest of his demands. He prodded me, his words as pointed and pained as a hot poker. But I would not lash out. I couldn't. If I did, it would give him the excuse he needed, the ability to get rid of me for good. No one would blame him for removing a threat that couldn't be contained.

Was Vanir mad? How could he ask me to do this, to take care of the human woman and coax her into marrying him? Me. *Why* would he ask me to do it? Did he suspect that something drew me to the human woman already, and he saw a chance to act against me? Was he counting on my needing to please him, so that I would do whatever he asked, no matter what? Or did he expect me to fail, knowing that I would hate the thought of any woman being bound to him, much less one who was alone at court?

Whatever his plot, he would be disappointed. I would continue to do my duty. And the last thing I needed was to become entangled with a mortal woman beyond what was absolutely necessary.

I stopped outside the door to where the woman was recovering, a private suite near where the rest of the minor nobility stayed in the palace. Taking a deep breath, I was relieved to hear, through the closed door, Siliana discussing the finer points of our skeleton hands. The woman wasn't screaming. No, she seemed...curious, if mumbling every other word. The medicine she was given would take a day to wear off and for her mind to return to its prior functions. In fact, I was surprised that she was already conscious—even elves typically needed a day to recover from that dosage.

Good. This was all good. This meant that the hardest part was done. The human woman had already been told that she couldn't go home, and that now she was living with nightmares.

I gripped the cold metal knob, opened the door, and let myself inside the room. And I lost my breath.

Both women stopped talking and watched me, while the woman's mouth dropped open as her eyes took in my skeleton hand. I didn't bother to try to hide it—she had seen our true natures anyway.

"You," the human woman said, her eyes flickering with recognition.

"You remember me?" I asked.

"Yes. You were the guy from the bar. The one who was all moody and disappeared."

I raised an eyebrow while Siliana politely covered her mouth. "Moody?" she asked.

That was all it took. The woman went into a tirade about how she noticed me, sitting and watching the crowd, apparently standing out more than I thought, all while I tried to get my nerves under control. While I tried not to stare at her.

The woman was worn and exhausted. She had dark circles under her eyes and her hair was a mess, but she was brilliant. That same feeling that I had when I saw her before, that inability to look away, returned, striking me hotter than ever. Her wide eyes, curious and sharp, took in every gesture, her body shifting in a way that was so *alive*. She missed nothing, taking in our expressions, our gestures, seemingly even the things we left unsaid. She didn't fit in this place, in its balance between life and death, no more than a rose belonged in winter. Her supple lips beckoned to me, and I wondered what it would be like to wrap my hands in that hair and pull her to me and consume her. No, my feelings weren't because she was human. By this point I'd been around hundreds of humans, if not thousands. Their novelty never attracted me. None of them sparked the urge to pull her against me, to devour every bit of her while she begged me for more. She was the star that flickered in the black night, the fire that overwhelmed everything it touched, consuming until it was changed forever.

And now I had to watch her marry Vanir.

CHAPTER SEVEN

AMBER

The skeleton hand was unsettling. Alright, it was terrifying. The elves all had a hand/lower arm that seemed to work perfectly, that could touch and move and grab, without a single muscle or tendon connecting the bones. That wasn't right. Whatever it was, it wasn't right. Yes, it had to be some sort of magic, but it still wasn't right.

And here I was, in the last place in the state I had ever wanted to be—with *them*.

What were the elves going to do to me? Siliana seemed to be trying to calm me down, but why? What did they hope to gain from me? Because they definitely wanted something from me. Otherwise, why go through all the trouble? Yes, they wanted me to join/bond with the barrier, but this was something more, something they hadn't told me. There were layers at play, evident in the way that Siliana carefully picked her words. I was not about to believe that I was kidnapped into a happily ever after—there was no way it was going to be that simple.

I had to take one thing at a time. I was still alive. And I was being taken care of. For now. And after being bit by a giant spider that still had a chance to kill me, the skeleton hands were something I was able to overlook.

What I could not overlook was the man, Eldrin, who had stepped into my room with a presence that took every word out of my mouth. That is, until Siliana prompted me to explain how I remembered him from the bar and I started to ramble. All while taking him in.

His silver hair was cropped close to his head, hovering above pointed ears and revealing a graceful white neck. Slowly, he shifted and took a seat on another unoccupied wooden stool, his posture as contained and graceful as a cat. His limbs were covered with a green tunic with long sleeves, but what I could see hinted at a muscular forearm that was no doubt as toned as the rest of him. The movement drew attention to his chiseled cheeks, and his strong jaw that was as sharp as the bones of his left hand—yep, he had one of those skeleton hands, too. How hadn't I noticed that he was something other at the bar—how he hid his ears—was beyond me. Though I really should have noticed something was different. No human moved with that grace, carried themselves with that surety.

And when he looked at me with those silver eyes, the ones that seemed to stare into every bit of me, I was suddenly very aware I was wearing nothing but a glorified bedsheet.

"Eldrin," Siliana said with a polite nod of her head once I finished talking, "this is Amber. We were just discussing what she can expect living here."

"Amber," he repeated, his voice low. He blinked fast, like he was remembering something. "How much have you told her?"

"Everything. Except for Vanir."

"Vanir?" I asked. That's right. The king. The king who apparently shared a name with a race of Norse gods. That was interesting.

From the way Eldrin and Siliana looked at each other, the king was not well-liked. It was like asking two co-workers what they thought of a manager. "You understand the bond with the barrier, correct?" Eldrin asked me.

"More or less," I replied. "In theory."

"And how it has to be made willingly?"

"...Yes."

"Well, in order to make bonding with the barrier more acceptable to you," Eldrin said, "Vanir would like to offer you marriage."

"...To?"

"Himself."

Siliana coughed, covering her mouth and turning away from me. Neither of us paid her any attention.

My own mouth was wide open. "Marry. The king. An elf king."

Eldrin nodded, watching for my reaction, other than the obvious surprise. What was he looking for? Was I supposed to be happy about this? Though, was my exhaustion making me see things, or was he watching me too, for more than just to see how I felt about the king? When I saw Eldrin at the bar, I felt something drawing me to him, even in that crowd. That feeling had not lessened, though it was being pushed aside by other things. And it couldn't be mutual. Right?

"The king couldn't tell me this himself?" I managed to ask, and I could've sworn I saw a flicker of a smirk on Eldrin's face.

"He will not," Eldrin said firmly. Yep, not my imagination. Eldrin really didn't like Vanir.

"Wait. Um, do I have to give an answer now? Because I have...a lot of thinking to do." And naps to take, a nap that was getting increasingly difficult to fight off. But I couldn't avoid the thinking. Siliana had pointed out that the existence of the barrier had, in effect, stopped me from leaving these woods. And I would be stopped by elves before I managed to get far, even if I didn't get lost. More than that, the poison effectively stopped me from leaving, even if I managed to get out. And now the elf king was offering marriage to get me to stay? I didn't trust the fairy fuckers before, and I definitely didn't now.

"You do not, Amber," Siliana said, shooting Eldrin a look I couldn't interpret. "But I would counsel accepting immediately." She lowered her voice. "You do not want to anger the king."

Oh. That. They *really* didn't like him. And I was inclined to trust Siliana, in this matter at least. The look she exchanged with Eldrin had not been an act, and the nerves in the room were so tight, waiting for my reaction, that it felt like strings about to snap.

"In that case," I said, "I would be pleased to accept."

They both nodded, having clearly anticipated no other answer. Little did they know that they were lucky I was too tired to put up a fight. Was I going to marry an elf I hadn't seen before? Hell no. But he wasn't standing at the edge of my bed with a priest and a ring, so I had time. Maybe marriage meant something else here. Maybe I would manage to find a way out. I really didn't have to stay here forever, did I?

"Uh, what now?" I asked, trying not to stare at Eldrin as much as I wanted.

"You will rest and be presented to Vanir within a day or two," Siliana said. "And then we have a month to prepare you to bond with the barrier."

"Prepare? Can't I just...do it?"

"No," Eldrin said. "The magic will sense what is in your heart. It has to be willing. Of its own accord."

"What happens if I don't have the right...heart?"

Siliana and Eldrin looked at each other once more. "We don't know," Eldrin said. "But I cannot imagine it would be pleasant. This is a forest that thrives on decay and death. I cannot imagine that if the barrier rejects an offering that the rejection would be pleasant."

"Oh," I said. "So not giving me the final antidote..."

"Is to motivate you to try," Siliana said.

"Yes. Nothing motivates quite like death," I said sarcastically.

"I'm sorry, Amber," Siliana said, bowing her head. "I know that this is a lot. And I know you will need time to grieve the loss of your old life and home. But I think you will like it here, with time. And we will do everything we can to help you."

"Why?" I asked. "Why are you two being so helpful to me?"

Siliana was the one who answered. "You did not choose to be here, but we need a human to succeed and protect us. And my conscience would not allow me to act otherwise." She lowered her voice. "Not when Vanir is guiding this."

Eldrin, the beautiful bastard who brought me here, was biting his lip while Siliana spoke. He also owed me an apology. He owed me more of an explanation—at the very least admit what he did to me. I could barely keep my eyes open, yet I wanted to wring an answer from him. But all he said was, "Rest. I will see you soon. When it is time to meet my brother."

With gentle farewells, the two elves left me alone, which was probably for the best. I needed rest, and I needed to figure out how I was going to handle the king—my new fiancé. The last thing I needed to think about was Eldrin—impossibly gorgeous Eldrin. There was no way he would want anything to do with me like *that* if I was promised to his king. Even if he would settle for a human.

And I had to focus on staying alive.

CHAPTER EIGHT

AMBER

Rest was hard. Oh, my body slept alright, and my vision had this bucolic fuzziness that made it nice to just lay back and let my attention dance along the winding curves of the window trim. The wood darted in and around itself, over and over forever. Like a white pretzel. Or spaghetti. Spaghetti with skulls. I contented myself for hours like this, staring at the art while I floated in and out of sleep.

Unfortunately, my eyeball activity made me realize that I may never have pretzels or spaghetti again. Did elves eat either of those things? What about Mexican food? Did they have cilantro here? Or coffee? No electricity was a given. Oh, please, *please* let them have hot water. I wanted a steaming hot shower more than I wanted anything in my life.

And then there were my friends and family, and everyone else I left behind. Would I see Emily and Phoebe again?

What would their reaction be if I told them that I *did* find a man—an elf king? See, Emily, that was much better than an accountant, or a lawyer.

My chest constricted. For all my failures, I would miss home. Terribly. But I had to work on staying alive long enough to miss it. And with my blackmailing husband-to-be, that seemed to be easier said than done.

Occasionally, footsteps in the hall woke me after the sun set, and Eldrin's and Siliana's familiar muffled voices carried through my door. Or was I just dreaming, pretending that they were there and watching over me, that I wasn't as alone in this place as I felt? Or was I truly alone? Despite what Siliana told me, I knew better than to believe that I was safe. Despite how I wanted nothing more than to cling to Eldrin and Siliana for safety, who knew if they could even protect me from the king?

While I slept, with the city's haunting music reaching into my dreams, I dreamt of a familiar shape in the shadows, and of silver hair and eyes that stayed with me in the dark.

"How are you feeling?" Siliana asked me when I woke, and I rolled over to find her sitting next to my bed. Dawn streamed through the windows, illuminating a carving of a golden skull hanging on the wall. The music from the night before was gone, replaced with the chirps of small birds. A cool breeze worked its way through the open windows, carrying with it the fresh taste of fall. The chilly air prickled my skin, and I wrapped the blankets tighter around myself.

"Fine," I said, groaning as I pushed myself upright. My head still hurt, my arm was stiff under the padded bandage, and I still felt that odd weight in my veins, but other than that I felt fine. Physically, that was. Mentally, I was still as tangled as Phoebe's latest attempt at crochet, but that was another matter.

"Good. Eldrin is going to take you through the city after breakfast," she said. "And tonight, you will meet the king."

"Why...not you? Can't you take me?"

Siliana gave me a kind smile, reminding me of a statue of a saint. "I would, but our king has ordered otherwise. Eldrin is responsible for your care over the next month. And for helping you become acclimated to living amongst our people."

"But the king is the one who wants to marry me..." I frowned. "Wait, why Eldrin?"

"Is that a problem?"

"No, but I'm confused." I was hardly going to complain about having to spend time with a handsome elf, if I was forced to be around one, but Eldrin had barely spoken to me. Eldrin was also the one who had brought me here. Eldrin was *also* the one who made me have such complicated feelings. I had lots of reason to wonder why it was Eldrin.

"Eldrin knows the king best so he can help you learn about Vanir, and he is in a unique position to look after you," Siliana said, though her tone made me wonder what she wasn't saying. Especially since her knowing gaze told me she had a lot to say. People in this forest needed to start speaking plainly, or I was going to lose my patience soon.

"I...see."

"Dress." She motioned to a chair that had a long green dress draped over it, along with a silky shift that I remembered from a video on historical clothing that was meant to be some sort of underwear. "Eat. Food will be brought to you in a moment. When you are done, Eldrin will be waiting for you at the bottom of the stairs. Go straight down the hall to the left and you will find them." After a few more pleasant platitudes and reassurances, she left the room, and thus I had to figure out how to tie on the elf robes on my own. She did offer to stay and help me, but I didn't feel like having company. I needed a chance to ground myself before I explored this new world. I needed the normalcy of dressing myself.

I ate the bread with butter and fresh apple slices that was sent to me, along with a glass of some sort of juice I can only describe as "zesty." When I was done, I left my room for the first time since arriving, trying to still my racing heart as I walked past elves who happened to be passing through the hall. They all paused and turned as I walked by. Apparently, red heads weren't common here. I stood out, especially since I was vertically challenged compared to them and had ears as sharp as a basketball. But no one stopped me. No one bothered to say anything to me. But they definitely stared, and the stares weren't welcoming.

I crept down the stone stairs, grasping the railing to avoid stepping on acorns and wet leaves and thus slipping to my untimely demise, but I managed. And then, once I was halfway down, I saw *him*.

Eldrin waited at the base of the steps, hands clasped in front of him, his posture as straight and unyielding as the trees around us. Unlike the conservative tunic he wore yesterday, today he was wearing brown breeches with black knee-high boots, and a gray linen shirt that was open at the top, showing just enough skin to catch my interest. My breath caught in my throat. What would it be like to rub my hands over those muscles, to be gripped by those gloved hands? Who cared that one hand was skeletal when the rest of him looked like *that*?

And then there was me, trying very hard not slip and highlight just how un-graceful I was. I wasn't particularly klutzy, but compared to elves, everyone was.

He raised an eyebrow expectantly when he saw me, and I decided I had to say *something* to him. Something that did not involve discussing his muscles.

"Are we going to battle?" I asked once I reached the ground, nodding towards the knives he wore strapped to his sides.

"Not intentionally."

"Then what's with the weapons?"

"The veinwart is not the only thing that lives in these woods."

"Ah. Yeah, I guess knives would be better than a Stabby Tabby."

"A what?"

"Never mind."

He began walking down the leaf-strewn path, which was lined with young saplings, gesturing for me to follow. He didn't have to tell me twice. What else was I going to do—let him wander off and leave me?

With little else to do during our walk, I focused on the scenery, especially since I didn't want to be rude and stare at him. He slowed his pace, allowing me to catch up with him, and we walked side by side, allowing me to take in the sights of things that were definitely not from our world.

The palace we left appeared to be a massive network of buildings, made of bleached/whitewashed wood facades carved into delicate poles, like long apartments winding through the forest. The effect was as if the birch trees themselves bowed down and formed themselves into houses for the Woods' people. While the palace had a foundation and lower levels made of hewn stone, that was not the case for most of these smaller buildings, which, as far as I could tell, eschewed metal and stone entirely.

"What are these buildings?" I asked.

Eldrin glanced at what I was gesturing towards and said, "Homes, for the most part. For people who are not well-connected enough to reside inside the palace, or who want more space than it can provide. We will see more modest dwellings the farther we go."

"And what about those that are not homes?"

"Storehouses, and a few specialty businesses." I should've guessed that people lived in these buildings. Elves of all ages went about their lives around us and ignoring us. At least, they pretended to.

A few minutes' walk took us to a change in the city's layout, and some buildings now stood alone, away from the bases of massive trees. Now there were also some that rose above the tree-tops and were wrapped around the trees and in their branches, their spires as white and delicate as the accents in the room that I recovered in. I gasped. I had seen nothing like this before, a city that embraced the forest like a treasured lover, one that was somehow both ancient with wear and pristine at the same time.

"More houses?" I asked, gesturing above us.

"Yes. Some elves prefer the heights, and the trees in this part of the forest can support it." He was right—some of the trees here had trunks as thick as a single-family home. Not all of the trees, of course, but enough that they were a regular sight through this city.

"How old are the trees?"

"Thousands of years," he said. "That one" –he pointed at a towering trunk near the palace behind us– "was planted by my fifth great grandfather. And we are a long-lived race."

"I see." I did not see. I couldn't imagine the passage of time that was necessary for a single seed to turn into something so monstrous.

We strode along a dark red cobblestone road, the stones worn from years of travel, and our own footsteps were lost among those of the other pedestrians who were going about their day. Each step took us further into a bustling market, though the atmosphere was still eerily refined, like each being was gliding through life as opposed to rushing through it, oblivious to anything but their ultimate goal.

It was strange to see elves doing things as ordinary as carrying food, talking to companions, and shopping at stalls. Yes, there were now lots of stalls selling everything from fall vegetables and pungent herbs, to rolls of brilliant fabrics, to weapons, and even things that looked suspiciously like dehydrated squirrels. I couldn't figure out whether to focus on the wares—or the elves. Their movements were something other, fluid and measured, their expressions carrying the weight of years that humans almost never saw. Yet, here they were, living lives, guiding children, assisting the elderly, and working and tending to the million necessities of life. A child lost their ball as it rolled under a stall, and the nearby adults stopped their tasks to retrieve it and hand it back to the jubilant boy. A young male elf offered to help an elderly woman carry her package. These small gestures, the bits I happened to see, were so...human. Well, when humanity was at its best. I had always pictured the elves as sitting in their woods, working dark magic and lounging, with their meals appearing and disappearing with a wave of a wand. I blamed them for delighting in ruining my world. This was nothing like I expected.

But I couldn't let myself forget that I was a stranger here, that I was not one of them, and that there were threads between the people involved that I didn't understand. As we passed other elves, their eyes raked up and down my body, their faces unreadable. Once in a while they turned and muttered something to a companion, or gestured at us. Their eyes said everything—it didn't take a mind reader to guess that they were wondering what we were doing and who I was. More than one fierce scowl was directed at me, and even more at Eldrin, but I looked away every time. Eldrin never strayed more than three steps away from me, his hands near his weapons.

"Ignore them," he said softly. "You are safe."

"Am I upsetting them?" Did they hate that I was here?

"Everything upsets them. But we should not talk about this here."

I knew already from the news that there were humans in the world that the Darkening Woods originally came from, but I didn't see a single human in this city. Were humans allowed here, back in their world? Or was I the first? Either answer left me uneasy. If there were humans here before and now they were gone, something happened to make them leave. And if I was the first, there was no telling what the elves could or wanted to do to me.

"I'm surprised it's already fall here," I said, desperate to break the silence with something other than crunching leaves. Though, it was nice how people gave us a wide berth because of him. A lot of the elves seemed to know him, which didn't surprise me—he knew and served the king. I needed information, anything he would tell me, and the fact that he had saved my life told me I could trust him a little—more than the others here, at any rate.

"It's always autumn," Eldrin said. "This is the Darkening Woods."

"But how...? Don't the leaves need to be green at some point?"

Eldrin shook his head slowly. "No. Not here. Once these leaves are done, the trees will bud golden leaves, and the cycle begins again. And our crops aren't tied to the season as strictly as the trees, but we grow what thrives in cooler weather. Back home we would also trade with peoples outside of the Woods, who lived in warmer climes, for our other needs. Death feeds our magic and our life, and in exchange we always live right at its edges. Including with this." He raised his left hand, the one that was skeletal. How far did the skeleton part go?

"I...see."

Again, I did not see.

"So, why don't you interact with the other humans, or try? I mean, it would make the barrier less of an issue. You wouldn't need it."

He paused, seemingly choosing his words. "There is a chance that this realm will return to where it belongs. If it does, we all want to be here. And we don't want others coming with. At least, not without an invitation."

"It *can*?"

"Possibly. It's happened before."

"It has?"

Eldrin turned to look at me, his silver eyes lit with amusement. "Surely, you've heard rumors of cities and peoples appearing, some disappearing. This is the way of worlds. In their way, they are living creatures. Nothing is stationary." I thought of missing things, some real, some little more legends, with such a presence in lore that it was suspected that they had some basis in fact. Atlantis. Roanoke. Avalon. The Lost Army of the Cambyses. Not to mention so many individuals who had mysteriously disappeared without a sign and had spawned a plethora of late-night cable TV specials. Did all of those mysteries stem from the worlds fluctuating? And did that mean there was a chance that everyone who was lost would come back?

"When could it happen?" I asked excitedly. "This can all be undone? Really? How long does it take?"

Eldrin gave me a long glance, and I tried not to fidget under his gaze. He turned forward again before he answered. "That we cannot know, and we desperately wish we had the answer. So many traveled from our world this time, in so many differently sized pieces. The ones who arrived on tiny parcels, their lands may have already shifted back and no one would have noticed." That I knew—some creatures had arrived in our world with little more than the ground they had been standing on.

I stepped along the road, which was slowly becoming more rugged, careful not to get dirt on my gown's skirts. I couldn't decide what was harder to wrap my head around—the conversation, or the gorgeous city. Granted, I hadn't asked anything *too* prodding, but Eldrin seemed willing to answer my questions, which was promising. My eyes drifted to a group of elderly elves, who were using their tall sticks to balance, their movements so smooth and practiced that it seemed like the sticks were a mere formality.

And here I was, trying not to trip on my skirts.

"I didn't know elves had children," I said, watching two boys with the signature pointed ears play with a leather ball.

"Of course," Eldrin said. "Did you think we always existed?"

"I thought maybe you sprouted from mushrooms. You're all so pale and waxy."

Eldrin slowly turned to look at me, so serious that I couldn't help but chuckle. "I'm kidding. But I am surprised to see them here. There aren't too many legends about elves having their own children, and it seems like they always struggle to reproduce in stories." A corner of Eldrin's mouth quirked up. Alright—he found me slightly amusing. That was also promising.

"I assure you, we have no issues with having the children we desire to have. We are currently in our capital city, Great Glen. Families will live in the cities, and very rarely anywhere else—parts of the Darkening Woods are not safe for children."

"Great...Glen?" I asked, frowning. "That's a name that's to the point. Shouldn't it be something like 'Greenfalafaliel?'"

"When the worlds merged, our language was lost," Eldrin said. "We took on your tongue and lost everything else. It seems all we retained in our original tongue are our names."

"Oh. How?"

"We do not know."

Silence descended between us, noticeable, yet not entirely unwelcome. I didn't think this would be a good time to offer that there were lots of legends about fairies and the magic in their names, since he likely knew all that and more besides.

Though we had walked several city blocks at least, tree roots the size of cars still lined the road, and buildings were

wedged around the massive trees, many of them still lurking high above the ground. Everything was cased in autumn, from the leaves falling around us, to the floral motifs
decorating the buildings' fascia. Everywhere I looked were
more leaves, acorns, fall flowers...and lots of bones. Once in
awhile, what appeared to be real bones were used in the
motifs, along with the expected carvings and paintings.

Despite the many people we had passed, their reactions
were still much the same—awe, curiosity, and revulsion.
In short, that hadn't changed. Though now their dress was
becoming simpler. We had obviously progressed to a less
wealthy part of the city, where garments were made of plain,
solid fabric and less embroidery, while shoes were crafted of
sturdy leather. A group of guards paused their conversation
as we passed, their heads rotating to mark our path. I swallowed. Hard. They weren't exactly hostile, but there were no
smiles.

"Do not fear them," Eldrin said quietly, repeating his earlier assurances. "They will not harm you. I will not let them."

"Do they want to?" I asked softly, ignoring the forbidden
trill of pleasure that worked through me at the idea of him
protecting me.

"No," he said, but he paused a little too long before saying
so. "This change has been difficult for everyone, and they will
wonder what your arrival means. Our people were indifferent to humans, before. They only rarely passed our borders.
And soon, everyone here will realize that you're the one who

is going to save us. Word will spread, and then they will greet you as their future queen."

Queen. That was right—at least one of them wanted me as a *queen*. My attention roamed to the elf at my side, the one matching his steps with mine so as not to leave me behind. Who was he? Why was he doing the king's bidding? What were they not telling me? There was the sense that much was still unsaid. For elves who were allegedly indifferent, their gazes told a different story. And worse, I needed that potion from the king. Yes, staying here was worth my life, but was there no other option than marriage? How did one turn down a marriage proposal and not anger a royal?

"Remember that my task is to make you as pleased about this as possible, so that your joining with the barrier will be true," Eldrin said. "And for that, we need to leave the city."

"Leave?" a male voice asked lightly from behind us.

We turned to find a young elf with night-black hair, who was around a half-head shorter than Eldrin. This one was dressed in a simple tunic and breeches and boots, and a healed cut on his cheek shone a brilliant white against his already pale skin. Simple clothing, yes, but everything was well made and clean—whoever he was, he had means.

"Oristan," Eldrin said, seemingly unconcerned at our new companion.

"That's it?" Oristan said, scanning me. "You have the most notorious guest in your care, and that's it?"

"I do. And yes." Eldrin glowered. I tried not to cross my arms and betray how uncomfortable I was, but I took a step closer to Eldrin out of reflex. Eldrin had saved me once, apparently at a cost to himself. He wouldn't let anything happen now. I hoped.

Oristan grinned, by far the friendliest reaction I received all morning. "Aren't you going to introduce me? Your favorite friend in the whole world?"

"You already did."

Oristan scoffed. "You used to be fun, remember? Human, did you know that he used to be fun?"

"No, this human didn't," I said. "My name is Amber."

"Ah, Amber. A delight to meet you." Oristan did a dramatic bow while Eldrin glared.

"There's a reason," Eldrin said sternly.

"Yes, yes. Reasons, so many reasons for being the most depressing elf in the Woods. Maybe come up with a new one?"

"Maybe you should come up with a new place to be."

"Oh, don't worry, I'm late for meeting Father. But I couldn't exactly resist the chance to say hello, could I?" Oristan winked at me, and then turned and waved goodbye. "Best of luck, Amber! See if you can get something resembling a normal reaction out of this one. It would be more than we've managed lately. It would be good for him. Bye, *Your Highness*!"

I bit back a smile, liking Oristan already. He seemed to goad Eldrin and show a new side of him, one that wasn't the stoic elf warrior guiding me through an unfriendly city.

The two of us watched Oristan walk away, until Eldrin placed a hand on my arm, guiding me along the road once more. His touch was light, but it felt heavy, in the way that it made every nerve sing. Wait, did Oristan say "highness"? I tried not to stare at the elf next to me. A member of elven royalty was my guard? Why?

I felt like Oristan was trying to tell me a few things with his little encounter, and yet he only gave me more questions.

And was it my imagination, or was Eldrin looking at me as much as I was stealing glances at him?

"Who was that?" I finally asked.

"That was Oristan," Eldrin said. "An old friend."

"He seems to like you."

"Yes. He can often be a fool." That last sentence was said in such a way that it didn't invite further conversation. Eldrin obviously had some backstory, and between being a "highness" and the sneaky looks Eldrin and Siliana gave each other when discussing the king, it was obvious that there was a lot more involved in this than I had initially thought.

But where did I fit in?

Great Glen was larger than I expected, though in human terms it didn't take up much space at all, maybe that of a small town. Probably because, unlike human towns in the

Midwest, the elves didn't hesitate to build up. Way up. And few of the roads were straight.

After around a half hour of walking we reached a place where there was more space between dwellings, and then suddenly we were in the woods, without a building in sight. As far as I could see, maples, oaks, and long-leafed trees I didn't recognize—like willows, but a brilliant red—filled the forest. The weather was temperate, enough that I was comfortable in the light layers, but the air warned that a bite of cold would come at night.

"Are all the lands in your world like this?" I asked. "Seasonal, I mean."

"No," Eldrin said. "This is our magic, our bond. Other lands have their own rules, and their own surroundings."

"Oh? Like what?"

Was that another hint of a smile? "The angels live in winter, in a place where they fly amongst the ash." That I knew—there was a very vertical angel mountain in New Jersey that was so hostile that they didn't need a barrier—the place's natural winds and ash clouds worked as one all on its own.

"So, they are like Christmas angels?" I asked. When Eldrin raised an eyebrow, I explained, "Like, wise servants of god that are often depicted as musical or as babies with trumpets."

"Only if those angels brand themselves with runes and drank blood, even that of their fellow angels." Nope, not even biblically accurate angels did that.

"Have you met these angels?"

"No," Eldrin adjusted his hair so that it curved behind his pointed ear. "While they are far more open to other races than we are, we haven't had the best relations. And they lived rather far away from us."

"I'll consider myself lucky, then, that they are far away still," I said. Nothing about branding or blood drinking sounded pleasant. "Besides, I like fall. Do you have pumpkin spice?"

"We have pumpkins."

"...Alright. That's better than nothing. I think." Pumpkin spice and autumn went together like cat hair and black dress pants. I wasn't about to miss out on the glorious combination, that delightful melody of human tradition and ingenuity in beverage form. I was going to do whatever it took to be able to enjoy it here.

Enjoy it here.

There I was, already resigning myself to staying here forever. Damn, that spider bite was really getting to me, and in more ways than just the heavy feeling that now resided in my blood.

"Where are you taking me?" I asked. "They're just letting us leave?"

"This is my home. *Our* home," he corrected. "And I have been tasked with making you desire to stay. You will never have that experience in your room, so I thought I would show you some of the beautiful areas of the Woods."

"The entire place is beautiful." And it was. Unlike the human woods, these trees and earth seemed to hum with something bright, something that made it sing and rejoice in just being. No matter that it belonged to *them*. No matter that every bit of it was edged with death.

Eldrin smiled, obviously pleased. "I'm glad you think so. But there is more to come."

CHAPTER NINE

ELDRIN

I had to stop looking at her, trying to use a mere glance to learn everything that I could. I told myself that I was looking only because I was tasked with watching her—with protecting her—but I couldn't stop my eyes from drifting towards her, like a bloom seeking the sun. The graceful slope of her neck and shoulders. The way her dress hugged her curves. The way her eyes lit up with the wonder of everything before her. The way her lips quirked, showing every emotion. How, despite the danger, despite everything that had happened, she was going to seize what enjoyment she could.

And my first impression wasn't wrong—she missed little, even if she didn't say much. She asked questions and seemed excellent at reading between the lines, the things I left unsaid. I could tell she wanted to ask me more from the way she watched me expectantly after I spoke. However, she didn't ask further questions if I didn't immediately offer a full answer. Knowing when to speak was a necessity for surviving at court. A spark of hope lit in my core that perhaps this human would manage to survive here, if she already showed such wisdom so soon.

But for her to survive, she first had to *want* to stay here in the Darkening Woods, and thus far, she was pleased with what she saw. That was good. I was doing my task. I chose not to see the fear that clouded her expression when she thought I wasn't looking. The way she stayed closer to me than necessary when we passed those who were not as circumspect with their gazes. I was going to do everything I could to make that fear disappear, but that would take time. To start, I was going to take her to a place whose beauty was impossible to resist. For that, there was only one place to take her—the Chain of Lakes. Again, that likely sounded better in our original tongue.

The northernmost part of the lakes was only around an hour's walk from the city and down a gentle slope, the forest's distant haunting melody singing in my ears while we traveled. The journey was a series of abrupt transitions, in the city one moment and then the forest the next, and it felt like but an instant before we came to the crystalline waters. At least, the journey felt short to me. Our speed was not an accident—I knew the paths to get to these lakes better than most, and the way to take that would be the easiest for Amber to manage. This was not the only road—there was also a way for braver elves to dart through the tree branches to the lakes, their feet never touching the ground, but I was not about to suggest such an impossible path to her. It would've been a waste of time for us both.

The Chain was a series of six lakes and many more ponds and marshes, but the largest was impossible for most mortals to swim across. Even elves struggled, though occasionally some tried and succeeded. We were not alone at the lakes—this one in particular was never completely isolated—but the other visitors would stay in the areas known for their pebbly beaches and wide spaces for families to play and relax. I knew these waters, and I knew which lagoons would be deserted. And while I knew of other locations that most would struggle to find, I wasn't about to take Amber any place truly private. Not while I had something to test first.

"This is gorgeous," she said, sitting on a massive rock and looking over the lake's water. The surface rippled in the wind, sending waves of brilliant blues and greens that reflected in the sun. As she watched, her green skirts were splayed out around her, resting over the tall grasses. "Are there a lot of lakes here?"

"There's more, but this is not a watery land." I stood next to her, arms crossed, my eyes searching for any sign of life, and ignoring dozens of animals in doing so. Considering everything that had happened to her over the last couple of days, Amber was remarkably self-assured. Was she in shock? It was possible. The venom would make its presence known sooner or later in a way that she couldn't ignore—if it hadn't already—but that day was not today. I told Amber that I wouldn't let anyone hurt her, but I was painfully helpless against the venom, which was the biggest threat of all. Not to mention Vanir.

"Eldrin," Amber said softly, her hands clasped on her lap, "since it seems like we're alone, will you answer a few questions I have? About...everything."

"Of course," I said. And I would. We were finally away from ears, and she had to have a lot of questions, ones that I couldn't safely answer in the city. As far as I could tell, there was no one close enough to hear. And it was going to stay that way.

"You're a prince."

Damn. She didn't hesitate in addressing poignant issues. "I am," I said. There was no point in denying it.

"So, the king, Vanir, is your...father?"

"Brother." As much as I wanted to talk about anything else other than him, I decided I may as well tell her the truth now—she would hear the stories herself eventually. And possibly much worse that wasn't true. "Vanir is my younger brother," I explained. "We have different mothers." Both of our mothers were still alive and mine was the only one who was queen, but my father's romantic betrayal didn't seem to be an issue to discuss at this point. "The fact that our father was king was enough for Vanir to be a contender for the throne—the throne passes through the hereditary royal, and the position of their spouse is largely irrelevant."

"Younger? And a contender?" She frowned. "Do elves have a different pattern for succession? Because in the mortal world, the crown would go to the eldest. Usually."

"It is the same for us," I said begrudgingly. May as well tell her my greatest shame, and accept being lessened in her eyes. "I am the oldest, and I was the original heir. My brother took my place."

"Oh," was all she said. But her clenched fists and rigid posture told a different tale. "But you're here. With me. How...sorry, in our history, most humans didn't like possible challengers to the throne to be so close to them. Lots of royal siblings met untimely, suspicious deaths."

"Again, it is the same here." I looked away. I could not bear to see her reaction to what I would say next. "My brother challenged me for the throne upon our father's death, as is common amongst our kind. The rules of succession are often suggestions. And I let him have it."

"Why?"

Why? That was a question I asked myself every day. And I often gave myself different answers, many of which danced around the truth. "Our lands were never at peace, even back in our original home. Vanir, for all his faults, is better suited for warfare. He is more ruthless."

"War? But you're here. What war is there?"

"There's always war waiting for our kind. Give it time," I said. "Once the peoples settle into their home here, they will remember the old feuds and find a way to bring them to life once more, this time with the humans choosing sides." I sighed, catching the worried expression on her face, the wide eyes that locked with mine. "No, Amber. We never wanted to harm the humans here. Instead, we were afraid that they would bring war to us."

Amber nodded, biting her lip. "Alright. So, Vanir is king, and you were the original heir. And he just...is keeping you around? That's awfully confident of him, from the impression I'm getting."

Hardly. "The change of the worlds interrupted things," I said, resisting the urge to pick at my sleeves, a nervous habit of mine. "It was deemed more practical to keep me alive. And near him."

"Practical?"

"I have my own allies, such as they are, including those who never respected Vanir. With the Woods in chaos, the last thing Vanir needs now is angering the elven who still support me, not when our resources are stretched so far. We need to stay united." It was a situation that vexed him daily, most likely.

What was she thinking? It was impossible to say, since she was staring off at the distance. Good. Yet another sign that she thought before she spoke and acted. She would have a chance here if she managed to maintain this circumspection.

As much as I was tempted, I didn't let myself consider what she thought of me. To admit to her that I had given up the crown...it pained me. Did she think me lesser for that? Could I let myself care what she thought about me? No.

"Do elves often marry mortal women?" she asked, deftly changing the subject. "Based on today, I would have to guess that they don't. Isn't there an elven match for the king that would be better? One that is not...me?"

She echoed my earlier protest to Vanir, and I had to find a way to answer her that couldn't come back and hurt me. "It's not unheard of," I said, "but it is rare." Once. It happened once that I knew of. "And I'll be honest—I am surprised that he made marriage part of his offer to you. I'm assuming he wants to entice you into completing the bond with the barrier, and maybe he thought that the idea of being a queen would be enough to do it."

"Because who wouldn't want to be queen?" she asked sarcastically.

"That is the idea," I said, biting back a grin.

She scoffed and shook her head. Again, I was struck by the intensity of her gaze, how she was seemingly searching for answers without a single word. She was truly stunning, in a way the elves could never be. Elves were like the trees, proud, graceful, and unchanging. She was like the wind, which moved and adapted and took in everything the world had to offer. Her brilliant green eyes often met mine, making my heart leap into my mouth. Her hair complimented the surrounding leaves, both of them a vibrant red that demanded attention. None of the humans I had met before had ever made me want to take a second look. None of them were her.

"I've never met him," she said. "And he expects me to want to marry him."

"You will meet him tonight."

"Will you be there?" She cocked her head.

I hesitated. Did she want me there?

"Yes," I finally said. A warm heat worked its way through me at her smile, how her posture relaxed. Yes, I would be there. I was not about to leave her to face an elven court alone. They would be polite enough to her on the surface, as long as Vanir insisted on her being treated with respect, but I knew better than anyone that manners could be used to hide cruelty. And this woman, who was primed to steal away the most eligible man in the kingdom, would attract an endless number of barbs. If not worse.

"What if I don't want to marry him?" she asked. "What if I don't like him?"

Inside, I groaned, though outwardly I stayed calm and offered her the best advice I could. "I suggest giving the idea of marriage some time before voicing any such thoughts. Vanir is a proud man. It is possible he may change his mind himself regarding marriage, if the two of you find yourselves unsuited. He can be fickle with his favor. But it is best not to anger him right away."

Amber nodded, wringing her hands.

A figure shifted in the distance, a shadow that flickered between the thick trees. Another elf, watching us, unmoving.

I stiffened, my hands hovering over my daggers. Would Vanir attack me here and claim that the human did it? Would he kill us both and blame it on the monsters that lived in these woods?

The movement caught Amber's attention, and she quickly found our visitor. We both stared, waiting. For long moments the elf stood there, his focus never leaving us. What was he looking for? The fact that he stayed there long enough for even Amber to notice meant that he wanted to be seen. Vanir *wanted* us to know that he was there.

And then the elven intruder was gone with a blink, leaving nothing more than the memory of a shadow. Out of some unspoken instinct, I wanted to comfort Amber, hold her in my arms and destroy anything that came near. For she was afraid. She trembled, her hands clenched at her sides, her teeth worrying at her lip. Painfully, I banished a budding treasonous thought, even as I stepped closer to her. Even if—*if*—such a thing as her and I could be, I had nothing to offer her. A life with me would be nothing but danger and regret.

"Who was that?" she whispered.

"*That* is why we have to be careful," I said. "Whatever happens, no matter what you want to say or do, never assume that we are alone."

CHAPTER TEN

AMBER

W ell, I really did it. Phoebe was right—I seriously should have settled for a lawyer.

Somehow, I not only ended up essentially being held hostage in a death-obsessed elven forest, I had also apparently ended up shoved between the king and his brother—who arguably should have been king. While I knew nothing about elven politics, as far as I was concerned, Eldrin had one massive advantage over the king—he had actually spent time with me. Unlike my future husband.

And to make things worse, I couldn't stop thinking about Eldrin.

Oh, this was going to be a spicy pickle to get out of.

For the rest of the afternoon, as I settled for a late lunch in my rooms and prepared for the impending, important evening audience, I did my best not to think about Eldrin's other advantages. The strong and elegant way he moved. The angle of his jaw and cheeks. The way he stared at me when I spoke, listening to everything I said. *Really* listening. The way I thought he moved closer to me when that elf snuck up on us, startling me and reminding me again that I was not safe in these woods, even if Eldrin's warnings weren't enough.

Nope, I didn't think of Eldrin's advantages at all.

At least the political debates distracted me from the fact that I was essentially in a gorgeous prison, the intricate carvings of my room's windows and doors walking that fine balance between beauty and death. Based on the conversations Eldrin and I had on our way back to the palace, death was the consequence of their magic, and how these elves managed to obtain their long lives. Thus, their eventual mortality would be at the forefront of their minds, even fused to their bodies. Any elven child of the Darkening Woods was born with the reminder of the bargain their ancestors had struck in the form of their skeletal non-dominant hand.

"Are you in pain?" Siliana asked me, looking at my shoulder as she stood near me in my bedroom. Another long green dress was draped over her arms, which I assumed had something to do with the royal audience tonight. Though, the dress was essentially a shrub attached to skirts, and I had no idea what it was meant for. "The veinwart is known for providing painful bites."

"I thought it didn't harm elves."

"The poison doesn't harm us to this extent," Siliana corrected. "That doesn't mean its fangs hurt any less."

Siliana was obviously waiting for me to answer her question. "It's not bad," I assured her. "I'd let you know if it was worse." The pain really wasn't bad. The sting from bite itself was dulling, to the point I was mystified at how it had managed to heal so quickly. However, the eerie weight that seemed to have settled in my chest was another matter, matched with the chill that constantly worked its way under my skin. However I felt otherwise, no matter how well the bite healed, I was not cured. And I wouldn't be unless I did what they wanted.

Siliana took a deep breath, as if she was restraining herself from saying something she'd reget, and then said, "Let me know if the pain becomes worse. We have remedies that will help."

"I will. Thank you."

She looked down at the garment she was holding and then back at me. Again, I was struck by the aching beauty of her features, the way she seemed to be a statue come to life. That was not an uncommon feature among the elves, but Siliana seemed painfully beautiful, even for them. "I am sorry, Amber," she whispered. "You did not choose this, and I do not fault you for not trusting us."

"What? Of course—"

She shook her head abruptly, cutting me off. "I can tell. I haven't lived this long without being able to understand what people leave unsaid. And you're wise, for not trusting us. I am sorry, Amber. We do need you for the barrier, but I wish it was someone who *wanted* to be here, someone who had a choice. And...I'm sorry that you're becoming embroiled in whatever Vanir is plotting for Eldrin."

"What do you mean?" My brow furrowed. Eldrin spoke some about their arrangement, but he didn't make it sound like Vanir still wanted to harm him. At least, not immediately.

"I've said too much." She took a deep breath. "The only other thing I will do is caution you to watch. Listen. I know you have no reason to trust me, but trust your instincts. When you meet the king—not to mention the rest of the court—you will understand what I mean."

I nodded in acknowledgement when I realized Siliana really wouldn't say more on the subject. What was going to happen tonight? What did she think that the king, or someone else, was going to do to me? At least Eldrin would be there, and I wouldn't be entirely alone.

Matter apparently settled, Siliana moved as if awakening from a dream and went back to the task at hand—preparing me for meeting the king. "I hope you don't mind," she said, "but I selected a garment for you to wear tonight. If you don't like it, I can find something else." She held out the dress towards me, like she wanted me to take it.

"What? No. Wait, *that* is my *dress*?" It didn't quite occur to me until that moment that she absolutely intended for me to wear the "garment" that was on her arms. A garment I had hoped was for a statue.

"Of course." She pursed her lips and chose that moment to drop the skirts to the ground, revealing the garment in its entirety. "I can choose something—"

"No. I just" –I shook my head– "I cannot believe that's for me. It's wonderful."

I never saw another dress like it, to the point that I thought it was either a prop or something for an effigy when Siliana brought it in. Surely, such a creation couldn't be meant for me.

The dress was made of dark green silk, long enough that the hem would surely touch the floor. Its neckline was cut in a square, low enough that my shoulders and chest would be rather bare. The bite from the veinwart would be visible on my shoulder, but that was no matter. Siliana told me they had ointments that would smooth its appearance if I wished to use them. And it was hardly like my bite was a secret at this court.

But that wasn't the amazing part—the dress's sleeves and neckline trim were made of a thick edging consisting of yellow flowers and green and red vines—real ones—hovering over the top, much like a thick fur. I was going to be wearing autumn itself to this audience.

"How are they intact?" I asked, pointing at the flowers. It was impossible that something crafted from living materials would be able to be constantly handled in such a manner, and it was especially impossible that they appeared so fresh.

"We have skilled craftsmen," Siliana said, motioning to me to turn around. "Preserving life, staving off the appearance of death, that is something that our magic is meant for." Still in awe, I did as she bid, unlacing my dress while I faced away. She had warned me earlier that I would need her help getting into tonight's dress, and it appeared that she didn't exaggerate. Thus, I would have to get over my initial shyness.

When the first touches of the cold silk hit my skin, I thought that, no matter what else I faced, I was well dressed tonight.

Hours later, after my hair was loosely styled, makeup applied, and that garment somehow placed around my body while remaining intact, I walked down the halls to where the king waited. Siliana did not come with me—she warned that this part I'd have to do alone. She had royal favor and was welcome to attend, but she said that this part would earn me more respect if I did it without her at my side. I suspected there were other reasons she wasn't going to attend—perhaps she just didn't want to. Lucky.

Alone, I trudged through the halls—those forbidding halls—where nature and death were displayed hand in hand, vines and leaves as much as part of the art as skulls. A monument to the fact that all beauty, even that of the long-lived elves, was fleeting.

I took the directed turns, and far too soon I came to the audience hall, where dozens, if not hundreds, of elves gathered together for the event. Hundreds, if not thousands of eyes turned to stare at me when I walked in.

I refused to wipe my sweating palms on the dress and instead focused on what was around me, namely, the spectacles that were the other elves' outfits. I wasn't the only one whose clothing took the word "natural" to extremes—some women wore dresses and skirts made with branches and fronds and nothing else. Others wore fabric seemingly crafted out of bright red leaves. One man wore a cloak edged with birch bark. All of this was seen in addition to the draping garments that were similar in cut and cloth to what I saw in the city with Eldrin. The court had its share of brocades, silks, and velvets, yes—and it also had so much more.

Eldrin. Where was he? He said he was going to come with me. He said he was going to be here. No such luck—I was still very alone.

Siliana told me that elves saved these types of garments for special occasions, which made sense. It would be hard to chop wood while wearing sticks. She also told me that the clothing could be even more dramatic, depending on the occasion. I had a hard time believing that it could be more than *this*.

I tried not to look at the parts of anyone that reinforced how I was the only human in this land. That was impossible—I was the only one in the hall who didn't have pointed ears. I was by far the shortest, other than those who were obviously children. And more, every single one of the elves had a skeletal hand, a mark of their deal with death. Not that I needed reminding of that fact—as I traveled, the halls became even more grisly, carved with skulls, bones, ravens, and gargoyles. Gargoyles? Were they real too? Sigh. Probably. I heard rumors of them appearing in North Carolina, but there were so many rumors, so many pockets and creatures pressed upon our world, that it was impossible to tell fact from fiction most of the time.

When I stepped into the throne room, which was packed with elven nobility and enough pine boughs to open a pop-up holiday store on a Manhattan corner, I gasped. The hall's architecture reminded me more of a cathedral than a palace, with its rising walls, balconies, and columns. Everything was done in the soft, swirling accents and forms that permeated the rest of the place. Except these accents and forms came with what could only be very real bones. Skulls, femurs, ribs, teeth, and more—all of them were used to decorate the walls, ceiling, and occasionally the floor. Three massive chandeliers hung from the ceiling, the candles shining through what were likely ribs arranged in a starburst pattern.

I took a deep breath. And another. And another. I wanted to ask Siliana about the bones I had seen in other parts of the palace. Were they real? I was afraid of the answer. Eldrin had warned me that I needed to keep my composure, that

I couldn't let anyone see that I was afraid. I would listen. Fear was weakness, and weakness invited predators, of all sorts. Thus, I would assume the worst so that I wouldn't be surprised later—until I was told otherwise, I'd believe that these were the bones of humans who had angered the king.

Even after the initial moments passed, everyone was still staring at me. Everyone. Every move I made, every single movement, was watched like a hawk hunting its prey. And based on the sneers and eye rolls, few liked what they saw. Tears welled in my eyes. This was too much. I couldn't do this.

The crowd rustled around me, and suddenly Eldrin appeared, bringing with him a steadying presence. I could breathe. Relax. Think. That is, before I really saw him.

Eldrin was dressed as fine as any of the nobles. His breeches were tight against his muscular thighs, giving me too much of a chance to admire what was hidden underneath. His green doublet was decorated with black gems and seemed to be embroidered with black feathers, and it carried some of the vines that were similar to what was on my own dress. A doublet that probably hid a sculpted core that was as strong as his legs. An unexpected heat worked through me, a desire to see and admire everything. Some of the elven men wore long draping open robes that revealed a long surcoat, but not Eldrin. What he wore, despite the layers, somehow left little to the imagination.

I swallowed. Hard. And remembered that we were far from alone here in this calcium-dense monument.

But he was here, with me. He was here. I could breathe.

He could help me.

"You look well," Eldrin said formally, his posture rigid. He frowned at the bite on my shoulder, which Siliana's cosmetics failed to cover perfectly.

"You...too."

Long moments passed. Was I supposed to say something? Damn, I had no idea what I was supposed to say.

"Would you like to meet the king now?" he asked.

"He's already here?" I looked around, seeing no one particularly distinctive in a sea of elves. Shouldn't people be prostrating themselves or something if there was a king?

"Yes. He is on his throne, receiving guests."

"Alright." I shook myself. "Yes. I should meet him." This wasn't going to get any better the longer I waited. And from Eldrin's nod, he seemed to agree. I followed Eldrin through the crowd, which didn't quite part for us as dramatically as I expected, though a few people bowed to Eldrin and called him "Your Highness." He moved confidently, acknowledging certain people with a bow of his head, and blatantly pretending that others weren't there.

However, I wanted to crawl into a hole and hide. My skin prickled from the weight of everyone's attention. It was oddly violating, like the elves were looking into the deepest parts of me, every secret laid bare. And there were so many eyes. If this was only a fraction of the court, the elven lands must've been massive. No wonder they were desperate to protect the sovereignty they still had. I had only been here a day, but I understood the elves more, my earlier anger shifting to the worlds' decision to merge and not the people who came with it—they obviously didn't want to be here, either.

And then, just when I was starting to get used to being inspected, I saw him. Vanir. King of the Darkening Woods. Lord of a Chair That Was a Carnivore's Dream.

And my fiancé.

Once we approached the king, making our way through one last group of elves, I bowed—or tried to. My dress defied gravity, but I didn't want to leave anything to chance. Eldrin bowed from his place next to me, far deeper than I managed. But the king didn't seem insulted by my lack of spinal dexterity. In fact, he seemed curious, rubbing a strong chin that graced a face that was as angular as Eldrin's and just as unnaturally beautiful. Though unlike Eldrin, this elf's gaze carried no hint of kindness when he looked at me.

I had felt more amorous advances from that dishwasher.

And I now understood why Siliana told me to trust my instincts—every single one told me to run.

"Amber," the king said in a heavy lilting voice. "Welcome to my court."

I bowed again. "Thank you...Your Majesty."

Was that the correct title? If it wasn't, he didn't seem to care, for he continued, "I am sorry that the way you have come to us has been so...unexpected. But I am sure we can as of yet make a good thing of an unfortunate situation."

I tried not to squirm. The king's voice reminded me of one guy from the East Coast that I had dated, who spent far too long lecturing waitresses for mispronouncing wines. He wasn't a date for long. Regardless, that characteristic—egotistical and condescending—wasn't attractive in my date, and it was not any more attractive in an elven king.

"Thank you for providing for my care," I said. Really, thanking him was the least I could do. And he did provide for a means to save my life, since the spider was hardly his fault.

"No need," the king said with a flick of his wrist. "I would be amiss if I did not care for my future wife. One who has so much to offer." His eyes raked over me, and a smile curved on his lips. Whatever he found in me, he was pleased.

I wanted to put a potato sack over my head and hide in a closet.

"A true sign of your caring and your love would be to give her the antidote now," Eldrin said. The crowd stilled. If we weren't the center of attention before, we were now. The bite on my shoulder, which I so far managed to ignore, went cold, as if ice poured into my veins at the mere mention of the poison. Was the spider's poison always this uncomfortable? Or did it somehow sense that people were talking about it, about how to get rid of it? Figured that something like this would be more magic than science.

The king frowned and he leaned to one side, gripping the throne's arm with his skeletal hand. Bone rubbed against bone, the light grinding audible, as he remained silent. "Who are you to tell me what wedding gift is fit for our queen?" he finally asked.

Queen. He intended me to be *queen*? Of here? Damn, it wasn't some mistake.

"No one, Your Majesty," Eldrin said with a stern bow. "Merely someone who does not see the need to postpone the inevitable. She will be your wife—how better to show her the care you will provide for her in the future?"

The king and Eldrin stared at each other. I didn't know the full scope of what was happening, but I knew that this was a challenge about far more than me. The way the court gasped told me I was right.

Wasn't Eldrin in danger from the king? What was he doing?

The king was Eldrin's younger brother. Eldrin should have been king. The king had only reluctantly allowed him to stay. And here he was, prodding at that same monarch, seemingly with no fear of the consequences.

Vanir was gripping the throne arms so tight the bones in his right hand were visible. Guards stepped around the side of the room, their hands hovering over their swords' hilts.

Somehow, the barely contained anger burning in the king's eyes showed that something was restraining him, something was holding the king back from murdering his brother here and now. And then I noticed it, the subtle shifting in the room, elves moving—some behind Eldrin, some to stand near the king. It would take one word, one movement, for violence to erupt.

What Eldrin said was true—he did have too many supporters for the king to kill him outright. With the lands in chaos from the worlds shifting, Vanir needed to keep his court calm. And he couldn't do that with Eldrin murdered.

But was all of this over me? No, not me. Not me at all. I was just a casualty, someone who had the misfortune of being placed in the middle of dueling royals. And I was someone who needed to try to stay alive, no matter what happened.

"Your Majesty," I said, doing my best to execute a feminine bow. Vanir looked toward me, an eyebrow raised, while Eldrin didn't take his eyes off the king. "You have honored me with your pledge. Please, let us not taint our first night together with such disagreements." Thank goodness I had read a lot of fantasy novels and knew how to play the pleading princess when the need arose.

The king licked his lips and smiled. And then laughed, a cold sound that rang hollow in the hall. Everyone relaxed. Except Eldrin.

"Of course, my dear." The king said. "You're right, why ruin our first meeting with something so tedious? Please—enjoy this court. And soon, we shall have more time together." He cocked his head. "I look forward to getting to know you better."

CHAPTER ELEVEN

ELDRIN

He was lucky.

Vanir was so lucky I didn't want to risk Amber's safety. She did nothing to get involved in our petty politics, and she didn't deserve to pay the price of Vanir's resentment. I gritted my teeth, watching Vanir leer at her, even as she walked through the court, meeting and speaking with one courtier after another. She was seemingly oblivious to how the monarch was still focused on her. I had been ready to start a rebellion then and there just from how he looked at her, like a possession that he wanted to tear her apart and consume. A thing. And in the face of his musing, she had stood regally before him—human, helpless, and perfect.

I couldn't react again, not in a way that would insult Vanir. I couldn't do anything other than follow her through the court, doing what I could to protect her from the courtiers.

Vanir may have had a budding obsession with her, but that didn't mean he would do anything to shield her from the insults that would inevitably come. I had acted reckless-ly already, challenging Vanir like that in front of the entire court. Foolish. I didn't think before speaking. I'd had enough of enduring Vanir's humiliations, but I could handle them when they just involved me. She changed everything.

I had been entangled with other women before—I was hardly a celibate prince. But they were women of the court and knew how to conduct themselves. By and far they were women who saw a title first, a man second, and I was more than willing to take advantage of the blatant exchange they gave me. Some entanglements lasted longer than others—a couple lasted for a few years—but they were all temporary and understood to be so. I considered myself far too young to wed, and I hadn't yet met anyone worth the turmoil any choice would stir. Unavoidable for a prince. Of course, my father had his own ideas and plans about my marriage, but they were irrelevant now. Vanir had taken my place, and no one would risk tying themselves to me, unless they wanted to risk themselves.

But Amber...she was outside all of this, in every way. Every smile she gave me was not because of who I was or who I could be. And unlike the women from before, Amber was on her own, without a lifetime of understanding the conflict she found herself in.

Hopefully Vanir thought my prodding of him to be merely a political challenge and nothing more. If Vanir knew my thoughts that were stirring about her, everything I was thinking of, he'd kill her—or worse—just to torment me. He'd likely sacrifice the barrier and let her die just to hurt me. I already suspected that he had engineered the deaths of two of my former lovers out of spite, women whose families weren't important enough to cause him trouble—why should I except him to treat Amber any better?

While we made our way through the gathering, with its light music singing on the air, my hands stayed near where my daggers were hidden in my doublet, ready for anything to happen. Anything could happen—tonight wouldn't be the first time someone was stabbed at a royal gathering. I would not put it past Vanir to have me protect her, just to cut her down in front of me. I should know—he already did that to my horse.

But for now, she had different foes to contend with.

"How old are you?" Lady Marciel asked Amber, peering down her nose. I stayed back, as I had done much of the evening, stepping in only when absolutely necessary. I didn't need anyone reporting that I was shielding Amber in a way that may hint at something more. Since I had seen Amber navigate an identical encounter only an hour earlier, I knew this one wouldn't give her any difficulty.

"I am twenty-four," Amber said.

"So little," Lady Marciel said. "You're a child. And a human. And for you to have the burdens of rule placed on you so soon..." Lady Marciel had two unwed daughters and a blatant desire to see one of them wearing a crown—much like every mother here tonight.

Amber's mouth dropped open and she covered it with her slender hand. "You actually said *that*?" she asked, in a tone I've since learned not to take seriously. Instead, I watched with as much impassiveness as I could muster, biting back budding laughter.

"Yes?" Lady Marciel said.

"You think the king is a fool!" Amber hissed softly. "How could you think such a thing of His Majesty?" Amber spoke quietly enough for mortals, but the sound carried.

"I didn't—"

"Yes, you did," Amber said. She then shook her head regretfully. "Oh, the king is going to be so upset when I tell him—"

"There's nothing to—"

"You're second-guessing his decisions. Mortal kings severed heads for such slights—and I'd expect nothing less of an elven." Amber chose that moment to point at some skulls on the walls to prove her point. Lady Marciel left us, scurrying away with an impressive speed. A few curious heads watched her flee and stared at us, but no one darted to replace Lady Marciel.

"How long do we have to stay here?" Amber asked me in a low voice after Lady Marciel was gone, the woman scandalized in a way I'd never forget. Amber held a goblet of red wine in her left hand, but she didn't touch it. She touched nothing. Ate nothing. Another sign that she was wiser than many likely suspected. The food was probably safe to eat, but clear wits were always necessary.

I took a few steps towards her, and immediately fought with myself to look away. The leaves and flowers of her dress graced her neck and chest, accenting her beautiful curves. I longed to trace the delicate skin underneath her garment, to push the boughs aside and explore as far as she would let me.

I cursed to myself. Such thoughts would get me nowhere.

"We can leave whenever you want," I said. "As much as I've been enjoying this."

"Really?" she asked hopefully.

"Yes. You have met the king and most of the court. There is no reason to stay."

"Yes, please. I want to go." She found an empty space on a wooden table, set down the goblet, and turned to me, relief evident. "*You* may find this funny, but I'm tired. And running out of ideas. I can't keep using the same lines on everyone—they'll be comparing notes soon."

"I understand." I gave her a small smile, one that would hopefully be written off as polite.

I was just about to offer her my arm to escort her from the room when I noticed the crowd shift, and one of the last people I wanted to see strode towards us.

The newcomer was a tall elf, taller than me, with night-black hair that went to his shoulders and unnaturally pale skin. A long-healed cut graced his lip, framed by a pointed nose. Long draping black robes hung from his frame, like a wraith haunting this hall. Gold embroidery, no doubt a gift from my brother, lurked at the garment's edges. He wore the gilt embellishment as if he were a beautiful fruit, whose insides were full of corruption and rot. This was my brother's best friend. And a bastard. Figuratively and literally.

"Eldrin," Ivas said, ignoring my title once he reached us, his lips curled in a smirk.

"Lord Ivas," I said, refusing to so much as nod, but leaving his slight to me unacknowledged. I wasn't going to start a fight tonight over a petty courtesy. Not when it could risk her. Not after I had been so foolish once already. I had been careful—so careful—but who knew what story would reach Vanir?

"And this is...Ember?"

"Amber," she said, straightening her back. "Are you another prince?"

"No." Did Amber intend this, or did she not realize that she forced Ivas to admit that he wasn't royal? Ivas may have had the king's favor, but he didn't have the blood. His rank was owed entirely to Vanir's whims. "I am Lord Ivas, advisor to His Majesty."

"Pleased to meet you."

Ivas let his gaze drag over her, lingering on places that no polite person would stare at. Was he jealous of her? Possibly. As queen she would, by default, be competition for Vanir's attention. Did Ivas desire her? Absolutely. He would never forego an opportunity to indulge in a novelty. "I have been meaning to say," Ivas said, "it is kind of you to give so much of yourself for a people you haven't met. Marry someone you don't know. Very admirable."

"I know that without Eldrin I would have died," Amber said, stealing a glance my way. "And without the aid of the elves, I would have died. I am happy to do what I can to repay that debt."

Ivas's lips curled once more. "As I'm sure you will. But surely, we are asking a lot of one such as you."

"It is the least I can do after the generosity shown to me by His Majesty."

"As I said," Ivas said with a predatory smile, one that made the hand by my dagger twitch, "what you are doing is very admirable. You are to be commended. Admired." His eyes made no secret of how they were raking up her body, inspecting every curve.

"Thank you, my lord." Amber swallowed hard.

"Should you find yourself in need of company, I am more than happy to oblige."

"Thank you. As queen, it will be best to be acquainted with important courtiers such as yourself." She lingered a little too long on the word 'queen,' subtly reminding Ivas of her role, that she wasn't just any mere captive to be played with.

"Be safe, Amber" –Ivas raised an eyebrow and suddenly turned to walk away– "these woods have many dangers."

I exhaled. Thank fuck that was over. That could have gone so much worse.

At least she knew how to handle Ivas—to address him boldly, to flatter the correct parties, and refuse to fall for his traps. I couldn't help the tinge of pride that worked through me, watching her manage the various courtiers. She was clever. She knew how to hold her tongue and when to use it, as I had seen many times this night. Maybe she did have a chance of surviving this court. I would've been more than satisfied if my partner was able to help me with the politics of governing as Amber had hinted she was capable of doing. Unfortunately, Vanir would not appreciate it. He only appreciated when people paid him compliments.

"Now can we go?" she whispered to me once he was gone.

"Gladly."

We stole through a side door, taking the long way back to her rooms. Yes, I was selfish in taking this longer route, but I wanted her to see as much of her new home as possible. Maybe she would come to love it.

And yes, maybe I wanted to spend a little more time with her, too.

"What was wrong with *him*?" Amber asked once we were outside, the courtiers' chatter now a faint hum. "It's not often I meet someone so...pissy. And there were a lot of irritated people tonight."

I bit back a laugh. How was she so good at getting them out of me? I hadn't wanted to laugh like this since before Father died—I've had little reason to do so since. If Oristan was to be believed, I was known for being light-hearted and jovial. Was.

"That is a good way to describe him," I said, first checking to make sure no one was near. "He is...greedy. He doesn't like the thought of anything—or anyone—stealing the king's attention away from him."

"He's worried the king will focus on me?" Amber squirmed as she spoke, which made me almost smile. She seemed to like the idea of Vanir touching her almost as much as I did. "The king barely spoke to me. He doesn't know I left the party."

"He does. Even if he isn't in a room, assume he is watching. He likely had people spying on you all night. And he was watching you himself for most of it."

Amber paled. "All night?"

"Yes. Don't worry," I said, "you insulted no one Vanir favors. I would have stepped in were it otherwise. And with the ones he does, you were assertive but not offensive. Which is a necessary skill for a ruler."

"Oh. Good. I...may have gone too far with some of them."

"No. They deserved it. And it is better that you taught them now that you're not one to be cajoled. They scent weakness like a bear can scent blood. If you hadn't, the next event would have been worse."

"Good. I think."

Maybe my words didn't have the comforting effect I intended. I had tried to assure her that she was capable of the role thrust upon her, when it was a role she had no interest in. But there was nothing we could do about that situation. Amber had to learn, if she hadn't already, that this court was as dangerous to navigate as the Darkening Woods itself.

CHAPTER TWELVE

AMBER

I didn't say anything after Eldrin's warning. Not about the king, not about Eldrin comparing this court to a den of rabid bloodthirsty bears. Nothing.

My head pounded. Something was wrong with this place, so very wrong. I was right not to want anything to do with the elves, or anything from those other worlds. If not for Eldrin, I would have dreamed about trying to run away by now—who cared what happened to me after? I couldn't stay here. This place seemed too dangerous for me, even without the poison. Siliana and Eldrin were the only ones who didn't make me feel like a stupid toy, something to be tested and broken. Or to be desired and then destroyed.

And during the audience, Eldrin stayed close to me, his presence a precious anchor as I was whipped from one elf to another, pressed and prodded in a way I could never have imagined. Everyone wanted to meet me, and no one was happy about the fact that they had to. It was merely a matter of how upset they were. Their dislike was no secret, even if their false words were hidden behind smiles.

But Eldrin wasn't upset that I was there. I didn't know if he thought of me as a friend, but his words didn't have that superficial ring to them, and his looks never had that condescending sneer. And his budding laugh—it was such a hard-won sound, but entirely worth it. I had to admit it to myself—if I left, I would miss Eldrin, too.

Silently, I followed Eldrin back to my room, through the macabre winding halls that were just starting to be familiar to me. The spaces were silent, with most courtiers likely still with the king, or so I assumed. Any servants were probably done with the bulk of their tasks for the night, or were occupied with the gathering. The isolation was welcome after the crowds, where I constantly had to wonder how my behavior would affect me in the future. Maybe I should have been more careful.

When we came to my door, Eldrin stepped aside, waiting while I fumbled with the thin metal key Siliana gave me. It clicked open easily enough.

I stepped inside the doorway, and just when I turned around to say goodnight to Eldrin, a skeletal hand grabbed my face and dug into my skin, pulling me backwards and into the dark.

I tried to scream. I couldn't. My voice was caught under my attacker's grip, my beautiful dress smashed against this foreign body.

But before I could think to try anything—as if I could do anything other than thrash—there was a blur of movement, the sting of fire against my arm, and then a loud crack. The attacker let me go and then dropped to the floor. I whipped around and found the man—an elf—laying there with his neck broken, staring wide-eyed at nothing. A dagger laid on the ground next to him, stained with thick red liquid. Blood.

My blood?

Eldrin stood over him, hands in a fist, and other than the blatant wrath in his gaze it was as if nothing had happened. He had killed someone—and likely saved my life—with as little effort as it took to breathe.

He saved me.

I collapsed on the ground, shaking, covering my mouth with my hand.

Oh my god. Oh my god.

It wasn't until the third time that I realized I was saying that out loud. That elf just tried to kill me. Why? Why me? I had been warned about the dangers of the Darkening Woods and this court, and they were real. Real.

The next thing I knew, Eldrin was kneeling next to me, rubbing an ointment on my arm that soothed the pain I barely registered. Yes, that was my blood on the knife. The fucker had cut me. Not deep, but enough that it dripped fresh fluid over my arm, ruining what was left of my dress. A knife cut—what a lovely thing to go with my spider bite.

I blinked hard. Somehow, Eldrin already had bandages on his lap, ready to stop the bleeding.

"Can I look?" He asked.

I nodded, holding out my arm and letting him bind the wound, his hands deftly wrapping the bandage around my skin, stopping once in awhile to place some other ointment between the layers. While he worked, my heart settled and my stomach calmed, his mere presence doing more than a million words could ever do.

Eldrin...he was focused entirely on me and on his task, his eyes narrowed and lips pursed. An unexpected pleasure trilled through me at having him so close and dedicated to such a small part of me. What would it be like if he were focused on other things, things that were far more pleasurable? I leaned into his touch as much as I could, even with his skeleton hand dancing over my skin. It didn't matter what part of him touched me, so long as it belonged to him. Was he being extra mindful not to let the bones touch my skin, using them only as necessary? He was taking care of me. He didn't have to, but he was.

He killed that elf to save me.

He saved me.

"Where is he?" I asked, blinking hard and looking for the dead elf. The room was empty, besides the two of us and the blood stains on the floor. Just how long was I sitting there in shock?

"Outside," Eldrin said. "He can be dealt with later. Are you alright?"

"I...yes." I abruptly shook my head. "I'm just...that was worse than the time I opened the AC filter at my first apartment and found mice skeletons."

He stopped wrapping my arm and raised an eyebrow. "What?"

"Nothing." I took a long breath. "Not the same thing. Not even close."

Methodically he wrapped my arm, and the rest of me ached for touch. I needed a hug. Bad. But I didn't think the elf would be up for that. Not with the way his eyes were narrowed and mumbled curses rolled out of his lips in a stream. His eyes focused on my injury, a growing fury lurking within them much like a gathering storm.

"Why me?" I asked. "Why did he do this? Was I too rude at the party?"

Eldrin huffed. "Hardly. Elves can and do much worse to each other all the time." He reached for another bandage, using it to secure the others around my arm in place. "I don't know why he was here." From the way his brow was furrowed, I guessed that he was trying to figure it out himself. "You are under the king's protection—notoriously, I might add. Our attacker was young and inexperienced. And foolish. Anyone who had known anything about you knows that you are accompanied at all times. So, either he or the person who hired him were fools, or it was meant as a message to me."

"You?"

His eyes went downcast. "My brother has the crown, but there are many who resent the fact that I am here at all."

What would killing me have to do with Eldrin? If they hated that he was here, why would hurting me be used to hurt *him*? I was nothing to him—right?

"What is the other option?"

Eldrin lifted my arm and moved it, checking to see how it responded under the bandages. "Well, not everyone is pleased with the idea of strengthening the barrier. There are some who think that we should let it fall and assimilate with the rest of the mortals." Figured. Of course, elves wouldn't be a monolith in that regard, if they were anything like humans. Some people thought that low-fat mayo was a perfectly acceptable substitute for the real thing. Sometimes people were very very wrong.

"If it's me," I said slowly, "I'm not safe here, am I? You told me—I have to be careful." I wiped my eyes, careful not to smear my cosmetics, or what was left of them.

"You are," he said with an intensity that shocked me. "I told you the things that I did so that you would be careful. I had no idea that..." He shook his head, as if even he couldn't believe what had happened. "I'm not letting anything happen to you, Amber. Do not worry."

I locked eyes with him. His hand was still on my arm, and who cared that the other one didn't have flesh? I hadn't had a chance to look at him so closely before, to be close enough to smell him, that woodland scent mixed with a faint note of apples. His lips parted a tiny bit as he stared at mine, and that earlier fire surged to a familiar yearning that worked its way through me, urging me forward. To him. There was nothing but him and his silvery gaze, drawing me in and refusing to let me go.

"What now?" I mouthed, barely above a whisper.

He blinked hard, the moment suddenly broken. A coldness from the unwelcome world rushed over me, right as I remembered that my question was about more than just us. "I will make enquiries," he said.

I had to stop thinking like that. There was no *us*. It was the shock. It had to be.

"You're going? Now?" My stomach twisted. The thought of him being pulled from me, leaving me alone *here* after *that* was too much.

His gaze softened. "I will have to, but not yet. I will not leave you alone until Siliana comes. Do not worry, Amber. You will be safe tonight. I promise."

CHAPTER THIRTEEN

ELDRIN

Safe, I had promised her. I was keeping my word and would continue to do so. I promised her that tonight she would be safe.

But what about tomorrow?

I sat on a bare wooden chair next to the door in her room, letting her obtain what sleep she could. Thick blankets were draped over her, her hair spread loose over the pillows. The moon cast its glow, illuminating her in an otherworldly light. Her even breath was hypnotizing, lulling me into a dream.

But this was no time for dreams. I had to determine who was behind this attack. It could not happen again. If it did, and I failed... I closed my eyes and took a deep breath.

The attack could've been meant to hurt me, if not directly, then by making me fail at the task my brother assigned me—of protecting the future queen. My failure would be an excuse for my brother to get rid of me. Amber had as-tutely noticed the difficult situation around me. My brother wanted me gone as a potential threat to his throne, that was no secret. The only issue was *how* he could do so without alienating critical members of his court.

Though, the attack could also truly have been for Amber. Humans were merely tolerated at best in the Woods, and there were more than enough fanatics who didn't want the barrier to stand. There were others who were repulsed at the idea of a human joining with our magic. However, it was common knowledge that I was protecting her, which indi-cated that the idiot was hired by someone with more power. Someone who stood to gain from Amber's death, one way or another.

I rubbed a hand through my hair, resting my head on my skeleton hand while an elbow braced on my leg, the bones pinching my skin.

What was I supposed to do now? There were few options available, and none of them good. And no matter what I did, the ultimate tragic outcome hovered in front of me like a lurking nightmare.

Even if I kept Amber safe, she would have to marry Vanir. She would have to be alone with Vanir. Lay with him. Touch him. And he would touch her...

Would Vanir be kind to her? Was Vanir kind to anyone? There were many rumors of discarded mistresses, bastard children who had disappeared, and serving girls who were suddenly never seen again. Why would he treat her any better? While kings and royals always attracted rumors, when the same rumor kept reincarnating itself, it was best to pay attention.

I fought down the urge to clear my constricting throat. I flipped one of my daggers in my hand to steady myself, the familiar leather hilt a comforting presence. The thought of what was going to come next was a bitter taste on my tongue.

Regardless, I couldn't pretend that everything was fine, that there wouldn't be any more threats. I couldn't allow myself to be around Amber, only to betray her by giving her to Vanir. Every inch of my body recoiled at the mere thought. And if I felt this way about her so soon, how would I feel as the days and weeks passed, as I spent more time with this beautiful creature who placed absolute trust in me?

No, I had a sinking feeling that, no matter what, the dangers we faced tonight were only the beginning.

CHAPTER FOURTEEN

AMBER

"Why am I doing this?" I asked Siliana while I held up a bough of red maple leaves. The leaves shook, dancing in the wind and from my trembling arms, yet they were hanging on much more admirably than me. I was ready to chuck the branch aside and be done with the whole endeavor. "There's enough trees in these woods, why do I have to be one?"

"It's tradition," Siliana said with a grin. Her golden skirts spread on the ground around her, like a resplendent sunbeam in the heart of fall. She regally surveyed the scene, watching and advising me much as she had this entire session, not bothering to hide how much the spectacle amused her. "Unwed maidens dance in a circle, holding the boughs. Whoever is the first one to lose all the leaves on the bough is crowned the queen of the festival."

"I already have a husband. Apparently. Isn't that close enough?"

"You're betrothed, but you're not wed. It would be strange if you were an elven princess and did not take part." She glanced around her before whispering, "And the king has requested it."

Ah, that explained it. Lovely of him.

We stood in a palace courtyard, the grand trees towering over us and showering red and gold with each breeze. As always, the air was still comfortable and not too cold, so long as I stayed out of the wind. Impossible with this bough.

I shook the branch with my uninjured arm. Hard. Nothing budged off the damn stick. I couldn't use the injured one yet. The injury from the spider hadn't healed, and the venom was making itself known more often now, a distracting numbness that pulsated out of the wound, seemingly radiating further each day. Not to mention that the cut from the attacker's dagger still smarted, days later. Though it had responded well to whatever Eldrin did, all things considered.

But this branch was surprisingly heavy. "Um, how long is this dance?"

Siliana laughed at seeing my expression. "Don't worry. It's magicked to only last several minutes. Even we elves would tire watching the same dance for much longer than that. And everyone is very excited to see the outcome."

"So, this is competitive?"

"Very."

"Wonderful." Last thing I needed—an elven girl whacking me with a stick because I shook my bough too hard and she wanted me out of the competition.

Rough laughter sounded from the trees. It belonged to a few young elves who huddled together, watching me through the spaces between the thick trunks. My cheeks reddened.

"Ignore them," Siliana said, sending a stern glance their way.

The young elves moved to leave, but not before one called out, "You're wasting your time. This dance is for elves, not humans."

"What should we expect?" Another asked. "Eldrin's involved." More laughter and talk I couldn't hear, though the mocking tones said everything. Not soon enough, the figures faded from sight.

"I'll say it again," Siliana said gently. "Ignore them."

I resisted the urge to run back to my room and instead held my head, and the branches, higher. The elves were right. None of this was meant for me, and I was never going to have a place here, even if I managed to do whatever needed to be done with the barrier. Eldrin and Siliana had given me friendship and protection, but even their influence was limited.

"Are they wrong?" I asked. "You said yourself that this is meant for an elven princess."

Siliana shifted, gracefully re-arranging her skirts around her. "As far as they are concerned you *are* an elven princess. Banish them from your mind. Anyway, do not be concerned about trying to perform well. You're going to be queen in truth, so it would be considered bad form if you did win. It would be seen as greedy, since you are already guaranteed a crown."

A crown that I didn't want, with a man who made me uneasy.

"So, I need to dance and shake, but not shake too hard."

"Correct."

I did not have the arm strength for this.

I focused on what was in front of me—partaking in this dance and earning my hosts' goodwill. It was now a few days after the attack, and Siliana had decided that it would be best to get ready for the harvest festival that was in two weeks. I had mostly recovered, and it was time to settle in. Though whether practicing now was Siliana's idea, or Vanir's, I couldn't say, and no one enlightened me. Eldrin was off doing...something, and he insisted that I was safe with Siliana, as he often did these past days. Not that I was in a position to argue otherwise, but I decided to defer to his judgment and focus on the gymnastics Siliana foisted on me. As best as I could tell, this festival was a combination of Thanksgiving and Mardi Gras, but with lots of leaves and skulls. From the blushing hints Siliana divulged, I had a feeling that topless women was another thing this festival had in common. With Mardi Gras. Not Thanksgiving. Hopefully.

"Are you dancing?" I asked, wanting to discuss anything else after the taunting elves.

"No," Siliana said, shaking her head. "I cannot dance. I have a spouse."

I almost dropped the branch. "You do?"

"Yes. She is still at our home. The one in the other world."

"Oh," I said. "I'm sorry."

"Don't be. All of us have lost someone. Some of us have nothing left." I didn't mention how true that was—I myself had thought the same thing many times. Siliana picked a fallen leaf off her dress and tossed it to float to the ground. "I can only hope that I live long enough to see the worlds return, and hold her again."

I never thought of it that way. I had lost a friend when the worlds merged, and some humans lost their whole families. I never thought to consider in detail that maybe those who arrived had left their own lives and loves behind.

Did Eldrin lose someone when the worlds shifted? I was afraid of the answer, both for his sake and because of what that would mean for us. Not that there was an "us." Or that there could be. Or that he even wanted there to be.

Did I *want* there to be?

I was both excited and terrified of the answer. Caring for Eldrin in that way would make things even more difficult—I was engaged to his brother. A brother who had made it clear that he would use any reason to harm Eldrin. Interfering with an engagement would likely be a good enough reason.

Yet, Eldrin was the one who made me smile. The one who I thought of as I fell asleep at night. The one I couldn't wait to hear from, to be near. The one I dreamed of holding me, touching me with the tenderness he showed me the night of the attack. In the Darkening Woods, he was my light.

It wasn't fair. I had finally found someone I wanted, someone I craved. And being with him would all but guarantee my death and his.

But Siliana's comment caught my attention. "Can that happen? Can the worlds reunite, that is." Eldrin had mentioned it, but I was curious as to what Siliana had to say.

Siliana picked a few fallen leaves off her dress. "It has before. But not always, and not always at one time. My guess is that the larger pieces are more likely to snap back somewhat intact. In which case...I think we're lucky, to be ruptured in this way. The smaller pieces tend to just fade, whether from blending into the current world or going home or somewhere else, I cannot say."

"You're not lucky. You've lost so much."

"It could be worse," Siliana said. "I've lived long enough that I've seen far worse. You forget, Amber, that the Darkening Woods was not always at peace. Skirmishes and wars have been a constant in our lives as much as the constant fall. I know that my wife is alive, and that I left her healthy and safe. That is a kindness not given to everyone."

"I'm sorry."

"Don't be." She took a deep breath. "This is not a situation any of us ever thought we would find ourselves in, and as such, we are each trying to determine things as we go. It is all we can do."

I nodded, but didn't want to press Siliana on understandably hurtful events. I didn't want to think about the worlds anymore anyway, what it might mean if this world snapped back and I never saw Eldrin again. As things were, I wouldn't see my family and friends again, and my heart ached to think of that, but Eldrin was quickly becoming a piece that would hurt to lose.

"What happens to the losers?" I asked instead. "The ones who don't win the leaf shaking contest?"

"Losers?" Siliana's eyes twinkled. "There are no losers. As the maidens dance, eligible men vie over the fallen leaves. Each leaf entitles the catcher to a dance from the maiden in question."

"The leaves are marked?"

She hummed in agreement. How much black-market leaf bartering occurred, with people trying to get repeated turns with their favorite partners?

"Will anyone want to dance with me?" I asked. "Or will my leaves just get tossed in the compost?"

Siliana chuckled. "Don't worry. I don't think you're going to have a shortage of partners."

"Because they want to flatter their future queen?"

"Hardly. You'll attract that attention on your own."

"But so many elves don't like me. Human and all."

"Some are not everyone, and not everyone is a fool." Siliana gracefully rested her hands on her lap. "Don't worry—they may not be as outspoken as certain parties, but you do have plenty of admirers here."

I grimaced. "I can only hope. I think I terrified the court at the audience."

"You did, in an admirable manner. It takes a bold personality to manage this court. For all of our grace and manners, we elves can be as vile a creature as you can imagine. And you did very well."

Though I didn't believe her, I accepted her compliment with a nod. I shook my branch extra hard, both to distract from my burning cheeks, and also see if I could force the damn leaves off. After one big shake I felt a pop in my shoulder and watched, victorious, as a leaf floated to the ground. There—I managed one. Only...fifty more to go. I shook that arm—working out the lurking spasm.

"You've made him smile a lot," Siliana suddenly said.

"What?"

"Eldrin. He hasn't smiled like this in some time."

"This is him smiling?" Sure, I caught smirks here and there, but he exerted extreme control over his facial muscles.

While the beginnings of pleasure burned through me at her words, doubt remained. "He is doing as the king commanded—that's all."

Siliana let out a little laugh. "I forget you never saw him before. Before Vanir, and then before you. Trust me, Amber, if Eldrin didn't want to be doing this, with you...you'd know."

Why was she telling me this? I was betrothed to their king. For now. But what if she was right? What if Eldrin really did like me like...that...

Was it actually a possibility? My heart lept, but then it crashed to the ground, overwhelmed at the reality of what it faced.

"I think I need a nap," I said. "It is a truth universally acknowledged that a young woman in possession of a shaken maple branch must be in want of a long nap."

"What?"

"Nothing." I really had to stop talking.

There was a rustling, and then suddenly Eldrin was there, so quickly that I hadn't noticed until he stood right behind me. He was dressed in a familiar outfit of brown breeches and a tunic, with the daggers I had come to expect, these garments being much more practical than what he had worn to the party. Yet my breath caught. He was brilliant and perfect and devastating. "Are you done tormenting her, Sil?" Eldrin asked.

"I've done no such thing," Siliana said with a grin. "I'm merely preparing her for the dance."

"When is this dance?" I asked. Elves tended to work with vague time frames, I noticed, probably because they lived for centuries.

"When is the moon..." Siliana mumbled, "ah, that's right. Sixteen days from now." Sixteen days. I will have been here for over three weeks by that point. And I would be here for so many more.

Forever.

Eldrin must have noticed something in my expression. "We could try to have you excused—"

"No." Siliana raised her hand. "You know as well as I that unless Vanir suggests it, it will not happen." Reluctantly, Eldrin nodded in agreement. Damn, it looked like twirling leaves was going to be my fate. I eyed the branch, preparing myself for a long afternoon of...shaking. I needed the practice.

"Would you like to leave the city?" Eldrin suddenly asked me. The afternoon light caught the angles of his face, as firm and radiant as the trees around him. "We can go, or we can stay. But I thought you would like to see something else. It's been a little bit since we've left the palace."

Did he...did he really offer me a way out of this?

"Definitely." I smiled, tossing the branch to the ground.

Sorry, Siliana. The arboreal torment would have to wait.

CHAPTER FIFTEEN

ELDRIN

I had a chance to have Amber all to myself, in private, and it was all I could do to restrain myself from taking her and darting through the city.

It was difficult to ensure true privacy, but I managed to lead Amber and myself out of Great Glen by losing the "guard," that is, whatever cretin Vanir found to follow us. And there was always one of Vanir's creatures trying to follow us. The trick to evading them was not acting like we were trying to escape—Amber and I didn't dart through alleys, wear cloaks, or cause elaborate distractions. All we had to do was go to the palace's communal dining hall, leave through the back door in the thick of the crowd, and then I brought her to a set of paths that led through a barely used gate. See, I had played in this city my whole life, and as a child I had spent every spare minute picking out the secret paths.

I knew which ones were not only deserted, but which were the easiest to conceal tracks, and which had confusing turns and crossroads that led even the most experienced awry. If questioned upon our return, why, I was only showing Amber her home by taking her on more scenic routes.

Alright, I did ask her to wear a cloak with the hood pulled up before we left. Her hair was rather distinctive.

When she first donned the cloak, I was struck by how much she had already affected me, after such a short time. I *had* to be alone with her—craved it. There were things I wanted to say that I couldn't with any ears near, even though reason told me that I should stay away.

Damn my reason. She made me feel like myself again, more like the prince I was before Father died. It was like I was a tree starved for water, and she was the one thing able to sustain me.

So, no. While I feared discovery of my deeper feelings, feared the danger that being alone with her could bring, I couldn't stay away from her any more than I could resist taking my next breath.

We walked along the worn forest paths, past ancient trees and thick brambles. And then I led her down smaller and more obscure trails that were little more than a line of worn dirt through the trees, until the boughs hid us from anyone who was more than a few feet away. I had no illusions that our pursuer wouldn't find us, but I wanted to steal precious time. I took no steps to hide our tracks, other than those that nature took care of itself. If I tried too hard to hide our path, then the king could have questions I wouldn't be able to answer. And what we were doing was difficult enough to explain.

All I wanted was some time alone, and not to be executed for treason. A small ask, no?

"Are you cold?" I asked Amber once we came to a glade. Rows of gold and red trees lined a field laden with tall, tan grasses and little yellow and pink flowers. The day's bright sun shone clearly, reflecting the brilliant golden tones in Amber's hair. Even for the Darkening Woods, this area was untouched, a place not often visited. Here, we had time. Enough time that I was able to indulge in looking at her.

Amber was still wearing the dress that Siliana made her practice that dance in, a sleeveless gossamer dark green gown that plunged low on her breastbone. She was so frail compared to the elves, her body curved where the elven were rigid and sharp. I knew she wasn't a weak creature, but it was a difference between us that was impossible to ignore. Her fragility meant that she was easier to harm.

"No," she said. "This cloak is enough. I'm warm."

"Good."

She looked at me, and I looked at her. Now that we were alone, and *here*, what was I supposed to say?

What did I want to say?

"We're alone," I said, stating the obvious. And then, once I realized how she could interpret that, I quickly added, "We can go back. If you prefer."

"No," she said. "It's nice not to have eyes on me. For once. In the city, I feel like they're always there. Even when I'm in my room."

I relaxed. "I understand."

Amber slowly stepped closer to me. Closer than how acquaintances or even friends stood. I didn't back away. I wouldn't have dreamed of it. My heart raced in my chest, sending hot blood pounding into my ears. She was glorious—radiant and lively. Her large eyes stared at me. I couldn't think. It was hard to remember that she was going to be my queen. Vanir's wife.

Vanir's wife.

I gritted my teeth.

"Will the eyes on me ever go away?" she asked. "After I'm…married."

A squirrel crashed through the nearby branches, oblivious to the painful scene below. "Not unless Vanir stops them. And I doubt he will. And even then, queens are not known for having privacy."

She nodded, apparently having expected as much. "I still cannot believe he wants to marry me. Is there any chance he will change his mind?"

"Always. But I cannot speak to what he is thinking now." I could only hope. But if I knew Vanir, he wasn't done playing this through yet. Especially since I was involved. And I saw how he looked at her—he would marry her, if only to give him an excuse to use her however he wanted. If only to see what it would do to me. Whether she lived long after the marriage was another matter. I didn't want to fully admit it to myself, but it was very possible that Vanir would arrange her death as soon as he tired of her. With lives as long as ours, elven rulers had never been shy about removing a spouse they no longer desired, one way or another.

"I will be here forever, whether I am queen or not, won't I?" Amber asked. Her hands clenched in front of her, worrying the fabric. "I can never go home."

"You can always go home," I said. "The barrier requires someone who is willing to stay. The choice is yours."

"And if I wanted to go now?" she whispered. "What if I wanted to leave?"

I hesitated. If she left now, Vanir would be furious. It would mean that the barrier was gone and we had no easy way to resurrect it. It would mean that so much of myself—including my life—would be at risk. And then there was the poison to consider—if she left, she could never be cured. She would die. But that wasn't what she was asking me, for she knew all of this just as well as me—she wanted to know if I would keep her as a prisoner, trapped for the benefit of a people who were not her own.

"If you wanted to go now, I would take you to the edge of the Woods myself," I said sincerely. "I'd never demand that you stay here against your will."

She smiled sadly and took a step closer to me. "I think you actually mean that."

"I do." She was close enough now that I could smell her. The distinctive floral soaps that Siliana liked to use mixed with Amber's own scent and took on an intoxicating air, making it all I could do to not lean into her. To devour her.

I clenched my fist. How was it she was to wed Vanir? Vanir didn't deserve her. More, she didn't deserve to be imprisoned by someone like him.

And every single moment that passed made it harder and harder to resist touching her, to claim her as mine. A sweet tension coiled in my lower abdomen at the mere thought of her skin against my bare flesh. My hands tangled in her luxurious hair. My mouth kissing her—

"I have nothing to go back to, even if I could leave," Amber said matter-of-factly. "I have my friends and family, yes, but I had nothing of a life. Just before I came here, I was actually about to move further north, and stay with my mother."

"That doesn't sound like you have nothing. Family and friends are not nothing."

"No, but they aren't *enough*, at least, not for me. I'm old enough that I'm supposed to have a job that's a career by now, a boyfriend who could turn into something more, *something* that's not an air plant that I keep replacing because I keep killing it." She smirked. "Trust me—my friends were not shy about telling me how my life is a mess. A lot. In fact, the night you took me, they gave me yet another lecture."

"You have no...partner waiting for you?" I assumed she didn't because she never mentioned one, but I couldn't be sure. How could she not have one? She was perfect, and I had seen the men at the bar flock to her myself.

"Ha." Her eyes twinkled. "No. Everyone I dated didn't last. I've just been picky. I haven't found the one that I can't live without, like they say. Sure, I found some I could live with, especially if they worked a lot and weren't home much, but that's not the same thing."

"That is something I think I understand perfectly." I examined her expression, searching for any sign that she was thinking about me like how I was consumed by her. "But would you go home? If you could?"

"Yes," she said without hesitation. "I'm the only human here. Why would I want to stay?" Her face searched mine while she asked her question, as if asking something deeper of me in turn.

Why indeed? Though my heart plummeted at hearing that she was willing to leave. She may have enjoyed our time together, and I was starting to think at times that she might feel *something* for me, but I wasn't enough to make her want to stay. How could one person be enough to give up everything and everyone you had known? And that was even *if* we found a way to be together with her pledged to Vanir. And even if we somehow found a way around her engagement, the fact remained that Vanir was king, and my life and hers would be in constant danger. At most, we could hope for a life of begrudging tolerance and constant humiliations. At worst... I had nothing to offer her. I was a Prince of the Darkening Woods, and I couldn't even promise her safety.

The wind gusted through the trees, scattering leaves through the air, and Amber clutched the cloak tighter around her. I listened carefully—there was nothing but birds and a few small animals in the woods. Our people were stealthy, but it was very hard to sneak up on another elf, especially if we were paying attention. And I was. I couldn't let myself be distracted by the red and gold foliage, the pink and yellow flowers, or how Amber stood so close to me, devastatingly raw and beautiful.

"What about you?" Amber asked, an eyebrow raised. "Do you have anyone waiting for you...anywhere?"

"No. If you haven't noticed, my position is complicated. I haven't found the right person who...Vanir would..."

"Ah. Yeah, I could see him being a soggy onion."

I chuckled. "Yes, he is."

"How did this happen?" Amber asked, gesturing with her hand towards the city. "People *like* you. I've seen it. People don't like Vanir. God knows I've heard enough about that. You could've been king. Easily, I think."

How *did* this happen? The how and why were something that had kept me awake more nights than I wanted to admit.

"A few things," I said, choosing my words carefully. "I didn't want to end the enjoyable life I'd had and I was afraid I would fail if I tried." That was the truth, formed as simply as I could. I couldn't bear the thought of lying to her—the truth was one of the few things I could give.

"I'm hardly one to lecture anyone on that," Amber said with a smile. "I just told you—I've been hearing the same things over and over from my friends."

Nothing changed? She didn't seem disgusted or angry. Instead, the same open, content expression looked back at me. Was it possible? She...didn't think less of me for that?

"As a prince, I had pleasures without the responsibility."

"Oh?"

"I could go where I wanted, when I wanted. I could disappear for days in the Woods and no one would care."

"Ah." She laughed. "*Those* kinds of pleasures." My heart skipped when I realized what she must've been thinking. At least she was corrected. I was no stranger to women, drink, or gambling, but I didn't enjoy them as much as being alone in the Woods with nothing but the trees' songs to keep me company. And maybe Oristan. Though, if he was along, our journey usually involved a lot of wine.

"There's more," I said, emboldened. "I foolishly thought it would be best for our people if Vanir was king. And he isn't a horrible ruler. As long as you aren't his family."

"You sure about that?" Amber asked.

"What are you speaking of?"

She shrugged. "Maybe people are more careful with you, but it sounds like he's been...how do I put it? A tyrant." She huffed. "I think some of your people don't think I speak the same language. They've been saying a lot of things around me."

What? How could Amber have heard of something like this while I hadn't? I heard murmurings, yes, but that accompanied all rulers. "Can you give me an example?"

"Yeah, apparently he has a pleasure house in...Red Grin?"

"Grove."

"That. And it's been staffed by people who aren't happy to be there. Or want to be."

I cursed under my breath. Vanir did have a pleasure house back in our old world, but it hadn't come with us to this one. The old one was staffed with courtesans who were trained and compensated well for their services to courtiers. That he felt the need to install one here, so quickly...

"And he's apparently had no issue taxing people within an inch of their existence here," she continued. "I didn't even know elves had currency, but it seems he's been doing his best to take as much as he can."

There *had* been displays of excess wealth on both him and Ivas in the last months. Was Amber right? Our people were fewer than before, and any gold in the land was drastically limited, even though we still had a burgeoning commerce that had adjusted decently well, considering. Did Vanir truly act so fast to claim what was left, not caring that it would destroy what economy we still had?

"Oh, and apparently he likes to cut off hands as a punishment."

"What?"

Amber shrugged. "I had the impression that was just something that was done here."

"No. No, it is not. Not unless the crime is severe. And if it was that severe, I would have heard of it."

Would I have heard if someone had committed such a crime? And if I had, what could I do about it? Vanir was the king, and I was not. And that was how it was going to be. There was no other choice.

"So," Amber said, "that's not normally done for failing to pay taxes?"

The blood left my face. "No. Absolutely not."

For the first time, I wished I had fought harder, fought at all for the throne. I would've been able to protect Amber, for one. And unlike Vanir, I wouldn't have been so focused on my own wealth to the exclusion of all else. I had my faults, but would I have been a better ruler? Now I would never know. It was too late.

"What is it?" Amber asked, taking yet another small step closer to me. Too close. "I've upset you."

"No. There is no possible way for you to upset me."

"Oh, give it time." She grinned. "I promise I'll manage it."

Time. Time we did not have, for anything. In a matter of weeks she would be bound to the barrier, and married to Vanir. She would be queen, and I would be a prince kept on the periphery, carefully managed or destroyed.

"Something is wrong," she said. Tentatively, she placed her hand on my upper arm. Her touch shocked me, forcing my repressed thoughts to the surface. My desire to take her for myself. To hold her. Treasure her. To make her cry out my name in rapt pleasure. I craved everything I could do with and for her. I wanted her to be mine. "You can tell me," Amber said softly. "I promise I won't say anything."

I raised my gaze. Her hand trembled slightly, even as it rested on me. Her breath quickened. How could I explain that it was the fact that someday I wouldn't be able to see her except at formal occasions, that soon, I would have to leave her to fend for herself, and *that* was what troubled me? The meager protection I could give would end too soon.

Her gaze locked with mine, and all of my fears fled. There was nothing but her—her steady breath, her delicate lips. Before I knew it, I had reached out my hand of flesh, moving a strand of brilliant red hair out of her face. Now my own hand was shaking from lightly touching her skin, from doing something so intimate.

We stood, watching each other, frozen in the moment. I could do it. I could lean forward and give into what I craved. She might let me. She might want me to. She—

And then she kissed me.

At first, I was so taken aback I stilled, and then all conscious thought stopped. The sight of her lost in the pleasure of her skin touching mine, the little sigh of contentment that escaped her lips, forced all else away. The touch of her was enough to send my senses dancing to the absolute edges of desire.

More. I needed so much more. Whatever she wanted from me was hers. Anything.

I'd had my first taste, and I was never going to be satisfied.

Her lips searched mine, hesitatingly at first, and then bolder as I reciprocated. I took her into my arms, relishing each angle and curve of her body, the way her breath caught with each movement. The feel of her supple skin through the fabric of her dress. How she yielded to me, letting my hands grasp what I had dreamed of doing since the moment we met. Her form, even down to her hips, was perfect in my hands. I was careful with my hand of bone, careful not to prod her unexpectedly, but she did not flinch. Instead, she pushed against me, her own hands exploring along with her lips.

This kiss—*her*—was nothing like I imagined. She tasted like spring, sweet and fresh, and full of life in the prime of bloom. She moaned against my mouth and I stirred, my attention drifting far lower as that sweet tension turned into an exquisite throbbing. I was content with this, just holding her and kissing her, but she made me already think of so much more. How she would feel with her legs around me.

How she would look with me inside her. What she would do as she was falling apart from pleasure in my arms. I started to harden as I pressed against her, and it was only the fact that we could be discovered and everything destroyed that I did not initiate more with her here and now.

She was meant to be with me. I knew it. Her sweet kiss was pulling me in deeper, sinking me into a world in which she was the only thing that mattered—but at the same time she was bringing me back to myself, like I was waking from centuries of sleep. I could change things. I could make a future for us. I could do that. For her, I'd be what I failed to be before.

Fuck Vanir. He was *not* going to take her. I wasn't sure how, but there was no possibility I'd let him have her, especially if she wasn't willing. If she wanted to be mine, she would be, no matter the devastation. For her, I'd risk everything, for what was life if I couldn't have her in it?

And then she took my hands—both of them—into her own. And I forgot everything.

CHAPTER SIXTEEN

AMBER

What was I thinking, lunging into that kiss? I had never done that before, with anyone. But there also had never been anyone that I wanted this much.

Yes, he was an elf—I never liked elves. But...Eldrin wasn't elves. He was Eldrin. He had saved me and protected me and helped me find joy in this realm that I had never wanted to see, much less live in. He was the one thing here that made me smile, that made me look forward to waking up.

I had been kidnapped and bitten and blackmailed. I had been taunted and mocked and trapped. But as I was pressed against his chest, his arms and hands holding me tightly, I realized that something good did happen despite everything. I had found the one person I was starting feel like I couldn't be without.

While we walked through the woods and into the glade, I wanted Eldrin—to touch him—so badly that it stung. I wanted him in a way that was getting impossible to ignore the longer we spoke. So, I dared. The worst that would happen was that he'd push me away and that would be that. And I wouldn't spend the rest of my life wondering. I wouldn't look at him, at that painfully beautiful face, and forever wonder—what if?

Hell, Eldrin could kiss. His lips took their time exploring mine, his fingers gripping me in conjunction with his movements. Now and then he stopped to nibble on my bottom lip and let out a soft groan. He wanted more, and the realization made me heady with excitement. Slowly, his hands explored my back, tracing a path of fire in their wake. I wanted him to touch me—everywhere. Now.

I didn't care about anything else—the poison, the barrier, Vanir. There was just Eldrin. His hands moving over me, chastely exploring each inch, even as I felt the urge, the extra friction that hinted at his yearning to go further. A sweet heat pooled in my core. His powerful form towered over me, and for the first time I truly noticed the size difference between us. He wasn't human, no matter how easy that was to forget sometimes.

I took his hand in mine—his skeleton hand. The bones were hard and strangely cool against my skin, but the fingers were deft, nimble. It responded to my touch as any other hand, his grip intertwining with mine. This hand was part of him, and I wanted everything.

And then he pulled away, leaving me breathless.

"Do you know what the consequences of being unfaithful to the king are?" Eldrin asked, gasping for air. His eyes narrowed, hinting at the seriousness of what he was telling me.

"No."

"The consequences to us both."

I didn't know for sure, but I had read enough about Henry VIII to have a pretty good idea of what disgruntled kings could do to wives.

I wiped my face slowly, out of reflex to steady myself and not to wipe off Eldrin. Wipe away Eldrin? He barely touched me and that was all it took to make me crave him. No one I had been with before triggered anything close to that sort of reaction, where the more I touched the more I wanted.

He was like the most intoxicating elixir that I would desire forever, no matter the ruin.

"You will not marry him," Eldrin suddenly announced, though there was no audience to hear.

"What?"

"I mean it—you will not marry him."

"We've discussed this—I can't say no. You're the one who told me I can't say no."

Eldrin took a few measured steps, slowly pacing the flower-covered ground. "The festival is in two weeks. A little more than fourteen days. If you perform well, you can declare to Vanir that you are overjoyed with being in these lands, and will bind with the barrier with or without his hand. He will be pressed to step aside and let you be free."

"He will?"

Eldrin nodded, the light catching his gorgeous silver eyes. "Yes, we have the perfect opportunity in front of us. The festival is a holiday where unmarried women are given a lot of leeway when voicing their opinions. A lot of engagements are made that day—and broken. And the king marrying a human woman isn't popular in the first place—you've seen it yourself. If you can convince the people that you are so overjoyed to be here that marrying him is unnecessary, then it will be hard for him to disagree. It will give him an opportunity to set you aside gracefully and keep his court happy." Eldrin placed a hand on his hip, and nodded. "I think he will do it." I couldn't tell if Eldrin was trying to convince me, or himself.

Did Siliana know about the dance, how it was a chance for me to escape everything? Was that why she was trying so hard to prepare me for it? Resting everything on this—on a dance and the king's favor—seemed risky, but Eldrin knew the customs. He knew his brother. And he wanted me.

Despite everything, my heart soared. He wanted me.

Eldrin took a few steps closer to me and wrapped me in his arms, placing a kiss on my head. I melted against him, a deep sigh escaping my lips. I could stay here forever, being held by him, breathing in his scent, feeling the thick panes of his chest under my head.

"Keep everything between us," Eldrin said softly, "and do as well as you can at the dance. That's all we need to do."

"That's it?"

"That's it."

"But what if I want..." I leaned my head back and kissed him again, nibbling on his bottom lip in a way that made him groan.

"Not yet," he said once he broke away. I felt him pressed against me, a silent reminder of how much it must have pained him to restrain himself. "Wait. We have to hide everything, but not forever. We can do this."

"Yes," I said. "I can."

I hoped.

"Come," Eldrin suddenly said, gently guiding me out of the glade, though his gaze now carried a heavier meaning, a secret longing now shared between us. "We won't be alone for much longer. Tell me about your favorite city." When I raised a questioning eyebrow he continued, "I'm asking something very ordinary so that when our minders find us—and they will soon—they won't find anything wrong. Because we are *doing* nothing wrong."

Fair enough. Eldrin wanted me to move on to an ordinary topic and forget the way that I wanted nothing more than to lay with him in this field? To take him for myself and feel every inch of his bare skin against me?

Alright then—Eldrin was going to hear all about the virtues of Las Vegas.

CHAPTER SEVENTEEN

AMBER

I took Eldrin's warning to heart. I didn't need to be a psychic to know that his being in a relationship with me could mess up everything for us in the worst possible way. Politics aside, Vanir didn't seem the type that would be alright with his betrothed being in a relationship with anyone else. His pride wouldn't allow it.

So, once we returned to the palace, I behaved like the ideal future elven queen. I danced. I learned what manners and culture Siliana could teach me. I even made an attempt to be friendly to the other courtiers. And I let Eldrin show me around the city to pass the time, with him constantly maintaining a respectable distance. Unfortunately. Every sight of him resurged the memory of his lips against mine, the feeling of his marble body under my hands. It all rekindled a very familiar ache.

And I had to wait.

I was on my way to meet Eldrin at our usual place at the foot of the stairs at the palace, when a familiar presence towered over me as I turned the corner.

"Good morning, Ivas," I said coolly.

"A lovely morning indeed," he said, his thin lips curling into a smirk, revealing oddly white teeth.

I looked around—we were alone. And Ivas was right in my way, hands on his hips, no doubt waiting for me to try to walk around him so that he could block me.

"Can I help you?" I asked.

"No...not yet."

"Alright, then." I waited for him to move.

"But you will."

A chill worked through me. "I'm sure."

His poignant gaze worked up and down my body, making me want to tuck my arms around myself. But I was not about to give him the satisfaction. "Vanir is a generous king," he said quietly, yet in a tone that managed to make me grit my teeth. "He shares so much with me. Everything."

"That's great for you two," I said. "Truly admirable." My throat was dry. I picked up on his meaning—with his leering I would've had to be dense not to, but my only concern was hiding my shaking. And get out of this encounter.

He opened his mouth to reply at the same moment that blessed footsteps sounded down the hall. I sighed with relief as he turned to leave and gave me a slick wave. "I'll be making your further acquaintance very soon, Amber."

As soon as I could—once I was sure Ivas was gone—I rushed and met Eldrin, stilled my racing heart, and did my best to forget Ivas. Ivas was a creep, and there was nothing Eldrin could do, other than help me forget.

"This is one of our art collections," Eldrin said to me twenty minutes later. "It belongs to the royal family, but its enjoyment has been gifted to our people."

"Wow."

That wasn't an understatement. We were in a room with ceilings that towered high above us. Ample light streamed in through the window, but there were no sconces, likely to guard against fires. The walls were carved with the same skulls and vines that could be found in the rest of the palace, but here the effect was muted. Instead, the designs were camouflaged into the white wood that made up the structure. Unless one looked closer, it was easy to miss all the signs of death. In Great Glen, that was an accomplishment.

The hall was crammed with art. Every few feet there was a new painting or sculpture, and each one seemingly depicted a different creature. Many were familiar-ish, like elves, fae, and orcs, but there were many more I had never seen before, including humanoid creatures made entirely of fire.

"What are those?" I asked, pointing at a picture of women who were seemingly made of lava, their skin cracking to reveal bright fires underneath. "Nymphs?"

"No. Elementals."

"What's the difference?"

"Those are nymphs," Eldrin said, pointing at a picture of beautiful women lounging in a grove, human except for the fact that their skin was dark green and they seemed to have moss for hair. In the back, a towering muscular man, who seemed to be half-tree, watched over the women like he was their guardian. "Nymphs can be trouble enough, but trust me—you don't want to encounter an elemental."

"Are there any in the Woods?"

"No. And thank the sun for that."

I took a few more steps and pointed at another picture. "I know them. Fae?"

"Gold Fae. Or Dawn Fae. Whatever they are calling themselves this century."

I frowned. "They're...metal." Indeed, one fae had golden metal panes on his face where his cheek should have been, and another had a torso that was open to reveal machinery, like a clock instead of entrails.

"Yes. They have taken liberties with their...inventions."

"But I've heard of them. They don't look like this."

"They're careful to hide it, as best as they can. Along with the humans who came with them."

We walked for a few more paces and we came across a statue of an angel, a brooding creature who had burning runes carved along his waistband like a belt. I had heard of angels in New Jersey, but they were aloof, even for creatures new to this world. I wasn't sure I had ever seen a credible picture.

Another turn brought me to a painting of a man sitting in a pond. Above the surface he was gorgeous, with stunning cheekbones and eyes that were a mesmerizing blue. Below the surface he was a skeleton, surrounded by death literally littered around him.

"What is that?" I asked.

"One of the rusalki," Eldrin replied bitterly.

"They're all women, I thought."

"They have to reproduce somehow," Eldrin said with amusement. "But you are correct, the men are almost never seen."

"Why?" I asked.

"The women make a better trap."

I nodded and kept walking. "It seems like you really don't like them."

"Back home, our lands bordered theirs. They have taken far too many of our kind. Even those who should have known better."

"They eat them, or...?"

"I assume so. But all we know is that they are never seen again." He shook his head. "And the rusalki we have captured have never stayed alive long enough to talk." When he saw my confused look he said, "They have a tendency to bite off their own tongues."

"Ah." Well, the rusalki were nowhere near here, so they weren't anything I had to worry about.

I looked around the room. Other than us, it was unoccupied. Now, it was very possible that someone was watching us somewhere, but this was the most alone we had been in days. We didn't dare have Eldrin come inside my room any more, because of the rumors it could start.

"Eldrin," I said, my voice barely above a breath. "After this—all of this—what happens to us?"

Eldrin skimmed the back of my hand with his human-like finger, that light touch igniting a flame that spread through my body, turning the latent ache of desire into full on agony. Then he said, just as quietly, "It will have to wait until after the barrier is in place and there is less attention on you, but I *will* have you. We will be together. But in the meantime, we will have to act as we are. We are too watched. Our time here could be interrupted at any moment." Then he looked me in the eyes and said, "If you will have me, Amber. If you are willing to stay here, I'm yours. If you desire it."

I trembled as he spoke, that familiar, all-consuming warmth filling me again. I could handle being trapped here, in the Darkening Woods, if I could have Eldrin.

"Of course, I will have you," I said to Eldrin. Before this, my yearning was a relatively small thing, but this moment ignited it to an inferno that pushed aside all reason. I wanted him. I would have him. I saw in him the mirror to me, the part that could turn me into something better than what I had been. Someone who would allow me to be me, even here, in a devastating land where everything was strange and cruel. The Darkening Woods were aptly named, for if one was not careful, it would consume your soul.

"I understand the risks," my mouth said, but every other part of me screamed in protest. As much as I wanted nothing more than for Eldrin to touch me again, it was not worth whatever punishment that awaited. I needed to be alive to be with him, and so I would do whatever I had to.

CHAPTER EIGHTEEN

ELDRIN

I kept my word to Amber—I hid what I felt for her. I had to, no matter how often our first kiss replayed itself in my mind. No matter how the lightest caress from her hand pushed me to the edge of losing my self-control. I didn't touch her, other than to occasionally take her hand in guidance, no matter how much the gentle curves of her neck taunted me, her laugh enticed me, and how the sparkle in her eyes as she wove story after story enraptured me entirely.

What if Vanir knew how we felt about each other? Worse, what if he was counting on it? What if he knew of my weakness for her from the start and was just waiting for the opportunity to use her against me? I didn't voice my concerns to Amber, but seducing the king's betrothed would give him the excuse he needed to remove me. No one could fault him for executing the one who had violated the future queen.

And my downfall would leave her in a danger I didn't dare contemplate.

"There's something wrong," Siliana said from her place next to me. We were watching Amber practice her dance in a courtyard, and she moved fluidly, as if she was born to it. It was entrancing, the way she swirled her hips to an unheard rhythm, gentle movements that I couldn't be sure weren't done to entice me. She twirled and met my gaze, giving me a broad smile that I knew was for me and me alone.

But I couldn't enjoy any of this. The festival was tomorrow. Tomorrow. It would take all the blessings of fate for things to work out for us.

"There's nothing wrong," I said to Siliana.

"What are you planning, Eldrin?" Siliana asked, her voice barely audible. "This isn't just wanting her to do well. I've seen how you are looking at her, and how she looks at you. Which means others have, too."

I crossed my arms, letting the bones of my hand dig into my sleeves. A cool breeze soared through the courtyard, the rustling branches making a music of their own. "I know." I paused. "There's nothing I can do for now. And there are many things I forbid to let happen."

Siliana let out an exasperated sigh. "You're going to get yourself killed, you know that, right? Your mother would never allow—"

"Vanir has wanted to kill me since the day he took the throne. I've been expecting it."

"That doesn't mean you have to hand the opportunity to him. And what about her?" She gestured to Amber. "Vanir is not one to forget a slight."

"It will be fine. I promise."

Siliana stared at me. "I hope you know what you are doing. Do you not remember the days before the worlds broke?"

"Always." I had been locked in my rooms, in what was essentially a glorified cell, with a heavy guard outside the door. Only Vanir's desire to avoid rattling the court—many of my extended family protested and he couldn't silence them all—made him delay as long as he did. It was only the twisting of the worlds that had stayed his hand.

I couldn't let the uncertainty of that time dictate my actions now, not when the stakes had grown so much. We were no longer in the same Darkening Woods, and things had changed. It would be fine. Amber would perform the dance, as she was doing now. It was beautifully done, and there was no doubt that she could beg a boon from Vanir at the end. Vanir would agree to release her from her troth to him, she would keep her word and bind with the barrier, and then she would be free. As free as she could be in a place she could never leave. Surely, Vanir wouldn't mind if I took her and left him and his rule alone, the human far from sight and me no longer a threat. He'd prefer it.

And Siliana, I didn't have to worry about her because she dared to be my friend—she was well-connected, and admired, one of the few courtiers who could flit between factions without so much as a ripple. We had shared certain tutors as children as our mothers were good friends. I was her escort at her wedding. Between her parents' connections and her own, she would be safe. Vanir wouldn't harm her. It would gain him nothing and lose a lot of respect in the process if he did.

I broke away from my stewing to catch Siliana watching me, disapproval writ on her face. "I'm not sure what you're thinking, Eldrin," Siliana said. "But I hope you remember that things with Vanir have never gone as planned before. And only a fool would expect it to be different now."

CHAPTER NINETEEN

AMBER

Time had never moved so slowly. The days before the festival were sluggish, long hours stretching into endless days.

I had to pretend to be something I wasn't and hide most of my feelings, no matter who I was around. Even Eldrin. I didn't want to end up as another skull on Vanir's throne.

Damn, was that how he got all those skulls? Bad breakups?

And then there was that awful dance, that testament to elven flexibility. I had practiced the dance many times until my arms ached and my feet went numb, Eldrin watching me with a small grin. With his eyes on me I came alive, exposed in the best way. And at the end of each session he would give me a compliment, step just a little closer than he should, and then back away, leaving me untouched in the cool fall air. Empty.

Sometimes I would go with Siliana and watch him train, and I saw again and again how he was able to deftly remove my attacker that night. He was able to duck a blow, take his opponent's arm, and throw him to the ground in the time it took me to blink. With unnatural grace he caught daggers flung at him in midair, and threw them back at another target, hitting it right in the center. His bare skin shone in the sun, a sheen of sweat covering him while he maneuvered his opponent. And yes, I couldn't but imagine myself in the opponent's place. I'd be wrapped around him, his glistening skin pressed against mine, his arms delving around and enveloping me. He could move me so that I was bent before him, my skirts hiked up, my legs—

"Staring at him won't make him come any closer," Siliana had muttered from her place at my side at the training ring. "This was a horrible idea."

"No," I had said, "this was excellent."

And when the matches were done and Eldrin strode towards us, it took all of my restraint not to embrace him.

"You did well," I said.

"Just well?" he asked with a smirk.

"'Well' is plenty enough for all of us," Siliana said, rolling her eyes.

I smiled at Siliana. I had to ignore the way Eldrin locked eyes with me, as if he was thinking the exact same illicit things.

Tomorrow it would all change. It *had* to change—I couldn't remain this desperate to touch him for much longer, to have him whisper his desires in my ear. To pin me underneath him, and feel his hard length against me. The dance had to accomplish what we wanted. Would it work? Siliana had instructed me as best she could, and by this point I could shake the maple leaves like I had been doing it my whole life. I wasn't as tall and graceful as the elves, but I knew how to make a leaf vibrate.

More practice wouldn't help me. It was time to rest before the day that would decide everything. Ha—as if I could relax. So much depended on tomorrow. If I tripped and fell, if I shook the branch the wrong way, that would ruin everything.

"Where are we going?" I asked Eldrin as we strolled through the city. Elves darted through the streets, which were decorated with hanging boughs and garlands made of vines and vibrant leaves, somehow making the place even more devoted to autumn than it had been before. Piles of textured gourds, brilliant yellow corn, red apples, and deer heads with flopping tongues sticking out of the sides of their mouths waited on the street for their custodian to swoop down and arrange them amongst the opulence. Apparently, decapitated animals were mandatory for this festival. Hopefully decapitated humans were not.

"Dinner," Eldrin said. "I thought it would be good for you to be seen in the city, so that when you make your request, more people will be familiar with you. Their support could push Vanir to grant it."

"Shouldn't we have done that...earlier?"

"No," Eldrin said, voice certain. "I want them to be familiar, but too much would..." He shook his head. "There are too many who might mean you harm. I didn't want to give them any opportunity."

Ah, that. The assassin almost no one mentioned to me again, despite that being the most traumatic event of my life. Even more than the spider. I was starting to get the impression that random assassination attempts were just a fact of life at this court. Hopefully, that wouldn't be the case once I was done with the binding and not engaged to the king. If I got lucky, they would leave me alone. The unhappy elves might decide that I wasn't worth killing. Might.

Eldrin guided me through the streets of Great Glen, where the gentle wooden curves meshed with constant reminders of death, until we came to a dark brown wooden structure with a weather-beaten sign hanging over the door. Lit by a lantern encased in orange glass and curved iron, the sign was written in a language I couldn't read. Apparently no one could. Not anymore. But the owners kept the sign anyway, a symbol of how they hoped to return home. I couldn't imagine losing everything about my native language except my name—that would be like missing a piece of myself that I would forever be searching for.

The inside was as worn as the outside and filled with elves of all ages. The walls were carved with the familiar skulls and bones, plastered against a backdrop of etchings of oak trees. The tables were made of fine—if worn—wood, obviously well-used potentially over centuries. Unlike a restaurant in the mortal world, everyone here was oddly...contained. Smooth. There was no carousing or spilling. Every movement was so gentle, as if everyone was a part of some dance. I wasn't sure I'd ever get used to that, a people who were so contained that even eating dinner was a tableau of grace. I surveyed the crowd, ignoring how elves looked at me with confusion and distrust. I took a deep breath. Their expressions were the point. That was why I was here. For the people. To change some minds.

There were children sitting next to frustrated elders, men and women conversing over their cups, and more men sitting at a table against a wall. One man looked awfully familiar. Oristan.

"Eldrin," he called out, beckoning to us and shooing his companions away, while simultaneously gesturing for more drinks. They begrudgingly obeyed, moving exactly one table over. "You can't avoid me forever."

"No," Eldrin said, guiding me forward with his hand on my upper back, "but I was hoping for a couple more weeks of peace."

I grinned. Anyone who could tease Eldrin automatically fascinated me.

"Ah, here is the famous woman," Oristan said, deftly raising a goblet to me while taking two more from a passing server. "I was wondering when you would deign to join us."

"We've been occupied," Eldrin said, taking his seat next to me at the table. I clasped my hands on my lap and foisted my back into an unnaturally straight position. No point in standing out more than I already did.

"With what? What could possible be keeping you so busy that you don't have time to visit your best friend in these whole woods?" Oristan asked in a way that said he already knew. He just wanted to hear someone confirm it.

"I've been practicing for the Maple Dance," I said, taking my wine from Oristan. And then frowned. During these weeks of practice I had made so many names for it that I struggled to recall the right one. "Oak Dance?"

"Ah, the Deathless Leaves Dance," Oristan said. I was 90% sure that wasn't what Siliana called it, but I nodded because that sounded just fine to me. "You're letting her participate?" he asked Eldrin.

"There is no 'letting' involved. You're assuming that His Majesty has need of the inadequate counsel of one such as me," Eldrin said softly.

"Eldrin, you're still a prince." He smirked and pointed at Eldrin with a bony finger. "Amber, if you're wondering if he's always like this, the answer is that he's usually worse."

I chuckled. "I guessed as much. I wouldn't expect him any other way." I wouldn't want him any other way.

Eldrin whipped his head towards me, the corner of his lip curved up. This didn't go unnoticed by Oristan, who reclined. "Well, and here I thought I saw enough of miracles for a lifetime," he said. "Forget the world being torn apart, here is Eldrin, showing happiness."

"Careful," Eldrin said, turning his attention back to Oristan.

"For what? Our future queen should know that she is having a positive effect on everyone around her. Life and death feed from the same hand."

"What?" I asked.

Eldrin answered. "It's an old saying—it basically means that two misfortunes can make a positive result. Ironically, it came from the veinwart." Yes, ironic indeed.

"Two wrongs make a right?" I offered. "That's what humans say sometimes."

Oristan nodded and sipped his wine. "I like her," he said once he wiped his mouth. "That's better than your explanation."

"And what are the wrongs?" I asked.

"The wrongs are twofold," Oristan said, counting with his fingers. "One, you were kidnapped. Sorry, Eldrin, but that is what happened."

Eldrin took a long drink, and I resisted the urge to place a hand on his leg. Instead, I said, "It's alright, it's like Beauty and the Beast. Without the Beast. Or the French palace. Or the library."

"There was a beastly veinwart and we do have palace libraries," Oristan chimed in.

"I'm not sure what Beauty and the Beast is," Eldrin said, "but I don't believe you are helping my case."

"You did save my life though," I said. "You didn't hold my family hostage until I agreed to take their place."

"See?" Oristan said, "Eldrin is an admirable man. He doesn't need to threaten women with their imprisoned family members. He just gets a veinwart to do it for him." Eldrin sighed and rubbed his eyes.

I barked out a laugh and asked, "So, what is the second wrong?"

"Two, the barrier is failing in the first place and some poor mortal is stuck fixing it for us. And then we get the positive result—we get you, my dear."

I smiled sadly. "I wish others felt that way."

Oristan flicked his wrist. "Oh, they'll come around in time. If this court isn't trying to murder someone or incite anarchy it wouldn't know what to do with itself. It might actually be forced to govern." Oristan lowered his voice. "Someone should, at any rate." Eldrin shot Oristan a glare and the topic was dropped. I had been insulated from most effects of Vanir's governorship, other than whispered conversations when other elves seemed to forget that I had ears, but it appeared that there was more to it than even what I had heard.

The three of us ate dinner and talked for some time about things that were suitable for eavesdropping, like how I found the Darkening Woods and if I was excited about the festivities. I wasn't stupid—I'd watched enough historical dramas—so I answered every question like it would be repeated back to Vanir. Because it probably was. From how Eldrin gave small nods once in a while, I think I did decently. There was a time and a place to be my sarcastic self, and it wasn't during this outing, and I was careful to barely touch the wine. While we ate, several other elves approached our table, were introduced by Oristan in boisterous tones, and then I promptly forgot them. Names and faces were never my strong suit, and everyone here looked very similar—tall and handsome. All in all, it was nice to be welcomed, such as it was.

Once night fell, Eldrin excused us, and we walked back to the palace. Now the city was silent, resting in preparation for the following day. The sky was empty of clouds, and even with the city's muted lights it was possible to see stars. The brisk wind was quiet, a fall evening that hinted at a promise of frost.

"Are they the same here as they are back home?" I asked. "The stars."

"No," Eldrin said. My cheeks burned—of course the sky would not have traveled with them. "Back home, the stars weren't just white—they could be every color, depending on the weather and the seasons. They were the first sign that something wasn't right. Before we realized..."

"The barrier."

Eldrin nodded. "We had one around our old home, around the entire forest. And when we moved it must have traveled and adjusted, albeit weaker than it was before."

"You really needed that barrier? I mean, we talked about this before, but was your home really that dangerous?"

"Yes. We were a land at war. Always. Most recently with the rusalki who share our borders, but they aren't the only ones."

"Over what? Why do you hate the rusalki?"

"Nothing that matters now," he said, clenching his jaw. "The short of it is that they took one of us, and refused to give him back."

"They didn't eat him?"

"No. We had...reason to think that he was alive. May still be alive. And we didn't want them taking any more of our people, for whatever reason."

"I think that's a fair request."

"But because of dangers like that," Eldrin continued, "we needed a barrier, for our allies seemed to shift with the seasons. Even though our enemies from our old world who made it here are presumably weak and distracted, we don't want to take the chance that they will use this opportunity to destroy us while they can. Not every people's lands here have their capital and ruler, but ours do. We are uniquely vulnerable."

"How did you learn about the others that came here with you?"

"Carefully. Fortunately, humans are very good at broadcasting news in public places."

That was an understatement.

I understood a little more about why the barrier was such an issue to the elves—it wasn't just about staying away from mortals—there were immortals who could cause trouble.

"If I can help, let me know," I said. "I mean, if there are certain groups you're wondering about or haven't been able to confirm. I might have heard something."

"I appreciate it, Amber," Eldrin said. "And I may accept your offer, once the barrier is settled and we are...free for other things."

Heat returned to my cheeks, for a very different reason. It was an innocent statement, innocently said, but there was a a secret meaning that was only too clear to me.

By this point we had entered the palace grounds and approached the steps to the hall that led to my room. Soon, we would have to say goodbye, though I suspected Eldrin never went far during the night. The assassin weighed heavy in my memory and I would've been very surprised if he let it go far from his.

"Wish me luck," I said, giving him a grin. "For the leaf shaking."

"No need," Eldrin said with a small smile that lit up his face. "You will be perfect." He leaned forward as if he was going to kiss me and then stopped himself. We were never truly alone.

Only one more day. Only one more day and this would all be behind us.

I was glad Eldrin had such confidence in me, because I definitely didn't.

CHAPTER TWENTY

ELDRIN

Finally, the day that would decide everything had arrived, and I didn't know whether to be relieved or terrified.

Our delicate balance was beyond tiring, wearing on me to the point that I would've despaired if I had to keep up this pretense forever. It was hard to protect Amber, while trying not to make it look like I was absolutely devoted to her. To be friendly with Amber, while not showing that she consumed every thought. To obey Vanir, while hiding that I wanted nothing more than to slam that crown into his throat. Not down it, into it, so that the blood and gristle and all rendered into a pulp and tore his life from him. Unfortunately, that dream could never become a reality.

Today could change everything. It *would* change everything.

After spending the early morning hours strolling near Amber's room, close enough to hear if anyone tried to enter, I was able to step away when the guards changed at dawn with those I trusted. Besides, the palace would soon be bustling and it would be harder for another murder attempt to take place. Luckily, elves didn't need nearly as much sleep as humans, and we could choose to rest in a state that was close to wakefulness if needed. Otherwise, I wouldn't have been able to watch Amber as I had these prior weeks. However, I still had a body, and that body had its needs.

While Siliana was preparing Amber for the festival, I took a few moments to eat and rest. After a short sleep, I sat in the palace's dining hall with other elves, many of whom were consuming the same cream-white bread with berry jam and herbal tea as me. Despite the crowd, I was left alone to gather my thoughts, and steady my heart that was threatening to lurch through my chest. There was so much that could go wrong today, and only a few paths for it to go right. Siliana was right—it was far too likely I'd be giving Vanir what he wanted.

"My, look what I found," Ivas said, strutting towards me. I tried not to frown. Ivas was my brother's "companion," who had decided to interrupt us during the party where Amber had met Vanir. I was just as happy to see him now as I was then. Other elves stopped eating and turned to watch. Encounters between us were rarely uneventful.

Ivas was dressed for the festival in a tight dark purple tunic and breeches and black leather boots. Around his torso was a jeweled ribcage, likely crafted from a deer. Vines and flowers gathered on his shoulders, spilling over a large cloak that covered the entire ensemble.

"Is this Eldrin, alone?" Ivas practically cooed. "Why are you here and not with your pet?"

I ground my teeth. It was not worth picking a fight with him. Not here. Not now. Not when we were so close. "She is preparing," I said.

"Ah, I suppose she has a lot to prepare for today, doesn't she?" Ivas said, jutting out his large chin. "This is only the first, isn't it? With so many important events to come."

"Indeed."

"You know," Ivas said, sauntering around the table, "I think I shall enjoy getting to know Amber. His Majesty is very generous, after all. He loves my ideas."

"Yes, His Majesty is generous," I said, eying a gold necklace around Ivas's neck that I didn't recognize. Another gift from Vanir? I remembered Amber's comments about Vanir's greed and cruelty. I had been so consumed with my own guilt and failures, so desperate to believe that I hadn't made a horrible mistake, that I hadn't seen what was in front of me.

"Well, I think Amber will learn to be generous with me, too, in time. Humans always are a little stubborn at first, aren't they?"

Taking a deep breath and digging my skeleton hand into my thigh until it hurt, I took a drink to buy myself time to think. Was Ivas behind the attempt on Amber's life? Unlikely. Vanir wouldn't have been so clumsy if he wanted Amber dead, and Ivas wasn't known for doing things without Vanir's approval. Vanir was cruel, but luckily, my brother was the mind behind their despotic union, a union that was rumored to be physical, though I had my doubts that was the situation.

Ivas wanted something from me, from this encounter. Now, what was it? To get a reaction out of me? If so, his comments about Amber were certainly a valiant attempt. No, there had to be something else.

"What is it?" I asked, setting down my ceramic cup. "Surely, you didn't come here just to speak in riddles."

"No, never," Ivas said, his smirk dropping into a sneer. "I just feel like you're putting so much effort into something so temporary."

"What is temporary?"

"Why, your little pet."

"Indeed, as it was always intended to be." I nodded respectfully. "She will be queen and then Vanir will be responsible for her care."

"Oh, Eldrin. Somehow you are both boring and too expressive. A unique combination." Ivas stalked off, giving me a little wave as he did so and ignoring the gawking onlookers. "You'll see."

Once he left, the chatter resumed, and I went back to my tea, though any joy I found in the flavor was gone. I sloshed the liquid around my cup, watching it leave a pale green layer on the sides.

That could have gone worse. Neither of us had to be restrained, and no one died.

But something Ivas said left my stomach uneasy, and not the part about him being with her. That was just talk. No, I was concerned about something far deeper. He was taunting me about Amber being a temporary ward, yes, but there was something more to it. Something I was missing.

A sudden chill ran through me, as if the fall winds were freezing my veins. I had to resist the sudden urge to flee the room and act on my suspicions, though my body seized, desperate to do *something*.

What if Ivas knew something I didn't? What if there was something more to Vanir's plans for Amber?

What if the barrier wasn't the reason Vanir wanted her after all?

I narrowed my eyes, watching Ivas stride out of the room, his dramatic cloak trimmed with expensive furs trailing after him. Another new gift, one of many, now that I bothered to notice them.

The sound of musicians tuning their instruments and preparing for the festival started outside, their strings and flutes carrying through the open windows. Laughter quickly followed, people already starting to celebrate before it officially began.

Whatever I was going to do, I had to do it quickly. I only had a couple hours before the festival events started, and luckily for me, Ivas was already dressed. His rooms would be vacant. Even servants had a day of leisure today, so most rooms would be empty. But even if I managed to make it inside, would his rooms have the information I needed to protect Amber? Did that information exist at all?

To avoid attracting attention from anyone Vanir may have sent to watch me, I went back to my own rooms and dressed, as everyone expected. These were the same rooms I'd had my entire life, even when I was my father's heir. Vanir didn't seem to feel the need to move me, since he took the king's suites. And he likely had other concerns than where I laid my head. I half-expected that Ivas would've taken my rooms out of spite, but Ivas had his own grand apartments—arguably better than mine.

Today, I paid the room's décor even less attention than I normally did, the onyx mosaic of skulls and vertebrae on the floor something that had welcomed me almost every day of my life. My clothes for today were laid out on a bench, three different options that my attending servant provided for me. By this point he knew me well, and knew that I changed my mind enough when it came to events like this that multiple options were a good idea.

Before I did anything else, I had to dress. The closer the time moved to the start of the festivities, the more that people would wonder why I wasn't ready to attend. So, yes, while I was going to be wearing ostentatious finery, somehow—just for today—it would help me blend in. The garments set out for me were simple compared to what Amber would be forced into—gowns with delicate layers that required a helping hand. As for me, I could get into my garments alone, and I ended up choosing something especially easy—they were basically just breeches and a robe that left my chest bare. On the shoulders rested a small skull of a primate that was treated with a hardened lacquer, and accented with real vines, flowers, and bones. I brushed my hair, changed my clothing, and that was it. Less than five minutes of work and I was now ready for a formal court event.

I confidently strode through the palace halls, making my way to Ivas's rooms that were located in one of the suites devoted to royal family members, careful to turn down a few other hallways first to make sure that no one was following me. No one was. Vanir likely assumed that there were too many eyes for me to get into too much trouble today, and he was likely right. And this wasn't trouble. I was...gathering information. There was nothing troublesome about it. Or so I repeated to myself. If caught, it wouldn't do to act flustered.

I was about to turn the corner to the hall to Ivas's rooms when my brother's familiar raw voice echoed down the hallway. Cursing silently, I leaned against the wall, hiding from view as best I could without looking too suspicious. As soon as I heard footsteps, I'd start walking the opposite way. I was doing nothing wrong.

Nothing wrong.

I had decided to take this path to the main courtyard—that was all. And I stopped to rest.

Several moments passed, my breath steadied, and then I listened. At first it was nothing of note, just discussions about whether the music was arranged for today and where Vanir wanted the visiting nobles to stay, not that the kingdom was large enough for much "visiting" these days.

"She's still practicing for the dance?" Vanir asked. "How quaint. I thought she would've decided not to attempt it once she saw the other dancers." There was only one "she" that they could be talking about.

"You did order her," Ivas pointed out.

"I thought she'd give up by now and plead illness. And she's still trying?"

"Yes. Trying hard, too," Ivas said.

"Admirable. But pointless, considering."

"You don't think she's attempting to gain your favor? I think Lady Siliana would have mentioned the role the dance plays, and the opportunities."

"I'm sure the answers to both of those possibilities is 'yes,'" Vanir said. "But like I said, it doesn't matter. It's pointless." A pause. "Remember."

"Oh. Right, the barrier."

"Exactly. Not like she will need my favor for long. Remember—they still think I have that remedy."

The two of them cackled and I clenched my fists, trying to recall what I knew of the magic that formed the barrier—and it was precious little. How did the barrier get strengthened? I had assumed that it was like any shielding magic—a prayer and a few drops of blood. The original barrier around the Darkening Woods took the lives of thirteen elves to create it thousands of years ago. I had assumed that since this was just a strengthening and not creating something new, and the barrier was much smaller, that it would, at most, just take some blood.

I should have known better—that it would require something more. A life.

I cursed myself, cursed the day I decided to let Vanir have all of this power. My fury was dampened only by necessity, my fists shaking.

Amber wouldn't need Vanir's favor for long, because Vanir didn't think Amber was going to be alive long enough for it to matter.

How many people knew the truth? Vanir and Ivas, for sure, and likely some of the sages who were devoted to the trees and listened to their secrets. Possibly a few archivists, bound to secrecy. Not many knew the details about the magic supporting the barrier, because that would open it up to being destroyed. By this point, the original thirteen were no longer mourned and were regarded as heroes, and no one likely suspected that any sacrifice of the sort could be demanded again.

But why tell Amber—and everyone who wasn't a sage or Ivas—that she was going to be queen...unless it was all to make her go willingly to die. Did they even need a mortal to support the barrier? Was that Vanir's lie too, to avoid the politics of sacrificing one of his own people, who were already discontented from the shifting of the worlds and his own abuses? From how Vanir was speaking, he didn't have the promised remedy at all, the one that would remove the poison from Amber's blood for good. Another lie to convince Amber to die with a smile on her face. I gritted my teeth—I had brought her here, only to be used and killed.

"It's going to be a long month for us," Ivas said. "I cannot wait for this to be done."

"Nonsense. It will go quick, the barrier will be restored, then I'll get my condolences at the sudden and unexpected death of my wife and all of this will be behind me. And if I'm lucky, I'll finally be able to do something about my brother."

"From what I'm hearing, he's doing exactly what you expected."

"Good."

I didn't stay to hear more. I had questions—lots more—but I had heard enough. And I had to act. Did Vanir really plan all of this? Was it all his idea? The king had counselors, ones sworn to serve the Darkening Woods, and Vanir wasn't necessarily the most clever man, even if he was ruthless. He had a tendency to banish or exile councilors rather than attempt to sway them. A few had died, suspiciously in retrospect, but Vanir had to be careful he didn't upset too much of the court too fast. I cursed my own folly yet again—I should have suspected more of Vanir. I shouldn't have thought that anything was beyond my brother. How many times would he have to harm or threaten me before I learned that Vanir would do anything to anyone if it suited his purposes? What was he doing to our people that they were so afraid to protest? The Darkening Woods was on the precipice of a reckoning, with sides already cast, and it was far too likely that many innocents would die in the process. Including Amber.

Regardless of who knew about the barrier, I couldn't stay in Great Glen. Neither of us could. If we didn't get that remedy, Amber would die from the veinwart's venom, whether Vanir sacrificed her or not. There was no path to life for her in this city. I would take her as far from here as I could, we would find a cure, and then we would flee, back into her world where no one could hurt her. Yes, our departure would break the barrier, but Vanir was on his own. He should have been honest with his people if he didn't want the consequences.

As quickly as I could, I rushed to Amber's room and pushed open the door, finding Siliana putting the finishing touches of cosmetics on Amber. I closed the door behind me and fished out some weapons that I kept hidden under the bed. Ones Amber didn't seem to know about by the way she exclaimed, "What are you doing? What's *that*? Are those daggers?"

"Eldrin?" Siliana asked warily.

"Siliana," I said, buckling the knives around my waist and hiding them as best I could under the robe. "I cannot tell you why I am here, because it will endanger your life to know. All I can ask is that you leave and go someplace for an hour or two. One that isn't associated with the festival. When asked, you can then tell them the truth—that Amber was ready for the festival, and you left her with me."

Siliana nodded, worry marked around her eyes. "I see," she said knowingly. "I will go to the tree to pray that our world is reunited. I won't be the only one there on a day such as this."

"The tree?" Amber asked.

"The shrines I told you about," Siliana said.

"Oh."

Good, I was pleased with Siliana's idea. That was an excellent way to get Siliana safely away, and kept ignorant of the treason I was about to commit. Sadly, this wasn't the first time we had to have a similar conversation. A nearly identical one occurred the night my father died, and I told Siliana that I was leaving to "see a good friend." That good friend happened to be Oristan and his father, who quickly notified the lords and ladies of what had occurred, and of the coup that was taking place. That was how—through extensive negotiations—I lived, provided that I swore oath of allegiance to King Vanir. My oath was brutal, but it was necessary—I vowed not to shed Vanir's blood. It was a bit more dramatic than Vanir's oath of kingship, in which he vowed that he would give of himself in service to the land. But I was a deposed heir, and drastic measures were deemed necessary. We elves of the Darkening Woods took our oaths seriously. The magic that fueled us required it. And exacted the price of breaking them.

Siliana gripped Amber's hands firmly and wished her well, gave me one more desperate look, and then left without another word, her soft footsteps fading on the stone floor. She knew better than to say anything else, and there was nothing she needed to say. Every goodbye carries the possibility of death, and this one was all too likely to come to fruition.

Once Amber and I were alone, I dug through the room and found her a light cloak, one appropriate for today's weather, and handed it to her. Anything more than that would raise suspicions, including supplies. I frowned at her shoes, those delicate slippers that were little more than fabric with a thin leather sole, but that was another thing that couldn't be helped.

"Where are we going?" Amber asked.

"You have determined that we're not going to the festival?"

"I'm naïve, not oblivious," Amber said. "Shouldn't we put on something...sturdier? I'm guessing you don't need daggers for a walk through the gardens."

"No." I put finishing touches on buckling the weapons while I talked. "If anyone sees us, and someone will, they need to assume that we're just going for a little walk until the festival. Anything else will be noted. Remember the path we took to the glade?" Amber nodded. "We will take that route again, but turning to go near the lakes instead. And then we will disappear."

"Why?" she asked, her lips pursed. "I'll go, of course, but...why?"

I lowered my voice. "He will kill you if you stay."

Amber's skin turned ashen. "Oh."

I took her hand, not daring to touch the rest of her. Not yet. "Don't worry," I said solemnly. "I didn't fight Vanir before, but I had nothing to fight for. Now I do. Until the last of my life is cleaved from me, I will keep you safe."

Amber let out a long breath and gave me a small smile. "I know. I trust you."

I smiled back, though my heart wrenched. I was going to put her trust to the test. If she was caught after today, it was very likely Vanir wouldn't keep her alive long enough to bond with the barrier. He would get rid of us both as soon as he could.

CHAPTER TWENTY-ONE

AMBER

E scape. Murder. Betrayal. Poison. Death.

Each word rang in my head with each step as I followed Eldrin through the palace, the reality of the situation sinking in. My eyes darted away from everyone we came across, worried they'd guess some secret just from looking at me. I could have stayed in my room and argued with him, insisting that he explain exactly what was going on before being willing to leave, but I had seen more than enough movies—nothing good came from a character dawdling when another warns them of impending doom.

Vanir had no intention of letting me live. I wish I could say I was surprised by this, but he didn't exactly give me a warm fuzzy feeling. And he had a throne of skulls. I was surprised that Vanir was going through the elaborate subterfuge at all, something that I'd ask Eldrin about later. Once we were safe.

Well, at least I wouldn't have to marry Vanir, nor would I have to perform the Little Leaf Jig for the whole judgmental court. There was always a bright side.

It was the bright side that I tried to focus on as I followed Eldrin through the crowded palace, staying unseen by staying in the open. I was dressed similarly to the other elves, in a gown of ochre lace that was accented with actual leaves and flowers. I had nothing on me that compared to Eldrin's skull shoulder pads—were those real bone? Judging from the belts made of finger bones and hair accessories crafted from ribs that festooned the other elves, my being bereft of bones was Siliana's choice. One that I appreciated.

We were just about to make it to the crowded hall, in order to slip out a side door and into the gardens, when a woman with an oddly tight voice called out "Eldrin! Come, visit with us." Eldrin muttered curses under his breath, but he managed to look properly intrigued by our newcomer. As for me, I bit my lip and lowered by gaze. This was a time to let Eldrin speak and try to get us out of this.

The woman rushed towards us, an unfamiliar cyclone of leaves and gauze. She was pretty. Of course she was—she was an elf. She looked at me, her expression as friendly and welcoming as a day-old gas station burrito. And that was the kindest phrasing I could think of to describe her. A lot of elves didn't like me, but most managed not to literally peer down their noses.

"Aren't you going to introduce me to your...companion?" she asked, eying my entire body. I stiffened and affected a noncommittal smile. "I've heard so much about her that I just had to see for myself."

"This is Lady Avalane," Eldrin said to me.

"That's it? That's how you're going to introduce me?" Lady Avalane asked. I could practically hear Eldrin's teeth grind together.

"She is one of my family's oldest friends," Eldrin explained. "And they have been good friends to me in turn. But she lives some distance from court." Ah—someone from a family that supported Eldrin, he was trying to say. That explained his manners...

"Yes, it pains me that we do not live closer. It seems that I missed a lot of interesting developments, until today." She eyed me once more, and I suspected that she was sizing me up for something. Eldrin said he didn't have any lovers here, but what about those who *wanted* to be? He was disgraced, but he was still a prince. A handsome prince. And if her family had its way, he would probably be king, right? Normally I would've been jealous, or vaguely insulted, but I had an execution to avoid—I wasn't overly curious about this woman's amorous adventures or ambitions.

"I need to escort Amber to the tree, but can I count on you to save me a dance?" Eldrin asked smoothly, though he had a tight smile.

"Of course. I shall look for you." The woman beamed, her smile genuine. For once. They exchanged curt farewells, the woman giving a sensual wave as she walked away, saving one last glare for me.

"What was that about?" I asked quietly once we were walking again.

"Nothing."

I raised an eyebrow.

"I mean it. I'm a prince. Sometimes people don't care about what branch they graft themselves to, as long as it's a royal one."

"So, you and her, you've never..."

Eldrin chuckled grimly. "We are a long-lived race, and she has already survived two spouses. Trust me—that is a spouse I do not desire." I didn't doubt him. I could tell instantly he had no more interest in her than if *she* had been a gas station burrito, but still, I was curious.

"Keep talking," he said softly. "It will make us more unremarkable."

Talking? Um...

"So, what is this tree everyone talks about? Does it talk? Is it really just a shrine?" While some of this Siliana had told me already, the tree was the first thing that popped into my head.

"No. The one we were discussing just now is a very old tree. The oldest. We go there to pray. Well, there are a few such sites in the Woods, but in Great Glen, that's what is meant by 'the tree.'"

"You pray. To a tree."

"Not the tree. The tree is connected to the heart of the Woods—technically they all are, but the oldest and largest trees have the strongest connections. There, we can use our magic to listen to the Woods, and its warnings."

"Literally listen?"

Eldrin frowned. "No. It's like...images, almost. Feelings." And then Eldrin went on and on and on about trees, magic, connections, and how basically the tree was some sort of Mother Nature telephone? Regardless, it kept us talking until we moved away from people and into the garden, where we fell silent as we snuck down the side path once more, slipping through the gate where we plunged into the autumn wilderness.

My heart thrummed in my ears. If someone was pursuing us, I had no hope of hearing them over the sound of my blood pounding and footsteps crunching leaves on the dirt path. Eldrin held my hand as he guided me, gently maneuvering me over puddles and branches that obstructed our way. I kept looking behind us—as if my mere human senses could detect an elf in time.

"If caught," Eldrin said quietly, "do not run. Do not scream. Our story is that I'm taking you for a walk before the dance begins. You were nervous, and I am helping you calm yourself."

"That's true enough."

He huffed in agreement. "That's why I'm not taking steps to hide our path, yet. I'll tell you when we need to run instead of trying to lie, and when we are going to have to watch where we step. But that time is not yet."

"Will they believe us?"

He paused before answering. "I hope we won't have to find out."

Despite the gravity of the situation, I couldn't help but admire the beauty of the Woods. The forest was the same as any other day, the morning sky clear and blue and the air temperate, just cool enough that I appreciated my cloak. A fresh breeze sailed through the branches, shaking another layer of leaves onto us. While the process of shedding leaves only took a few weeks in the human world, my understanding was that it could take months here for trees to lose all their leaves before spending a short time utterly bare.

"How much time do we have before they notice I'm gone? That *we're* gone?"

Eldrin paused before answering, his steps measured. "At least an hour. Maybe three. This is a massive festival, and Vanir won't expect us to leave in the middle of the day. Not when everyone knows you've been preparing for the dance, and expecting to ask a favor of him."

"A three hours' head start, from elves," I muttered, shaking my head. Yep, trying to run from elves in the woods. From what I've seen, the elves moved in the forest like dolphins in water. And I was basically a goldfish. A small, fat goldfish.

"I know these trails," Eldrin said confidently. "We have miles to gain on them before they even notice that we're missing."

"And then what? What are we going to do, even if we manage to hide from them?"

Eldrin didn't answer, and merely continued striding through the path, my hand gripped in his.

"Eldrin?"

"I'll explain it to you tonight," he finally said, in a tone that made my stomach churn. "Once we can rest."

CHAPTER TWENTY-TWO

ELDRIN

I did not lie to Amber—I could never lie to her. I knew these trails, these hidden ways through the forest, better than most of our people. I also knew how to cover our footsteps, to make it seem like we went in circles when Vanir's men finally hunted us. And they would hunt us.

For now, we didn't have to worry. For a couple days at least, while we carefully picked our way around the lakes, we would be fine. He wouldn't find us. I knew what we could eat, and I knew where we could rest. We wouldn't be comfortable, but we would live. And we would be able to hide.

We were not on our own. The Darkening Woods was dense and particular about who traveled on its hidden roads—it wouldn't be pleased with a large force plundering through its boughs. No, Vanir would be limited in who he could send, and how many. And it would take his minions some time to determine that we were gone at all. Vanir would search the palace first, the festival, and then the city. No one saw us leave the grounds, no one saw anything other than that we were with the other courtiers the morning of the festival, as expected. We likely had until nightfall until they realized we weren't in the king's domain at all.

We had time.

We had time.

But then, assuming that we successfully escaped, what next? I told Amber I would answer her questions later, but that was mostly to buy myself time to plan, for none of our options were good. I knew nothing about the poison that worked its way through Amber's veins. Elves were immune from the worst of it, though the veinwart's bite was painful and prone to blood poison, and the initial antidote she was given was used by our people to speed the healing from its initial effects. There was no point in trying to escape the Woods until we removed the poison.

We had no choice. I would have to take Amber to the most remote village in the Woods (ironically, Gold Glen) and beg a healer for help. Someone had to know something. And then I would take her back to her people. Where she belonged. Where she had a future. Where she would be safe.

At least, that's what I told myself would happen.

Two hours after we left Great Glen, we stopped. I had long ago told Amber that we had reached the point where we would have to run if encountered—no one would believe that we were merely walking any longer. We needed to keep going, but she needed rest. She didn't complain, but she was not an elf. She struggled as we went through the Woods, her breath racing and sweat gathering on her brow, her posture hunched.

"I'm fine," she said when I inspected her shoes after she slumped to the ground, the slippers already fraying at the seams. The small grove where we rested was off the tiny footpath we had been following, where I would be able to hear anyone coming long before it was an issue.

"Tell me if the pain becomes too much and you're finding it hard to walk," I said. Maybe I could steal something better for her to wear somewhere.

"Never."

"Please don't pretend—not with me."

"I'm tougher than you think." She cocked her head, flashing me a grin.

I nodded, defeated. It pained me that she would have difficulties during our journey, but there was nothing I could do. Besides, I had more pressing concerns.

I left her at a small shelter of intersecting trees while I looked for a meal. It didn't take me long—I found some berries and bitter nuts, and when I returned, I urged her to drink from the spring. Thus far, the Woods did not hint at anything amiss. The Woods wouldn't necessarily carry a song of alarm through its rustling leaves if we were being pursued, but there was always the possibility. And I had every sense strained to detect the first sign of pursuit.

And then, once Amber had a chance to rest and eat, we walked again, her steps more halting than before. But she still pushed on. We couldn't travel fast, dressed as she was, and a human at that. Tonight, I would have to trim the gown's hem and sleeves and hide the scraps, but for now I could admire her, the beautiful garment wasted with no one to see it.

"What's wrong?" Amber asked. "What are you looking at?"

"You," I said, and she blushed even deeper than her already flushed skin. We fell silent once more, focusing on a part of the path where the branches went low, making even Amber have to bend. We stayed quiet most of the day out of instinct, since my ears were our best defense to being alerted to being followed. There was so much I wanted to say to her, and I desperately wanted to hear her voice.

That all would have to wait.

There was nothing around us, nothing that didn't belong in the forest. Just Amber's steps on wet moss, her heavy breathing, and the rustling of leaves on the wind. This far from the city I could hear trees' songs, notes so faint it was unlikely Amber heard anything, though I was sure even she noticed that the Darkening Woods was alive. If I closed my eyes, I could pretend it was seven years ago, when my father was alive, and the world stretched before me, and everything I desired was only a voiced thought away. At that time I walked in the forest, trusting that I would be the lord of these lands when my time came, yet also fearing when that would happen. How much of my fear was that I didn't want to be burdened with the responsibility of ruling, as much as I feared failing at it? If I had done what I was supposed to, if I had fought to keep the throne, then Amber would be safe. Our people would have a ruler who was doing his best to protect them and not extract everything he could for greed. I didn't know what it would take for the barrier to be fixed, or if any human blood needed to be shed, but Amber was not going to be the one to repair it. I would watch the last drops of my life leave my veins before I let harm befall her.

And then, just when the sun was a rubescent orb hovering over the horizon, we rested next to one of the lakes. Small waves gently lapped at the shoreline, chiming as they ran over pebbles. Birds flew in the trees, snatching berries off nearby branches. The sun beamed its last rays on the water, cascading the surface with its glow.

And there she was next to me, taking in her first evening of freedom. With me.

"It's beautiful," Amber said. Her gaze was heavy, her head tilted. She could go no further tonight, and she needed to save her strength for the days ahead.

"It is," I agreed. "Rest. And stay close to the ground by these trees. I won't go far—I will find something for us to eat. She nodded and did as I suggested, landing on the ground with a soft thud. I would enjoy having her with me, as soon as her other needs were taken care of.

Leaving her hidden in the foliage, I searched nearby and found more berries and lily roots that grew in the waters. We were lucky—it was easy to scavenge in the Woods during this time of the year. And if we became desperate, I could hunt, if needed—I had my daggers—but these findings would serve as an adequate meal for the night. It was best to avoid hunting for another reason—a fire would be a risk, an unnecessary one. I doubted Amber wanted to eat raw game, and I wasn't about to try to make her.

Regardless, I had our meal.

It was time to rest.

We were alone, and for now, we were safe.

CHAPTER TWENTY-THREE

AMBER

We were alone in the woods, on dark paths that Vanir could not hope to follow.

At least, that's what I told myself when I narrated this to myself like an epic quest. I had to think of something, otherwise I would have been either paralyzed with fear, or panicked into running for the border. Neither option was smart.

Despite my fear, which made me jump at every sound that I didn't make, the scenery was gorgeous and pristine—nothing like my murky thoughts. The water at the lake where we rested sent its gentle waves to the shore, echoing the rhythm of my breath. Though there was no moon, I was able to see a little of my surroundings, thanks to how the trees and flowers seemed to carry a dim glow. This place was enchanted. Yes, the elven city was ethereal, but where we were now was nature, pure and untarnished in a way that our world never experienced. We were now in a place where nature itself seemed to cry out in joy.

Unfortunately, my feet were crying out in pain.

I stood at the edge of the water, soaking my feet in the gentle waves, while unbuttoning the top of my dress's outer bodice. The stays had rubbed my skin raw as we fled—the garment was not meant for fleeing through the woods. Since we were stopped for the night, then I may as well rest and let my skin get some air. We would be doing the same thing all over again tomorrow. The blisters would be—

"What are you doing?" Eldrin asked from behind me. "Stop," he said, his voice oddly deep.

My head whipped around, holding my garments in place. What was wrong? I hadn't intended to strip naked, but I could see how he'd think that. "I...of course." My cheeks flushed. "Sorry, I didn't think..."

The fire in his eyes, consuming me, told me that his objection wasn't out of modesty. A deep heat gathered inside me as his measured gaze roamed over my body. His expression was feral, animalistic, a single mindedness that told me that he wouldn't stop until he got what he wanted.

And he wanted me.

All the tension from the last few weeks rose, furious at being restrained for so long. The kiss. The glen. There were weeks of painful yearning. Now we were alone. And there was no elven fiancé in the way.

The morning's danger, the urgency that had pushed us to escape the city, evaporated like the night's mist, and it sunk in that I was finally alone with Eldrin, and there was nothing to stop us.

I drank in the sight of Eldrin, admiring him in a way that I hadn't had a chance yet today, since we had fled so quickly. Truly, he was dressed like elven royalty. His chest, revealed under that open robe, was perfectly sculpted, begging for my hands to run over the panes, which would then be followed by my lips. The robe's angles highlighted the rest of his form, all muscles and sharp edges. His dark breeches were mostly hidden by the robe's thick fabric, but they did a horrible job of concealing that his thighs were as muscular as the rest of him. His hands rested at his sides—both the skeletal and human—and I wanted nothing more than for both of them to explore me. His posture was rigid, yet he moved fluidly, a weapon that was able to maneuver like rain running down a mountain.

He was desire and danger, and I wanted all of him.

And now he wanted me to *stop*?

"No. None of that," he said, brushing aside my apology. "It's not you. Never you," he finished in a whisper, stepping closer to me. "It's that if you continue what you're doing, I won't be able to stop myself. And I can't resist you for a second time. And once we do this, there is no going back."

The dull heat in my core flamed into a ravenous inferno. No going back? Why would I *want* to go back? He was right—this would change everything. Us. We would be transformed from two people who were standing at the barest edges of love into something more. Much more, and it was unlikely either of us knew what that truly meant. Eldrin didn't strike me as one who did casual flings—not anymore, at least. If he was going to give himself to me, this was going to mean something. Be something. And today, he had sacrificed everything he had, every position at court that he still had left, for me.

Yes, there was no going back. But I only saw a path forward. With him.

I dropped the dress, letting it reveal the last layer over my breasts, which were still hidden under the thin tan shift. They immediately stiffened in the cool air, making my remaining clothes chafe against my skin.

"Good," I said.

"Amber..." My name was reverent on his lips, and he knelt down before me, taking my hands in his own. His skeleton hand was no longer strange to me, it was just another part of him. The bone was both sharp and yet smooth on my skin, ever so gentle despite the edges. Both of his hands encased mine as he placed two solemn kisses on them, this adoring touch making me close my eyes while I relished the feeling of his lips on my skin.

I hesitated. What should I do next? The last thing I wanted was to break the moment, to shatter this perfect dream. Still kneeling before me, Eldrin stilled, his lips hovering over my hands, warming them with his gentle hot breath. My own breaths rushed harder, and even the air around us felt charged.

And once either of us moved, it would unleash a thunderstorm that would consume us both.

Before I had to decide, he stood and leaned forward so that his mouth was now just above my shoulders. Something so small and intimate—his presence, closer than we had been in weeks—instantly awakened every nerve, anticipating what could come next.

I couldn't help it. I let out a long exhale, and an incessant throbbing echoed inside me, impossible to ignore. When he touched me—*if* he touched me there—he was going to find me desperate for him.

"You're not mine to touch," Eldrin said, lightly teasing. "This is treason."

"Treason?" I grinned. "You kidnapped me. Twice."

Eldrin smiled back. "You went willingly. This time."

"I'd follow you anywhere." I moved my hands so that my fingers entwined with his. His eyes roamed to my breasts, settling his attention on them, and a thrill rolled through me that I was able to create *this* much of a reaction out of him already—with nothing more than a slight touch.

"Give me this, Eldrin," I said, meeting his silver eyes. "Please. Give me you. Because everything is going to change, and I want to remember what it feels like to have you inside of me." Fuck that was bold, but I needed him. Who cared what it took?

Ages passed during the next few seconds, my heartbeat counting each painful moment that went unanswered.

What would he say? Would he change his mind? Did he still want me like that? I had caused so many problems for him, and there was no end to them. He had every reason to want nothing to do with me.

His jaw clenched and he closed his eyes, obviously dancing on the limits of his self-control. His chest rippled with his breath, revealing each muscle. I swallowed. Waiting.

One breath.

Another.

And another.

"Please," I repeated softly.

That was all it took.

CHAPTER TWENTY-FOUR

AMBER

E ldrin's eyes flared open, a predator homing in on his prey.

Without taking his eyes off me, he removed his garments, dropping the robe on the ground, followed by his breeches and boots. Within moments, everything covering him was gone, except for the fabric around his waist, though an unmistakable bulge strained against it. The curves and edges of his member were visible, showing just how much he wanted me. My mouth dropped open. He was a statue, chiseled and lithe, far beyond most human men. Deep rivets ran along his chest, meeting in a tantalizing v at his waist. Broad shoulders gave way to sinewy arms, which twitched as if he were restraining himself. For the first time, I saw that the skin of his left arm tapered smoothly into a skeleton near the elbow, as graceful of a transition as if it were a cat's claw.

He noticed me looking and gestured with it. "Does it bother you?"

"Never." Nothing of him could ever bother me.

He glided over to me, and I barely had time to gasp before his human-like arm wrapped around me, pulling me against his muscular chest. I inhaled his familiar scent mixed with something new—pine and...bergamot? The palm of his skeleton hand rubbed me through what remained of my dress, the bones tracing an eager path over my skin. His own breath rushed in my ears, the hot air heating my skin and sending fresh goosebumps across my flesh. His lips met mine in a frantic dance, the taste of him an intoxicating nectar.

My legs parted out of instinct, and he nudged a thigh between them, moving with a taunting friction against my core. He was as desperate for this as I was, and the knowledge did nothing but make the ache deep inside me stronger. The urge to have him plunge that hard length inside me, to take and ruin me, all but unbearable.

I bit back a groan that didn't go unnoticed.

"So responsive," he said approvingly. "I wonder what sounds you'll make when I'm deep inside you...here." His hand reached down and ran a finger between my legs, that little gesture enough to turn my groans into whimpers.

Slowly, he guided me over to where the grasses were tall and soft, and he gently set me down amongst them, letting them tower around me. Flowers surrounded the edges of my vision, their petals still a noticeable yellow in the muted light of night. We were in our own little world of unsoiled beauty, where time stopped and there was nothing but us and *this*.

And then, once we were on the ground with him poised over me, he devoured me.

His lips tangled with mine, pulling me deeper into him. His bare, hard chest pressed against my hot skin and made me writhe, while we both tried to tug off the rest of the dress without destroying my only garment.

More. I needed more. I wanted to feel every bit of him against me. It wasn't enough, never enough. I cried out, frustrated with the fabric, and Eldrin smothered my moans with his mouth, quieting every bit of my protest. He knew why I was fighting. He knew exactly what I wanted. And he was making me take my time. His lips consuming mine, he gently untangled me from the dress and then cast it aside, like unwrapping a gift that was just for him.

Now in nothing but the thin shift, the night air hit me, pushing me closer against him for warmth. Muscular arms wrapped around my back, holding me tight while he explored me with his mouth, sweet kisses occasionally leaving my lips to trail along my neck.

Once in a while his skeleton hand touched me, cool and firm, a reminder that I was with Eldrin.

And I was still wearing far too many clothes.

Fighting harder to get rid of everything keeping me from him, I lifted my hips and tugged the shift down, maneuvering the flimsy excuse for a strap down my arms, baring my breasts. His mouth opened the tiniest bit when he caught sight of the newly-exposed flesh, and then he cupped one breast with his hand, his tongue teasing and flicking the peak and eliciting a fresh groan from me. He kissed both of my breasts, followed by my neck, and finally my lips, his hands and mouth working all together in a frenzy.

Meanwhile, my own hands had worked their way down to his waistband before I even knew what I was doing. I needed to see him. Every last bit. My hands had explored Eldrin's every dip and curve, and my eyes wanted to experience everything for themselves.

"There's no rush," Eldrin said, nibbling at my ear, his solid member pressed against my thigh. "We have all night."

I bit my lip and ran a hand down the front of his undergarment and gasped, the outline in the fabric having done woefully little to prepare me. Eldrin wasn't a small man, and I expected that all of him would be proportional—and it was. "As I said," he whispered, "there's no rush. We will make sure that you're ready for me."

Ready? I was ready *now*. But then he kissed my neck and nibbled at the tender flesh that waited at the curve of my shoulder. I forgot what I was thinking, until I felt him tug my shift further down my hips. Now he was kneeling to the side of me, removing the shift while I kicked my legs to get rid of the fabric. Fabric that was In. The. Way.

"Amber," was all he said as he tossed the shift aside and looked at me, drinking in every bit of the sight. There was nothing left to shield me. Nothing between me and his hungry eyes that took their time roaming over me.

And then he was hovering over me again, his body a welcome respite from the cool night. His flawless bare skin pressed against mine, and I let my fingers dance over his arms and back, my palm coming to rest against his beautiful face. I tried not to fidget, but I flushed. He was so perfect, an unearthly creature, painfully gorgeous. Yet he looked at *me*...

Me.

"You're perfect," he said, answering my thoughts. Even as his eyes narrowed at the spider bite on my arm and the mostly-healed cut.

I couldn't help it—I snorted a little. An elven prince calling *me* perfect. He placed a finger over my lips and said, "None of that tonight. You're perfect, and you're mine. And I'm going to show you exactly what that word means. Mine."

His lips found mine again, while his human hand reached between my legs. I opened them, letting him explore where he wanted. And *fuck*, he knew how to explore. He moved delicately over the outside of my core, and expertly flicked his fingers against my sensitive flesh. He teased me, driving me deeper into this world where there was nothing but him and what he was making my body do.

He stifled a moan when he found the slick wetness waiting for him. "Fuck..." I ground into him, begging him to go further. Inside me.

"Touch me," I gasped. "More."

"Will you let me?" he asked, his finger circling my entrance. "With all of me." His skeleton hand, he meant.

"Yes." I would. I wanted all of him.

"Let's try this first." And then he placed a human finger into me. And then he added another, stretching me farther. "That's what I want to see," he said, grinning as I clenched and thrashed on his hand. "I want to see you fall apart on me."

Fall apart? I was already undone.

My eyes caught sight of his hand and fingers moving inside me, and all I could think of was the bulge between his legs, rubbing against my thigh with such delicious friction. I stroked it, back and forth through the smooth fabric, his shaft filling my hand. A tremor worked its way through him and he froze, watching my hand on his cock, even as his own was still exploring me.

"This isn't what I planned," he said, his silver eyes meeting mine with a challenge.

"Plans change."

"They do indeed." Suddenly his hand was gone, leaving a cold emptiness in its wake. A smug grin spread across his face as he pulled off his undergarments, revealing his cock. He leaned back, letting me see all of him, every majestic inch.

Yes, he was definitely not like most human men.

Still laying on my back, naked before him, I swallowed. Hard.

Any nerves about whether I could handle him turned to need as he hovered over me once more, his lips meeting mine in a frenzy. He settled between my welcoming legs, his hot weight resting on my core, glorious, and just a hint of what was coming. The grass underneath us acted as a cocoon, as soft and warm as any bed. The forest's rustling leaves carried a hint of music, a sweet song tantalizing the air.

And Eldrin...Eldrin was my friend. My lover. I needed to be a part of him, so that we were two halves made whole. As we were meant to be.

"Eldrin," I said, with more of a moan than a whisper, "I want you."

"I'm not ready to take you yet." He brushed strands of hair out of my face, although his body betrayed his words as his shaft rubbed against me, a drop of wetness brushing over my leg.

"Please," I begged again.

He trailed a finger of flesh down my cheek, my neck, and then my chest. Fuck, I burned. His finger dancing over my skin, his hot breath on my neck, his powerful form above me—all of it reduced me to a simpering mess, desperate for him.

"I wanted to spend so much more time," he said, trailing that damn finger lower and lower until it found my clit. He flicked it back and forth, and I gasped, spreading my legs wider, the aching to be filled growing greater by the moment.

"I wanted to draw pleasure from you bit by bit until you were numb from it."

"I already am."

"No. Not yet—but I can't resist you." His whole body moved between my legs, positioning himself at my entrance. Slowly, he rubbed himself on my wetness and worked his way inside the tiniest bit. I closed my eyes. He was already stretching me so much. Too much. "Don't worry—we're just getting started."

All at once, he moved, pushing inside me, in and out slowly and deeper with each thrust, drawing my thighs up to let him enter completely. And then, once he was fully in, the shock of him stretching me faded and was replaced with a perfect fullness.

He looked down at us and grinned. "I could look at this forever—me inside you." All I could do was whimper in response.

And then—thank fuck—he moved. I bit my hand, the rush of pleasure pushing me to the point where I could hold nothing in. He thrusted back and forth, stroking me with his fingers in a way that somehow made me want more, even as he had filled me to the brink. Always more.

Then, when my chest was covered with sweat and I had forgotten where I was, he leaned down and kissed me gently, using our closeness to rock deeper into me, as far as I could take him. I ran my fingers through his hair, gripping his short silver locks, and leaned my head back, faded into *this* perfect sensation. Nothing was better than this. Nothing.

Holding him was like embracing the life of the forest itself, strong and eternal. And he pressed me against him, his movements guiding my own, like he was determined that there be nothing separating us again.

I clenched around him, as hard as I could. Two could play at this. If he was going to delve into me so deep, then I was going to take him in return. I wanted to see him undone from pleasure. From me.

He grinned, like he understood what I was doing. And before I knew it, with one fluid motion, he was underneath me and I was on top of him. I stared at this beautiful man spread out under me, impaling me and jolting me gently. God, I couldn't take it. Even now it wasn't enough. I wanted even more of him. Everything.

He guided my hands to his firm chest. "Show me," he said. "You want to claim me? Do it."

I jutted my hips back and forth, moving in a steady rhythm. His abs clenched along with his jaw, and his lips uttered a stream of curses. "Amber, you're—"

I smirked. My hips gyrated, driving him to the brink like he did to me. It was his turn to gasp, and his skeleton hand gripped my ass, the points digging into my skin. It didn't hurt, not even close, but the sensation was so perfectly poignant that between my movements, his grip, and the way he thrusted underneath me, I felt my pleasure begin to build. I reached my hand down and touched myself, straining each bit of rapture from his movements. He nodded with approval, watched me, and the delicious agony pushed itself higher and higher.

Fuck, he was perfect. I could've ran my fingers in the deep indentations between his defined muscles. His features were so regal and elegant, a beauty crafted by the immortal forest. And the man behind them, the one who had risked so much for me and lost everything for me...

He was everything.

I leaned forward and kissed him, resting my hands on the grassy ground, and our lips resumed that familiar dance. Except this time, though, there was an urgency behind it, as he thrusted harder, so hard that I broke away from the kiss and hung my head over his shoulder to keep my balance, my voice was now senseless moans as my pleasure crested over me. His groans echoed mine, followed by the sensation of him utterly filling me.

We had fallen off the edge, and I didn't care how we landed.

CHAPTER TWENTY-FIVE

ELDRIN

She collapsed on me as I laid on the ground underneath her, struggling to catch my own breath. Her smooth, perfect body, the way she cried out with pleasure, the way she dared me to keep up with her, the bold way she took what she wanted...it was better than I had dreamt. Her body rested on me now, a delicate sheen of sweat over her, while I still filled her. My pleasure ebbed away, along with the thirst to claim her, content for now.

I was complete. Utterly. Perfectly. Complete.

I hated that the trees choose that moment to rustle, to remind me that this was not our paradise and our lives were still in danger. I pushed those thoughts aside, as Amber was still draped over me, nuzzling my neck with her sweet lips. Her disheveled hair was a testimony to what we had done, even as she still ground on me. I already felt myself hardening anew, ready to take her again.

But not yet. I wanted to enjoy this moment as long as I could. And we both needed a little rest.

Maybe there was a way we could be together after all of *this* and she would be mine before all the world. Maybe I could leave the Darkening Woods with her, if it would let me. Maybe...

Those plans would have to wait. We had to survive Vanir first. We had to cure her of the poison that was slowly consuming her. And at this moment, I had a beautiful woman in my arms. One whose eyes were heavy and sated with pleasure. Chuckling, I wiped my face and planted a kiss on the top of her head, breathing in the scent hidden in her red curls. "My ember."

"It's Amber."

"No." I shook my head. I could never forget her name. "The true word has been lost, but it means you are the spark that has ignited my life."

She paused. "Damn. I want to know what the original word is."

"I do too." We moved upright, and still sitting entwined around each other, I wrapped my arms tighter, tugging her close to me and moving her so that her back was against my stomach. I cursed to myself—she was definitely stirring me again, and from the way she reacted, she could feel it too. And then she ground against me harder.

"What are you doing?" I asked. She was making me lose all control.

"Nothing," she said and kissed me.

I returned her kiss. "That is not nothing."

"No?" She nuzzled my neck.

"No." I laughed softly. "I think you know exactly what you're doing."

"Then what is the problem?"

I bit back a contented sigh. She was going to be my undoing...

"Unfortunately, we need to settle for the night. Are you cold?" I asked. We couldn't risk a fire, but we had garments that we weren't using.

"No. Not if I have you."

"And you always will."

"Will I?" she asked.

"Amber, look at me." She listened, shifting so that I could see her brilliant green eyes, the ones that looked at me like she never thought of anyone else. "I cannot say what the future holds, or if we will even be alive when it is done. But as long as I walk on solid ground, I'm yours. The choice is yours if you will have me or not."

"Choice?" Amber frowned, but on her, that expression merely made her hauntingly beautiful. "I can't stay here."

"No." I kissed her hand. "But we will find a way. I was alone for decades, and spent the last years wasting my life serving

Vanir. Through my foolishness I lost everything. I refuse to lose you, too."

She turned around and shifted so that her back was against me once more, and I could no longer see her face. Her even breaths mirrored my own as we settled into the grasses, preparing to sleep bare amongst the leaves and the stars. I wrapped an arm over her protectively, holding her close, doing my best to shield her from the cold. We were hidden in the Woods, sleeping with nothing but the ancient forest to shelter us, but we may as well have been in the grandest palace, for all that there was nothing I'd trade this moment for.

We laid on the ground together, her chest heaving against mine, slowly steadying into rest. The exhaustion of the day could no longer be ignored. It may have been my imagination, but before sleep took me, I thought she whispered, "You may not have a choice."

CHAPTER TWENTY-SIX

AMBER

I had died. That was the only explanation that made sense.

Waking up tangled in Eldrin's arms was wonderful to the point of disbelief. At first, I thought that the whole thing had been a dream, until I opened my eyes and saw his silver hair and his angular face. His skeleton arm was draped over me possessively, the bones pressed into my skin. The arm twitched as he slept, just like a normal arm. When I trailed a finger over the bone of his forearm, his fingers jerked, as if the bones were connected with muscle and nerves and not some strange enchantment from the Woods. The two of us slept naked, but it was warm enough with his body against mine that I didn't notice the cold. I sighed. I could've stayed with him like that forever, as if we were one of the forest trees, our limbs forever entwined. The dawn had cast everything in a dim glow, making the world around us have a rosy sheen.

Unfortunately, all dreams end.

"I always meant to ask," I said to Eldrin after he woke and we were relishing the last moments of rest, "how did you manage to get to Minneapolis from here, and then bring me back, so fast? It takes around an hour by car."

"The Woods," Eldrin replied, his voice muffled by my hair. He nuzzled my neck, planting soft kisses. "It is one of the results of our gift. It can help us move outside the forest—with effort—and it takes only a thought and it brings us back. Like an arrow string snapping back into place."

"Can you travel anywhere, then?"

He shook his head. "The farther we go and the longer we stay, the harder it is. The Woods holds on to her children. Forever."

"How long are you able to leave?"

"Days. Maybe a couple weeks at most. It depends on the distance."

"And it will take you back, no matter what?"

He thought for a few moments before answering me. "There's...some situations where one of us can stay away longer. But trust me, Amber, you do not want to consider them. I would no longer be the man you know."

I'd take his word for it. He couldn't leave for good? No wonder these elves were so protective of their lands—the Woods wasn't merely a part of their home. This place was their only home. As I had seen time and time again, it was a part of them, even responsible for granting them their long lives. They weren't the only elves in existence, or even in the United States, but they were the only ones bound to something like the Woods in this manner. That I knew of.

There was a lot I didn't know.

"Eldrin?"

"Hmmm?" He nuzzled my neck.

I swallowed. "Before the worlds shifted, I had a friend. She is now in your world, where the Woods used to be. Do you...do you think she is alive?"

Eldrin moved so that he looked me in the eyes. "I'm so sorry."

"Thank you, but you had nothing to do with this—it isn't your fault."

"That doesn't mean I want you to grieve."

Words danced on my tongue. I wanted to tell him about Anna, how she loved campy horror movies, cheap macaroni and cheese, and seemed to have a sixth sense on when things were on sale. I loved nothing more than to walk small town streets with her, talking about our crushes, our fears, and what we would do if we ever managed to leave Grand Rapids. Turns out that we both left, in very different ways.

"It would help to know if she is alive," I said. "I've seen how the elves treat humans. And to have a city of them suddenly appear?"

"They won't kill them unless they attack, if that's what you're asking," Eldrin said. "The Woods are in chaos, no doubt. But we have records of this happening before—our people will know what happened and they will do what they can to manage the disturbance."

"That 'management' isn't to kill them?" I stifled my thoughts that some humans wouldn't survive—take tens of thousands of people and someone was bound to do something stupid.

"No. We don't want to live with any others, but we usually don't wish to harm them. They will probably want them gone—they would help them leave the Woods and go to where there are other humans. Either the human kingdom, or one of the groups that are in other lands."

"Oh? How many such colonies are there?"

He smiled solemnly. "Enough that I wouldn't worry for your friend. If she was a friend of yours, and treats my people with respect, they will help her find a home. Do not fear."

I nodded, blinking back old tears. It was not an absolute answer, but it was more of one than I had before. It would do. I wanted to talk leisurely with him all morning, but we had a king hunting us, and no time to waste.

Eldrin gave me a long kiss before we went on our way to start another day of rough travel, taking only a few moments to wash off in the lake. The day chilled as it went on, and I hugged my cloak against me, the exertion the only thing keeping me comfortably warm. The two of us barely spoke, mostly since I was too winded, and it seemed to be some unspoken agreement between us that it was for the best. No point in distracting us.

But Eldrin did more than walk and listen. He was skilled at picking out edible plants as we went, including ones we used to freshen our breath, so that we didn't have to stop for any meals, though only Eldrin would've been able to get me to eat a blood-red mushroom. It tasted like a mushroom, but, like, extra mushroom-y. Or maybe eating anything the color of fresh blood had that effect. Whatever it was, it was spending the rest of its prominent existence safe in my stomach.

A branch broke behind us. I whipped my head and my heart rushed into my throat. But Eldrin just curtly shook his head. It wasn't Vanir—we were still safe. This morning, Eldrin had told me what he had eavesdropped from Vanir, and I couldn't say I was terribly surprised that he planned on killing me. He did seem like a Bluebeard in the making. But some questions still remained.

My pained steps went easier today, after Eldrin removed the extra fabric from my dress—if i ignored the blisters. Unlike me, he kept all the items attached to his "robe," which I definitely appreciated. It was an attractive outfit, and it would've been a shame to destroy.

"Where are we going?" I asked after the sun was high in the sky. I had realized that we never spoke about the ultimate plan since we were interrupted by...other things.

"Gold Glen," he said. "It's as far away from Vanir as we can travel while still staying in the Woods, and I hope there are answers there. Or at least knowledge of where we can go to find them."

"...You're not sure?"

A pause. "No."

"That seems...unfortunate." We walked on what were technically paths, but they were little more than slightly trodden areas that wound between the trees, as opposed to maintained and smooth roads. The wooded paths were overgrown, leaving roots and brambles that required deft navigation and focus. Neither of which I had, as I ran straight into a low branch for the second time that morning, my throbbing head adding to my raw feet.

"Stay closer to me," Eldrin said. "I can help." He had taken a break from disguising the trail behind us, opting instead to do it only every half mile or so. Any more and disguising the trail would slow us down far too much to make it worth it, or so he explained.

"No, it's fine," I said, wiping the bark dust off my face. "Maybe one of those branches has magic and they'll give me powers."

"What?"

"What was it that Oristan said? Two wrongs make a right?"

"Life and death feed from the same hand."

"Yes, that." I took a few more steps, sniffling and rubbing my nose. "That's an odd saying. Do you know where it comes from? You mentioned that it referred to the veinwart, but how?"

"Actually, I do remember," Eldrin said, his expression determined. "I think. There's an idea that..." He stopped walking, his lips pursed. He looked off at the distance, at something I couldn't see.

"What is it?" I asked, placing a reassuring hand on his shoulder, setting aside the budding fear that lurked under my skin.

He shook his head and turned to me. "It is likely nothing. There's a legend. A myth associated with this tale."

"A story? I love stories."

He took my hand in his. "This one involves a hero who slayed a monster. A monster whose bite was poison, but the poison's cure was enduring a second bite."

"That's it?" I asked.

"No."

"Well, come on, I need more than that. I want elven stories."

He grinned. "Whatever for?"

"Because I've never heard them. Because it sounds like you grew up with them. That sort of thing is important to me."

He kissed my head and his lips lingered there. "Very well," he said, lowering our hands. "A long time ago, when the gods bothered to walk amongst us, there was a god who became angry with an elven city. See, he had heard that someone within boasted that he was a better craftsman, and that offended him."

"Ah, yeah, we have some legends like that. Wait, there's gods? They're real?"

"Unfortunately," Eldrin muttered. "But as I was saying, the god cursed the city by having the giant spider hunt anyone who left the city. The spider was larger than a horse, its skin was as hard as rock, and its poison deadly to everyone who tried to kill it."

"Sounds lovely," I said.

"It would be lovelier if you let me continue," Eldrin said, faux scolding me. I nuzzled against him, taking in his scent.

"Well," Eldrin continued, "many tried to kill it and failed. A young elf volunteered to kill the spider. He was so young that everyone mocked him for thinking that he could do what the most experienced warriors could not. But this elf paid more attention to what the god had done and said, and guessed what the god truly wanted—humiliation and subjugation. As you may have expected, those from the city did neither of those things.

"So, the hero left the city to hunt the spider, and when he found it they fought. And was poisoned."

"Bitten?"

"Yes. Fatally, according to the story. After he was bit, the elf fled just far enough to sneak around back to the spider and be bitten again and given more poison. After that, he was cured, and the spider was nothing but another animal—easy to kill."

"Is this true?" I asked. "An elf decided, while dying, that he wanted to be more dead? That makes no sense. Why would anyone do this?"

Eldrin shrugged. "I cannot say. I think that maybe he was dying and wanted his death to come quicker. Or the venom made him hallucinate. Or this story is just a story. But all myths tend to have a basis in truth—this one we use to explain why the veinwart poison does not harm us. It's a reward from the god, who changed his mind after he saw the elf's heroism."

I thought about what he said for a moment. It was true that myths and legends came from somewhere. And elves had long memories. But I was getting a horrible idea. "The spider. Do you think a second bite from the veinwart could cure me?" I frowned. "That seems like a stretch. And I have enough sense not to go back for a second time."

"The monster was a giant spider, and it is said that this was the first veinwart." He took a few steps forward along the path once more. "I told you it was nothing. We cannot consider doing it regardless."

"No, it's not nothing," I said, scampering up to him. "Could it work? What if I was bit again? What would happen?"

"You're not being bit again. I refuse to allow this." Eldrin's jaw clenched. "If we're wrong, it would likely kill you immediately."

"And if we don't find a cure, I'll be dead soon anyway." I pointed at my shoulder, where my veins near the bite were starting to be rather puffy, like nightcrawlers under my skin. The constant cold lurked in my veins, to the point I had accepted it as a part of myself. "And your other plan is, what, going to a remote village and asking for help? For a cure that didn't exist in Great Glen?"

He crossed his arms and resumed walking. "It is more elegant than that."

"Legends come from somewhere—you being here is proof of that." I grabbed his arm and he turned to me, letting me look him in the eyes. "This is my decision—my life. I want to try it," I said sternly. Yes, another bite was reckless, and painful, but what did I have to lose? It didn't seem like there was any medicine available that could cure me, if it existed at all. Eldrin's other plan seemed to be to beg a healer who would probably rub leeches or powdered maple leaves on it or something. And what was the spider going to do—make me more dead?

"No, you're not," Eldrin said, bracing his hands on my upper arms, careful to avoid my injuries.

I sighed. It seemed we were going to be doing this the hard way. "So...where do we find another spider?"

"Amber, no. I cannot let you die."

"You're not *letting* me," I said. "This is my choice. I will be doing this. You can either help me, or not. If we do nothing, either Vanir will kill me or the veinwart will. I want to decide what happens to me. Give me that. Please."

Were my words fair to him? No. It broke his heart, as evidenced by his despairing face. Eldrin wouldn't let me risk myself, no matter the reward. But I had to do this. There was *something* in that legend, I was sure of it. At any rate, it was better than waiting for something else to kill me.

"Please, Eldrin. Help me."

He paused. "You truly want this?"

"Yes."

He closed his eyes for a long moment, and then opened them. "I do not want you to do this, Amber. If you're harmed, I may as well cleave out my heart. I will have nothing."

I took his hands in mine—both of them. "I know," I said softly.

"There is a den," he said, resigned. "Near the border."

"That's good. Right? We're heading in that direction...right?"

"We are. But it will take us a week to get there. At least."

My eyes widened. Just how large was the Darkening Woods? The size of a couple counties. Around fifty miles across. And how fast could I walk? In these little cloth slippers, in this terrain? ...Eight miles a day was pushing it. And we had to be careful, and couldn't take the direct paths. Yep, it would take a week. Easily.

Now, Eldrin—he could've sprinted and been there by the next breakfast. But unfortunately, I wasn't an elf, able to run across counties in a morning. No, the contented soreness between my legs reminded me that it was definitely a good thing I was not an elven man.

"I can't lose you," Eldrin said.

"And that's why I'm doing this," I said. "Because I truly believe that this is our only option."

I gave him a smile, even though my heart cracked. Even if I was cured, there was no way that we could be together. I couldn't stay in these woods, not with Vanir, and it seemed that Eldrin was unable to go far from them for long. There was no possibility of him coming with me and starting a new life.

My heart was going to get broken, again. And this time there wasn't anyone who would be able to pick up the pieces.

CHAPTER TWENTY-SEVEN

ELDRIN

We walked in silence for another hour or so, her decision stifling any desire to speak.

Amber was going to die. She was going to die. She was—

I had to stop thinking like that. It wasn't going to do either of us any good.

Maybe she was right—legends and myths came from somewhere. *Something* had to have spawned it. Maybe the veinwart were creatures whose venom warred with each other, one in effect negating the other. The story did seem to indicate that. Though, another one of our legends was about a wolf who expelled diamonds with each cough, so it wasn't as if all of them were logical.

Amber had seized on this idea, her excitement adding a little more energy to her steps. She was right—this was her decision. And I respected the fact that the alternative was likely a matter of whether the poison or Vanir would kill her first.

Moreover, with this plan, there was hope, as fragile as it was. The Darkening Woods had many mysteries, and it was entirely possible that the secret to the veinwart's venom lay within the creatures themselves.

Or maybe this was all merely a wish and I was going to watch her die. The legend involved an *elf* who survived, after all, and Amber was very human.

In the meantime, I had to worry about getting us to the veinwarts' den in the first place. Amber and I were in a part of the Woods where there were thick trees that could have easily held a human home in its trunk, with branches that reached desperately for the sun. The leaves were as large as our faces, golden and resplendent in the light. I took a deep breath. This was home. Home. Even if we never managed to make it back to our world, at least we elves had *this* here. We would never be without a piece of the Woods. No matter that I could not live without the Woods, I didn't want to. I needed the Woods, and there was no other place I could envision being as content. It wasn't surprising I felt this way—the Woods and I were bound together, after all. But at the same time, being here without Amber was a life I did not want, and it was far too likely that would be my fate.

And then, right when Amber started to softly hum a gentle tune, the air shifted, becoming heavy. The trees' song stopped for a few heartbeats before resuming, something that would have been easy to miss if I wasn't paying attention. But I was. And thus, I knew what we had to do.

"Amber," I whispered, turning to her, "reach around my neck, and hold on."

She stopped humming immediately. "What? What is it?" she whispered.

I faced away from her and knelt down. "There's someone coming. Reach on to me, hold on, and do not scream."

She did so without protest, her thin arms latching around my neck while her slender legs gripped my waist. It would do.

I stood, and jumped. First, I leaped from a boulder to a log, and then reached and grabbed onto a low branch, pulling us up. Upward and upward I went, carrying us both as high as I could go without causing the branches to shake, until I found a spot in the wide boughs that could hide us.

"Here," I whispered, setting her down against the trunk. She let go, stepping backward and gripping the trunk, the rough bark giving her fingers a solid hold. She had done well. She had only made a little gasp when I jumped, and even now she silently stared at me, eyes wide. Any questions remained unasked. I nodded my head and moved next to her, holding her against me.

"Where?" she mouthed. I pointed below.

Her brow wrinkled. She couldn't hear anything. I barely could. It was two elves, younger men, judging by their steps. Were they Vanir's men? Unlikely. They could've just lived nearby and were hunting. Or they may have heard that we had disappeared and thought they'd find us on their own, desperate to earn favor from the king. It was entirely possible that Vanir offered a generous reward for our return.

Suddenly, Amber froze and gripped my hand harder. She heard them. She closed her eyes, leaning against me, and I held her. I would protect her from anything.

Would they think to look up here? I cursed under my breath. I could easily kill two of them, but their disappearance would alert others to this area when they didn't return. I also didn't want to commit murder, not for Vanir. Not when these elves could have just been pursuing their own affairs and had no interest in us. I would have to wait and see what happened.

They came closer, their steps becoming louder, their voices clearly carrying up to us. Hunters. They were merely hunters who were successful and talking about their quarry. Nothing about Vanir, or me, or any humans. Just hunters.

I relaxed, but made no move to leave the tree. Just because they weren't looking for us didn't mean they wouldn't betray us. And if they did stay silent, I couldn't ask them to risk Vanir's wrath if he suspected what they did.

"It's alright," I whispered in Amber's ear. "We're safe. We're just going to wait." She nodded and kissed me on the cheek and I adjusted my grip so that my arms enveloped her completely. It was only the fact that our lives were at risk that kept me from giving into the urges that rose with her so close to me. Her scent. The form of her body against mine. The caress from her hand. I had to pay attention and keep my mind clear, lest we lose everything.

It was an hour before I trusted that it was safe to leave the branches, dropping us to the ground with the lightest sound. The elves' tracks led away from us, and hopefully, since they had their prey, they wouldn't return.

Once on the ground, Amber and I looked at each other, at a loss for words. She gave me another nod, her expression serious compared to the mirth she had expressed so recently. She seemed to understand—for all that the forest was peaceful, safety was fleeting.

And there was no guarantee we would be so fortunate next time.

As the day and then the evening after our brush with the hunters wore on and the sun faded, my fear of being discovered mellowed, and once again I was left alone with my fear for Amber. Amber and her foolish plan.

I wasn't about to lose Amber to *this*. Vanir was a cruel enough fate, but the veinwart? Would it be a second, self-inflicted bite that killed her?

She turned back to look at me as she strode along the path, giving me her signature smirk. "Stop frowning," she said.

"I'm not."

"The trees are perkier than you."

I smiled, despite myself. "I am 'perky.'"

She cackled, stifling her laugh with her hand. "No. Sorry, Eldrin. But that is not true."

We bantered back and forth for some time, her prodding letting me forget that she would be taken from me, one way or another.

Her idea had to be the solution. It had to be. The second bite would cure her, because I could not imagine her dead. For all that I lived surrounded by death, the idea of Amber reduced to nothing but a skeleton grated at my being, for more reasons than there were leaves on a tree. She was so vibrant and alive—she deserved the long lives of us elves, not to be reduced to dust and then forgotten. Elves remembered their dead, and even used their bones to build our homes out of respect, but as a human, Amber wouldn't be given such treatment. Vanir would likely leave her in the forest, exposed. Or burned.

She was the ember to my life, the one who brought me back to myself, the one who changed everything. There was no life that I wanted without her.

It twisted my soul more that even if this plan with the veinwart did work, I would still lose her. Once she was cured and free to leave, I would lose Amber forever. I could not ask or expect her to stay, not with Vanir desperate for revenge. Not with me, an overthrown heir who was just now finding the courage to consider taking back what was his. A life with me, in the Woods, would be nothing at all but a dance between danger and ruin.

But I refused to think of such things as I watched her sway along the path, her filthy frayed dress hugging her curves. She was like a little nymph, darting between the trees she called her companions, with no concerns other than those of nature itself. Even now, it was hard to take my eyes off her—every single part of me was drawn to her as a moth to the fire, and I would relish being consumed.

And then the rains started.

The calm fall evening was gone and a torrential downpour flowed over us, dousing us within seconds.

"What is happening?" Amber called out, her voice smothered by the rain slapping the leaves and ground. Her red hair was already plastered against her face, the dress pushing against her curves even more tantalizingly. "This isn't supposed to happen. What sort of fall has rains like *this*?"

"This is a blessing," I said.

"Why?" She wiped her face. "Because we don't need to shower?"

I grinned as she pushed soaking strands of hair behind her curved ears. By this point I knew well the jests she made, the tone that meant she wasn't serious. "The rains are the best thing we could've asked for," I explained. "It will make it harder for Vanir to find our trail." I never stopped listening for him. Never stopped waiting for the whispers that announced that another elf was nearby. But we were still somewhat safe. We had time. And not even Vanir's men would dare to hunt for us in this rain. It would be futile.

"I still don't understand how this can be happening," Amber said, shaking her head and blinking hard. "This is beyond rain."

"It happens, sometimes," I said. "The Woods has its moods."

"Yes." She looked up at the darkened sky once more. "I can see that." Her arms were now wrapped around herself, rubbing her upper arms. The cold caused little bumps to form on her skin. She needed warmth, soon.

"Come," I said. "Let's find a place that is more sheltered." With my hand on her lower back, tracing gentle lines up and down her spine, I guided Amber off the trail. I knew these trees, I knew how they grew, and as I suspected, there was a place not far away where the trees grew thicker, a little grove where the branches almost blocked the elements, covering us like a little open-sided hut. Here the light was dim, with the same branches blocking the rain also blocking out what little light we had. The floor of our shelter was covered with ferns and soft grasses. It wasn't the most glorious bed, but it would do for a night. And it was relatively dry.

Now out of the rain, she wiped her face and eyes again and wrung out her hair, taking the chance to be free from the onslaught of water. "Here." I took off my robe and passed it to her, holding it above her and shielding her from what was left of the rain. The scent of pine needles filled the air around us, and the falling water was now merely light drops—a minor inconvenience compared to the deluge.

"This isn't what I expected. I didn't know it could rain like this here. I'm sorry, but I'm still surprised." Amber chuckled, leaning against me after we sat on the grass. She had taken my robe and had wrapped it around her like a cloak, but she huddled in front of me, her wet bare skin on mine. She shivered and I pressed against her, desperate to share my warmth. Her breasts made contact with my chest, and I resisted the urges that were budding in me anew. Though I wouldn't be able to hold back forever.

"It isn't common," I admitted, trying not to focus on how her hand was moving across my stomach, dancing in slow circles. I hardened already, thinking of what it would feel like if her hands drifted lower. "But as I said, this is good. It will obscure our trail, and wash away any scent."

"And he won't guess where we are going?"

"I doubt it," I said. "He likely expects us to go to one of the settlements and find someone willing to help. Maybe contact one of my allies."

"Like we were originally going to."

"Yes."

We listened to the rain falling. Vanir was no doubt hunting the woods for us, but he very likely didn't feel the need to hunt too hard. All he had to do was order that the border be watched, and bribe informants in the settlements. He probably assumed we'd need to go there eventually, for supplies and a cure. I cursed to myself. Maybe Amber was right—her idea was foolish, but the alternative could have easily led to Vanir's trap. Who was I attempting to fool? Vanir certainly had at least one trap set for us, and likely more.

"And in the meantime," Amber said coyly, "we get that free shower. And it gives me a chance to be next to you." Amber looked up at me and my heart stopped. Her green eyes with flecks of yellow met my own, like she carried the forest itself within her. An arched eyebrow was raised, a question. A promise. Her plump lips fell open, just a little, as her hand worked its way over my stomach to the front of my breeches. Where she would find that I was already far ahead of her in that regard.

"Can I?" She paused over me, her hand warming my cock through the fabric. There was a strange tone in her voice, deep and broken. Yearning.

"Yes," I managed to say. Whatever she wanted, she was more than welcome to it.

She dropped my robe on the ground, careful to avoid the mud. And then she turned her attention to me. Slowly, she untied the top laces of my breeches and pulled both them and the inner garments down, letting me free. The cool air hit me, a blatant contrast to the warmth of her hands, and the hot heat that I knew she had waiting for me.

Thinking of making it easier for her to touch me, I stood and gripped a couple branches that were nearby. I had to hold something—anything. Even the mere thought of what could be coming making me unbalanced. She stared at my cock, eyes wide, and wrapped one of her perfect hands around it, stroking me gently. I braced myself against the branches, gripping them harder—and then almost snapping them when she opened her mouth and took me inside.

Fuck.

I closed my eyes and saw lights. Her wet mouth consumed me, the poignant heat overwhelming everything. Her greedy tongue flicked around the tip, her mouth sucking, and she made this sweet little groan when she tasted me. Her other hand cupped me, rolling me expertly between her fingers as she took me to the root, her throat flexing around my crown. I bit back a groan as she took me deeper, the head of my cock hitting the back of her throat. My thighs flexed involuntarily as she swallowed around me, and I worked my hand into her hair to pull her back—but she flicked her eyes up at me and gave me an insouciant wink. "Is this alright?" she asked, slowly rubbing me in a steady rhythm that gripped me extra tight.

"Yes." I said, and she smiled at the croak in my voice.

Alright? I was dancing on the edges of oblivion. Every time I dared to look at her, her mouth locked around me and devouring me, I almost lost control.

Yet I couldn't stop looking at her. She was kneeling before me, focused on her task while her breasts heaved as she moved. That perfect mouth was so wonderfully tight. Her delicate hand was wrapped around my shaft, working me so hard in conjunction with her tongue. It was a sweet rhythm that was pulling me to release far too soon.

I couldn't have that.

Somehow, I found the strength to gently move her away, hissing at the cold air hitting my wet member after the warmth of her. I bent down to kiss her and whispered, "You're next."

A look of surprise crossed over her as I suddenly helped her up and braced her, both of us now standing, against a tree trunk, near where I had been mere moments before. She gripped the jutting branches, as I had done, while I worked my hand under her dress and pushed aside her undergarments, exposing her.

"You're ready," I said, unable to keep the pleasure from my voice at the slick sweetness I found.

She moaned in agreement, spreading her legs further apart to let me inside. I delved one finger into her, and then another, so that when I was done she was standing and yet resting much of her weight on my hand. I moved in and out, twisting and exploring, then she helped me pleasure her by pushing down and grinding against me. Her sweet arousal washed over me, begging for more. I added another finger.

"Eldrin—"

"Yes?" I did not stop moving, not while she firmly thrashed on me, taking what she needed.

"I cannot—it's too..." Her protests turned into fresh moans that send a fresh ache of desire through me. I had to be inside her. Soon.

She leaned against me while I attended her, my cock pressed against her thigh, her perfect heat and wetness coating my fingers. Her brilliant hair surrounded her like a halo, the perfect goddess she was, taking everything I could give her. I was in no rush. If she wanted to take an eternity spending herself on my hand, I would let her. In fact, I could think of no better way to use the time.

"Eldrin," she said, breathless. "I want you. Now."

"You have me," I teased.

"Not. Like. That."

"Oh? You mean like this?" I worked my smaller finger around, clumsily flicking her little nub, her resulting cries telling me both that she loved it, and that she was ready for something else entirely.

"Or do you mean like this?" I adjusted her and moved her a few steps to the side, where her back could comfortably rest against the branches. I knelt down before her, much like she did for me. But this was her turn.

Slowly, I lifted her skirts, and she took them in hand, giving me full access to her. She was perfect—swollen, inviting me to touch. To taste. A perfect feast. I licked her, and was rewarded with a shiver that worked down her body. Careful to only touch that part of her with my hand of flesh, I spread her lips and sucked on that nub that was practically begging me to taste it. My mouth filled with her. I sighed. I'd consume all of her if I could, take her into me and never let her go. She was sweet, a taste that was uniquely her, a scent that I would recognize anywhere. My mouth devoured her, sucking and flicking on every part of her in turn, while I plunged the two fingers back into her.

"Fuck. Eldrin." She squirmed.

I smiled, my mouth not leaving her. Instead, I moved my fingers harder. Her legs spread even more, her one hand desperately bracing herself behind her while the other held up her skirts for me.

"Fuck, Eldrin," she cried out and shivered, clenching rhythmically around me as her release took over her.

She was a goddess, and she was mine.

When she was done pulsating, I took out my fingers and leaned back. That would do. For now.

Seemingly exhausted, she crouched over, heavy breaths shaking her body. Sweet satisfaction worked its way through me, almost better than the pleasure she herself had given me earlier. Now she could claim to be utterly spent. *Now* she was ready for me.

Gently, I helped her to the ground and bent her over, moving her so that her knees were spread apart for balance, her elbows bracing herself. Anticipating what I had in mind, she moved up her skirt and presented herself for me. Her perfect, swollen self.

I couldn't wait any longer.

I spit on my hand and moistened my cock, hovering it at her entrance before I slammed into her in one swift movement. She cried out, her nails digging into the ground as her ass jutted into me. Her tight heat wrapped around me, urging me deeper into her, promising exquisite relief, if only I would seize it. And I would. Harder. Faster. I gripped her hips, my fingers digging into her flesh as firmly as I dared, working her and watching as she moved over my shaft, meeting my thrusts, pushing me ever harder. She was pushing me to take her, challenging me to see how hard I could go. I would never hurt her—never—but she triggered a primal part of me, one that was content to meet that challenge, to take it and give her everything that she wanted, and more.

Amber...

I had never known an experience like this, a wholeness, the sense that I was now complete. Before I had nothing. I wanted nothing. I was nothing. But she changed everything. The woman underneath me, sighing and gyrating, was the missing note of my song. And I would do anything—*anything*—to keep her safe.

"Eldrin," she moaned. "You're...you're..." My name was repeated like a prayer as she lost herself in me for the second time. The pulses of her release gripped me tighter, and with an animalistic urge she took control, working herself over me.

"Amber," I said softly, closing my eyes to focus on nothing but the sensation of her.

"I want to feel you," she said. "Claim me."

She was going to be my downfall.

Moments later I spilled into her in heady waves. I shuddered, lost. She heaved underneath me, damp from the falling rain, the skin of her ass red from where we collided.

"Did I hurt you?" I asked once I could speak, running a finger over a red mark on her hip.

"No." She turned her head back and smiled, and then moved, making me spill out of her and face the cold once more. Already, I couldn't wait for the next time I'd have that sweet slit around me. "It was perfect."

"Good." I took her onto my lap, where I sat on the ground, cross-legged. Her hot skin pressed against mine, her steady breaths comforting. My arms wrapped around her in a gentle embrace. She didn't care about my skeleton arm, which was clutched against her flesh. She treated it as every other part of me. As one, our breaths mellowed, and we sought each other's warmth against the cold damp of the coming night.

As if she read my mind, she moved and looked at my hand, the white bones stark against her pink skin. "What does it feel like? I mean, can you feel?"

"Yes," I said. "The sensations are there, but it doesn't feel pain the same way. It takes far longer to burn. And it can be severed, though smaller cuts are difficult to accomplish. It is bone—very strong bone—but not iron."

"Can I...touch it?"

"Of course."

Gingerly, she adjusted herself so that her back was flush against my chest, and traced a line along the bones. Her mouth dropped open in wonder as she explored. From the bones that made up my hand, to my forearm, to where they merged with flesh near the elbow, the transition as seamless as a dagger plunging into a sheath.

"It's cold," she announced.

"Probably for the best, don't you agree?"

She laughed. "Very good point." The laughter died down and she moved her hand so that she took my skeleton hand in her own, our fingers entwined. I reciprocated, meeting her live flesh with my grip. My breath caught, lost in the radiance of her life against the death magic that made up mine.

She accepted me. All of me.

"I'm glad I met you, Eldrin," she said gently. "Whatever happens. Know that I don't regret meeting you."

My heart ached. Her beautiful words soothed any doubt I had left, not that there was much at all. "I could never regret you, Amber, never," I said, planting a kiss in that beautiful hair.

CHAPTER TWENTY-EIGHT

AMBER

There was no end to the forest.

I could have stayed in that damp, branchy "cave" forever. Really, I could have stayed anywhere with Eldrin forever. But I didn't like the fact that now I had to keep walking, walking, and walking more in order for the days to pass before I could sleep next to Eldrin. We spent days like this. Weeks? We had to be at the home of the veinwart any day now. This forest couldn't go on forever.

Right?

Days of walking were followed by nights where we explored each other's bodies, and I learned his better than I knew my own. I learned that Eldrin's ears were particularly sensitive, and he discovered that there were few things he could do to my breasts that wouldn't have me begging for more. Little things, but these were the things that made us adepts of each other, worshipping with the same physical prayers every night.

The things that let us ignore how one way or another, we soon would have to say goodbye.

The joys we found in each other were almost enough to let me forget that the spider bite was growing stronger, its glacial poison moving with each beat of my heart. Every day, the coldness spread farther through my blood, reminding me that my time was limited. We couldn't try to find a healer, because we simply didn't have enough time. I could sense it. The poison was now a constant pulsating that felt like someone stuck an icicle against my shoulder and wouldn't take it away.

At my best guess, we had maybe a week—at most—before the poison would make me unable to function. And that was assuming that the poison didn't overcome some unknown barrier and suddenly devastate me faster. Despite my worries, I didn't say anything to Eldrin. He probably guessed my condition on his own, and telling him would do nothing.

Did Vanir know how quickly the poison would kill me? He had planned for our "courtship" to take longer. But maybe it was the exercise I was doing, spending my days fleeing through the woods, that was making the poison spread through my blood. Poison that wasn't my main concern at this moment.

I stretched my arms, hoping to ease my cramping muscles, looking at what surrounded us in this more southern part of the Darkening Woods. The forest was still an idyllic paradise, fall in a perfect, ethereal form, yet hiding nightmares in its shadows. The trees took on skeletal poses, decked in dresses of golds and reds, sheltering animals that were enjoying nature's bounty. Too bad I was too busy dying to enjoy them. Though in a way, it was fitting that I die in a forest devoted to death.

"What's wrong?" Eldrin asked.

"The same." I looked behind me. "How has Vanir not found us? Or anyone?" Other than that one incident with the hunters, we hadn't had to hide. We had barely seen so much as a squirrel, thanks to Eldrin's guidance. From what little I had seen, I could pretend that we were the only people in the forest.

"Are you so sure no one has?" he asked. My jaw dropped. He grinned, and then so did I. It was nice to see him smile and joke. "Don't worry—we've avoided everyone. I've been careful to keep us to trails that are deserted and avoid the creatures that live in the Woods. You are safe. I promise."

"Until I get to the spider." I slammed my mouth shut when a morose expression immediately took over Eldrin's face. Worry and fear. I was being sarcastic, trying to make some sort of joke, and failed. Even if he didn't say anything, there was no way he wasn't thinking about the spiders.

We kept walking along the trail in silence, our footsteps crunching the leaves underfoot. The weight of what I had said lurked heavy in the air. At least it was a sunny day, and at least we didn't have to deal with another downpour, though most nights still had light showers.

"It's my decision," I said gently, shattering the quiet. "The veinwart's bite is the only thing that has a chance of working."

"It also has a chance of killing you."

"So does just sitting here."

"But you're making your end—"

"I know," I said. "Better the veinwart than Vanir."

He huffed, his eyes glazing—a sign that he was drifting into a world of pensive thought of which he only allowed me an occasional glimpse. There was nothing I could say now, because there was nothing to say. Words didn't change the fact that we had to choose from a list of awful choices.

We had had this same argument so many times. And yes, I was aware I was asking a lot of him—would I have been able to sit back and let him poison himself deliberately? To have him die in my arms? But part of me suspected that he thought the same thing about the legends, that they had some truth to them, or he wouldn't have allowed me to attempt this at all. Though that did nothing to prevent his worry that I was doing nothing but ending my life too soon.

The feeling was mutual.

I watched Eldrin, whose attention was now seemingly back on guiding us through the woods. The forest was peaceful, with leaves floating in the air and beams of light breaking through the gaps in the branches, casting the world in an unearthly glow. Nothing like the turmoil in my heart.

When this was all done, what would happen with us? Assuming I was alive. Eldrin wouldn't want to go to the mortal world—he'd be miserable, and it sounded like he couldn't. And I couldn't stay here. Not with Vanir. This world wasn't meant for humans. Even if Vanir wasn't an issue, I would not fit in here. I didn't fit in back home, either, but at least I'd be around people who aged like I did. I'd have my friends. I'd have familiarity. And Eldrin deserved someone he could grow old with as an elf and live an elven life.

Eldrin offered me his hand of flesh and I took it, walking side by side with him through the forest. He gave me a small smile, one that I returned.

No matter what happened, our time together had a limit, and it would shatter me once it was done.

CHAPTER TWENTY-NINE

ELDRIN

The night was cold, which was a reason for Amber to push herself as close to me as possible while we slept under the stars. Not that she needed a reason. The hours we had spent together only made me crave more, like she was an ambrosia and I was desperate for every drop.

Her hair was spread over my arm, and she rested her head on my bicep while she smiled. Her eyelids were heavy, our lovemaking spurring her to contentedness.

I kissed her, as desperate for the taste of her as I had been a mere hour before, when she had taken off her dress and climbed on my lap, riding me until she climaxed. And then I laid her down and tasted the sweetness that dripped out of her, drove my tongue into her, until she shuddered and whimpered, begging for me. And when I finally entered her...

"Already?" Amber asked with a contented smile, grinding against my hips. "We just finished."

"Always." I nibbled on her ears and her neck arched in response, moving her breasts. I took one of the perfect mounds into my palm and massaged and cupped it. "Are you not ready?"

She kissed me in turn. "Always," she echoed against my lips.

"You're perfect." I moved my hand and traced the delicate angles of her face.

"I know," she said, and laughed. "And humble."

I shook my head, biting back a grin. "I see that. And I would not have you any other way."

Silence fell between us, and Amber snuggled harder against me.

"What would you do, if you could do anything?" Amber asked. "With us."

"What do you mean?"

"Pretend you are the god of this world, and you could do anything. Get rid of anyone. Bring anyone here. What would you do? Not Vanir or the veinwart, obviously. Something different."

I thought for a moment. "There is a glade in the Darkening Woods, in the part that is still in our original home. It's known for being one of the most beautiful spots in the forest."

"Is it?"

I nodded. "I think so. A special flower grows there, a sort of lily. And *only* there. It's said that it was a gift of a god to the elves. It smells so sweet, the flower has a rich nectar that has no equal anywhere else in the Woods. The honey made from it is used to heal, and it does so better than almost any other medicine." A soft look crossed her face, as if she was imagining it for herself. "Elves of the Darkening Woods often have their marriages there," I added.

"I can understand why," she said quietly.

I swallowed. "I'd like to bring you there one day." When she blinked hard, I continued, "I know it is impossible, but that is something I dream of doing with you—to take you there and make you mine. Forever."

"You would?"

I nuzzled her neck, my love for her—and it *was* love—rising in my being, an emotion that was as impossible to ignore as desire. Where lust was a wildfire, strong and fleeting, this was the sun, steady, constant, and necessary. "Without hesitation. No one, and I mean no one, was able to bring me back from the hell I put myself in. No one has made me find joy in this life, even before I lost it all. You are my heart, my ember, and should the fates allow it, I would keep you with me forever. I cannot find happiness in this life without you—it would be impossible."

She answered me with a kiss, desperate and urging. And when she moved to take me into her arms, and when I took everything she was willing to give me, I had no hesitation that I meant every word.

But we were almost to the veinwart, and soon, whether we were able to stay together, or be lost to each other forever, would no longer be our decision.

CHAPTER THIRTY

AMBER

"We're here," Eldrin suddenly said to me the next morning, his steps on the path coming to an abrupt stop.

We were only roughly an hour into our day's journey, and we were now at a place in the forest that was oddly...still. No breeze. No birds. Nothing. I looked above and around me, at the fallen leaves that blanketed the ground. Nothing moved. I half-expected skeletons to be propped up under the trees, this part of the woods carried that heavy of an aura of death and fear. Nothing like the tender moments we had shared with each other last night, when Eldrin admitted that his feelings for me were beyond even what I suspected, but were exactly what I had hoped. No, this wasn't a place to think of such things.

"You're sure they're here?" I asked. For all that the area sent shivers up my spine, nothing indicated that this was a home to giant spiders. Giant spiders with deadly poison and gruesomely sharp teeth.

"Yes." He gestured towards a dead oak tree. "They live there. Veinwart live underground in colonies, buried under rotting trees." He paused. "I can hear them. Under the ground."

The bark was peeling off the desiccated tree trunk in thick sheets, and the few remaining limbs it had were barely hanging on. This was where those massive spiders lived? It seemed doubtful to me. For one, the oak tree was far too small to hide a veinwart, even if the bulk of the colony was underground. And two, the area was too clean. Weren't there supposed to be giant spider webs, desiccated carcasses, or something? No, instead this was a bucolic autumn forest that was just a bit too...quiet. Eerie, yes, but just quiet.

My stomach flipped. The spiders were here, mere yards from me. This was a bad idea. I could change my mind—Eldrin would be happy if I did.

But if we didn't try this, what other option did I have that was any better?

The memory of the spider's bite surfaced, my original wound throbbing as if it remembered exactly what had happened to me. And I had to brace myself for it to happen again. I was going to put myself through that. Again.

"Assuming they're here," I said, not taking my eyes off the trunk, "how are we going to get one to bite me?"

"I'll catch it." He searched my face, as if looking for any sign of doubt. If he saw anything, he didn't say.

I placed a hand on my hips. "You're going to catch a spider that could eat a poodle for breakfast?"

Eldrin cocked his head. "That sounds like a challenge." A challenge? He was ready for one. He was ever the assertive prince, even all battered and alone in the forest. His robe hung over him, frayed and stained, the flowers long smashed or torn off altogether. The bones still hung onto the cloak, apparently being made of sterner stuff. His abs shone in the light, rippling with every movement. It was all I could do not to stay in one place and not see if he wanted to do something else before I died.

"What if it bites you?" I asked.

"It won't," he said confidently. "And remember, even if it does—elves don't react to the venom the same way you do."

"That's right, you're a chosen child of the forest," I jested.

"Correct." He smiled, but the corners of his eyes were weighed with worry. About me. There was a lot to worry about.

I needed a moment. Didn't Catherine Howard need some time before her execution, practicing how she would lay her head on the block? If she could take her time, so could I.

I sighed and sat on the ground, resting my aching legs, which were cut with a bunch of tiny little scrapes and scratches from plodding through the woods. My poor feet had it worse, the slippers all-but worn away. Blisters had long since formed, popped, and reformed baby blisters of their own.

Eldrin joined me, shrugging off that overdressed robe he still had with him. Wearing nothing but his breeches and boots with his daggers strapped around his waist, he was ready for a fight. My eyes were drawn to his arms, how they were nothing but evidence of raw strength. His silver hair was tousled, his skin scratched, but he was still regal—a king. He sat next to me, his presence an anchor against the storm of what was going to happen.

"Do you trust me?" Eldrin asked.

"Of course. I wouldn't be here if I didn't." Technically he did kidnap me, but there were extenuating circumstances.

He nodded, stretching his fingers. "I know this sounds impossible, but we *can* do this. I will catch one of the veinwart. We will have it bite you near where your original bite is, and then I'll kill it."

I appreciated that his tone changed from trying to talk me out of this to supporting me. "The other spiders won't attack?" I asked. "I'm surprised they hadn't already."

"They're cowards. They won't attack unless they're sure they can win." It didn't feel like a coward when that last veinwart had its fangs in my neck, but I assumed Eldrin had some esoteric knowledge of mythical spiders that was beyond me.

"...What happens after? After the bite."

"I don't know," he admitted, and I wasn't surprised. "I'm not sure how long it will take to see if the cure worked. But once it does, we're not far from the barrier. We can send you across immediately, if you want. Maybe your people can help." *If it works at all*, he left unsaid.

"If I want," I repeated softly. "You would let me go through the barrier?"

"Yes. I will do whatever you want."

"But the barrier will break."

"You are my concern."

I could do whatever I wanted? I wanted him. I wanted to live with him forever. But there was no home that would take both of us. If he could go to the mortal world, it would be difficult for him, fawned over and hated in equal measure. I couldn't watch him suffer the slow death of being away from the forest he so clearly adored.

What we had was like a snowflake in a warm hand, perfect and unique, but fleeting, impossible to hold for long.

And here I was, delaying the inevitable. Each breath had brought us closer to when we would have to say goodbye.

"Are you ready?" Eldrin asked, pulling his knives out of their sheaths, the sharp edges glinting in the light.

Ready? Was I ready to be chomped on by a giant spider again? Hardly. But if this was what it took to save my life, or at least avoid what Vanir had planned, then I would do it.

I nodded and we stood. It was time.

And I was the greatest idiot who had ever lived.

My fists clenched at my sides, and my heart raced in my chest, threatening to burst free. My feet, clad in those threadbare slippers, dug into the wet leaves. I should have been running. I shouldn't be standing *here*.

I shouldn't be waiting, staying put and merely watching, while Eldrin walked up to the dead tree and took his knife, slowly dragging it in the ground around the base. The leaves bunched around the knife, but he kept moving, gliding it along in a circle. What was he doing? It seemed like he was marking some boundary.

And then it struck.

A black shape suddenly rose out of the ground under the trunk, lunging at Eldrin. Before I registered that the spider was there, Eldrin already moved, clear out of the creature's way, its head caught under his arm, and its jaws clamped shut. I had watched him spar before, but those practice sessions were nothing compared to seeing him in action, that fluid dance with death that was as smooth as a river. I blinked once and found that he held the spider with one hand, and his knife in the other, and was approaching me, bringing me the creature that could kill me.

Would kill me.

Now that it was daylight and I knew what I was looking at, the terror from that night resurfaced, and it took all that I had to stay in place. To this creature, I was merely prey, something to be consumed. And I had to let it eat me.

The veinwart was the size of a black lab, its head like a fuzzy black volleyball. Red human-like eyes reminiscent of frozen blood looked at me, the hunger evident in its gaze. Its mouth dropped open, a sticky substance similar to black rubber cement dropping to the ground. When it caught sight of me, the veinwart tensed, and then opened its mouth wider, revealing horrendous fangs the size of knitting needles. The furious spider lunged towards me, only to be held back by Eldrin's grip.

Hell. No.

"Amber," Eldrin said, his voice calm, "hold out your arm."

Hold. Out. My. Arm. To *that*?

"Now, Amber," he said sternly. "I can't hold it forever."

"Fuck me," I muttered, exposing my arm, and slowly—so slowly—moving it towards the creature's mouth. I locked eyes with Eldrin, trusting beyond trust that he wouldn't let the thing kill me.

Eldrin adjusted his grip, and the veinwart's mouth opened wider as I stepped closer, hot breath spreading on my skin. A little squeal emerged from its mouth, like a pig delighting in dinner. Like it was tasting me from my scent.

Oh, fuck me.

This wasn't going to work. It wasn't just going to bite, it was going to bite my arm *off*. It was—

Fire and ice flooded my arm, and agony took over everything. My scream caught in my throat, stopped by the poison that froze my muscles and clenched around my neck. I was both frozen and burning, and I wanted nothing more than to have my skin ripped off, *anything* so that I didn't have to feel this.

Did it feel like this before? I felt ice after the first bite, but then my vision blurred, and I passed out. I didn't remember having my muscles seize in my throat. I didn't remember my heart feeling like it was splitting in half. My chest constricted, unable to let in air.

Oh, god. Oh, god.

We were wrong. *I* was wrong.

The bite was supposed to cure me. What it gave me was not life. Nothing I felt screamed life. Instead, we had brought me to my death. I was going to die. I knew it like I knew that the poison was thickening my veins, making it impossible for my wretched heart to beat.

I was wrong. I ruined everything.

"Amber!" Eldrin yelled. Somehow the veinwart was gone from his grip, no longer a concern. Somehow the trees were blurring, the forest becoming a wash of gold, crimson, and brown.

And then, just when black dots overtook my vision, there was nothing.

CHAPTER THIRTY-ONE

ELDRIN

F uck.

Fuck. Fuck. Fuck.

What could I do? What did I *do*?

"Amber!" I cried out. "Amber, wake up," I begged.

I shook her lifeless body as she stared in the direction of the sky. Her gaze faded, already focusing on nothing. Her heart was almost silent, the faintest thrum that threatened to stop at any second. I gripped her hand and nothing gripped me back, her fingers slack.

"Amber..." I bit my hand, stifling another cry, one that was doomed to go unanswered.

What did I do? I trusted a hunch, a legend, and instead I killed her. I let her follow some dream, some hope, that was nothing more than promises whispered like ash in the wind.

I killed her. It would have been better if I had left her alone and let the veinwart poison take her the first time. At least then she would have been with her family and friends. At least that way she would have a grave, and someone other than myself who knew what had happened to her.

I did this to her. Me.

I was right all along—it was a good thing I did not accept the ruling of the kingdom. If I did this to her, who I loved more than my own life, what would I have done to the Woods?

It didn't matter that this had been her idea, that she decided to pursue the veinwart—she wouldn't have been able to do it without me. I should have known better. I trusted some obscure hope, and now she was gone.

I failed Amber. I failed everyone.

Her weight was heavy in my arms as I sat on the ground, beyond caring that the damp ground soaked into my breeches. Her dress—that beautiful dress—was in tatters, its threads long unraveled. The veinwart rustled behind me, but I didn't care. Their bite wouldn't harm me like it did her, but they were welcome to try. they could cause was nothing compared to what I did to myself. To her.

I bit my hand, hot tears blurring my vision. She was dying, her face taking on the sweet oblivion of sleep. Her breath was weakening with every moment. Fading. Fresh puncture wounds graced her arm, dripping that crimson ichor over her skin.

There was only one thing left that I could do for her. I wasn't going to let her die here, not in the woods that claimed her life. She deserved to be taken home, back to the human soil, where someone would find her. A place where her memory and grave would be treated with respect. Her family and friends deserved to know what happened to her.

I could give her that at least. The Woods took her life, and I was not going to let it own her death.

Gently, I tugged my robe back on, lifted her up, and carried her away from the spiders and towards the barrier. The last time I carried her she was sated with lovemaking, whispering sweet promises in my ears. I had promised to keep her safe forever.

I had failed.

We were miles away from the barrier, and I rushed towards it, each thudding step heavy blasts against my heart. I went as fast as I could through the trees, darting through shrubs and gullies, no longer caring if I was discovered—it didn't matter what happened to me now. Nothing mattered other than getting her home before it was too late. I didn't care about the damn barrier any longer, even less than I had this morning—Vanir deserved its destruction after what he let happen.

Was that breath her last? What about this one? Or this one?

There was no way to know.

My tears dropped on her face, which didn't react to my tangible grief touching her glassy skin. Nor did she so much as blink at my sobs. And after I left her, what was I supposed to do? She was gone.

Why should I stay here? Why should I stay anywhere? There was no point to me.

Vanir had the kingdom. The kingdom didn't need me. I failed Amber. I had nothing. I resolved that after she was gone, I would leave. Whether I would leave this world or just leave the Woods as best I could, I did not know. I just had to get *away*. I couldn't think. All I could do was feel the loss that permeated me, delving into every part. I was nothing but a void where she had been my light. She was my ember, and now her spark was gone.

The barrier tingled over my skin long before I saw it, the iridescent haze that blurred the air, like heat rising off hot stones. I could see through the barrier, see the mortal farmer's fields beyond it, an abrupt line where the eternal autumn of the Darkening Woods broke into the mortal world. The barrier naturally pushed most elves and animals to stay within—and others out—but I had the ability to push through it. It would fight me—as it was meant to—but I would take her home, even though the barrier would shatter.

Others from our home had interacted with the mortal world and survived. Now that we were no longer the first, things would be easier for the elves of the Darkening Woods. We would endure. We had to.

I stood at the edge of the barrier and took a deep breath. Everything I had worked for from the moment Amber crossed my path had been a lie. And now I would destroy it all. Vanir could deal with the consequences.

"Look what I found," Vanir suddenly said from behind me. I whipped my head, finding Vanir and his henchman, Ivas. Both of them were dressed for battle, in simple tunics and breeches and light armor. Both of them sneered at me, at Amber dead in my arms. I looked around, seeing only the two of them, and hearing nothing to indicate that others were nearby. A small blessing. And a sign that they didn't expect me to be any trouble.

How did they find me so fast? Then again, I wasn't subtle this morning. Someone had to have seen, and the king was faster than me and had been searching for me for weeks. He had to have been watching the barrier, looking for any sign that we were trying to leave. I would not have put it past Vanir to have known where I was for some time, to make me think that we were safe until it was too late.

"Pathetic," Ivas said. "You had a woman trust you, and you managed to kill her after what, a month?" He was right.

I wanted nothing more than to carve that smirk off his face. It wouldn't bring Amber back, but it would feel damn good.

"How did she die?" Vanir asked, raising an eyebrow, looking at Amber's limp body. Her red hair trailed over my arms and hung over the ground. "I don't see any blood."

"Does it matter?" Ivas said.

"Yes," Vanir said. "We should have noticed if *this* happened." Then his eyebrow raised again. "A fresh bite? Interesting."

I clenched my fists, my breath tight.

"She was always going to die," Ivas said, as if announcing that trees had leaves. "One way or another." There was something in his smirk, something that told me I had missed something obvious, yet again.

"It was you," I said. "You're the one who ordered that she be attacked in her rooms."

"Of course," Vanir said.

If I had the ability to feel anything else, I would've been shocked. But as it was, I was just tired. The game had been stacked against us from the start, everything manipulated—no wonder we had lost.

"I knew the attack wouldn't succeed," Vanir continued, "not with you so devoted. But I knew it would push her towards you. And it did—how could it not, when the elf sent to guard her saved her life? And now look—my brother ran away with my betrothed, blantanly obsessed with her. And look here, I caught him trying to break the barrier, which would doom our people." Vanir pulled out a long dagger. "No one will blame me for what I'm about to do. And here's the best part—you can't kill me. Well, not easily. One must never be too optimistic."

"I think we can assume he won't be able to manage it," Ivas said, looking me up and down. "He's barely standing."

Vanir was right—I couldn't spill his blood, or the Darkening Woods would take its cost. And he was also right that are plenty of ways to kill someone that don't involve shedding blood. But Ivas was also right—it would be very hard to accomplish a bloodless death when fighting two skilled elves at once. And it had been a long time since I had a full night's sleep or a meal that wasn't berries and roots.

And I had just lost my reason for living, for fighting. Who cared if they let me join her?

Vanir nodded to Ivas. It was time. What had lurked between us our whole lives was going to be settled here, with only the Woods as a witness.

I could just let them kill me, to spill my blood and let my soul greet Amber's. But I couldn't let them win without a fight. I owed Amber that much. I wouldn't insult what she had given to me by cowering before the men who had taken her life from her as surely as the veinwart did.

As if they planned their movements, Vanir and Ivas spread out, their daggers now out of their sheaths. I had mere moments before they would be in position to attack, and it would take everything I had to meet it.

I shrugged off the robe, leaving my chest bare to the cool air. Carefully, I set Amber down on the ground in a pile of leaves next to my garment. I would bring this fight away from her. Even dead, she didn't have to watch me fight. She didn't have to watch me die. And they wouldn't bother with her—to them, she was already dead. They wanted me. With luck, they would forget about her and leave her body here to find peace in the Woods.

There would be no such fate for me.

Quickly, I stepped away from her, both of my knives out, my hands moving to a familiar grip. This fight would test me—there was a very real chance it would kill me. I was a better fighter than Vanir, and Ivas was more into the appearance of fighting than practicality, but it was two against one—and I was not at my prime.

Before I could take my next breath, they attacked. I feinted Vanir's blow and ducked Ivas's. There was a flurry of blades, blocking and slashing, and a mere second later we stepped back, all of us untouched. Each of us weighing the other.

That was just a test, to see what I was still capable of. Now the real fight would begin.

I blocked another flurry of attacks, not thinking—only moving. Always moving. I couldn't stop. One would attack and the other would move, aiming for where I was vulnerable. The three of us ended up in the fluid dance that was the signature style of our people—the first time either of us stepped out of line it would be our death. The first time either of us stumbled would be the last.

After a vicious flurry, Vanir and Ivas jointly stepped back, catching their breaths. I did the same, sweat gathering on my brow. We couldn't do this forever. I was tiring—it was only a matter of time until I slipped. Until I was too slow.

And I couldn't spill Vanir's blood. He didn't dare run into me because he knew that with the correct move, I'd be cursed, but he'd still be dead. But of the two of us, I was by far at the most disadvantaged. I was weak, weaker than them. All I was doing was prolonging the inevitable. Either they'd kill me, or the Woods would. I couldn't just win—I had to win in a way that wouldn't curse me.

"What do you think we're going to do to your little human after we're gone?" Vanir taunted. "All that pretty hair—there's still lots we can do with a corpse. And then look at you—a failure again. A failed king. You couldn't even keep a human safe."

"She's probably not dead yet, I think there's lots we could still do," Ivas said, a sickening grin on his face.

I steadied myself. They were trying to anger me. Trying to get me to make a mistake. It wouldn't work. I had heard all of Vanir's taunts before, and more besides. Amber wasn't of real interest to them—it was me. They wanted me. They wouldn't be able to do a thing so long as I lived.

Then Amber groaned.

Vanir and Ivas turned to look at her—and that little distraction was all I needed. I lunged towards Ivas, getting past his guard and slicing his neck. Small drops of blood coated my knife—not enough. He moved at the last moment and rolled away, avoiding the killing blow, though he was now left with a thin red ribbon across the tender skin. He touched the wound and looked at his hand, sticky and red. And then glared at me, gripping his daggers harder.

All of this happened in the space of a few heartbeats. Before I could steady myself, he attacked me with a renewed viciousness now that Vanir was gone.

Wait—

Where was Vanir?

I couldn't think. I couldn't look. I could only manage Ivas and his flurry of blades, the anger in him fueling his attacks. He slashed at me, managing to slice my shoulder. Not deep. I could tell it wasn't deep. But I was weakening. The next time I wouldn't be so lucky.

"I think we've had enough, haven't you?" Ivas asked, nodding at my wound.

"Never."

Darting, I broke through Ivas's guard just enough to land a blow to his face with my fist clenched around the dagger's hilt—he didn't expect me to switch to that style of attack. To his detriment.

Groaning, he stumbled back and knelt on the ground, stemming the gushing blood flowing from his nose, while I took in what made Ivas suddenly gloat.

King Vanir, my craven brother, knelt on the ground, holding Amber in front of him, using her to shield his body. To my surprise, she was awake but dazed, her eyes taking in her surroundings with a distant look. She clutched my cloak in her hands, worrying the fabric through her fingers. A knife was at her throat as she leaned back against Vanir's chest, unable to hold up her own head. He met my gaze, unable to keep the triumph from his eyes.

"Now, you're going to stop this," Vanir said. "You can't kill me. And I am more than happy to kill her. And look what you did to poor Ivas." Vanir shook his head. "You should have been more careful, Ivas. You insisted that you'd be the best to help me take care of this, and look at the mess you caused." Vanir turned back to me. "See, part of being king is handling one's own problems—the people expect it."

By now Ivas had recovered, his hands clutched around his weapons, blood still pouring down his face. But he stayed back, watching what Vanir would do.

"She has nothing to do with this," I said, knowing it would be pointless to argue. But I wasn't trying to convince him—I needed time to think. I'd keep him talking as long as possible. Ivas took a few steps away from where he had initially rested, and I didn't dare let my attention slip from him. He was still close enough to attack, but he seemed content to nurse his bloody face for the time being. And watch.

"She has *everything* to do with this. If you had listened to me," Vanir said, "the barrier would have obtained what it needs to survive. Our people would be safe."

"Safe? What about how you are ruining our people with your greed? And those you tortured? Imprisoned? A pleasure house, Vanir? You couldn't find anyone to tend to you willingly?"

"You cannot blame me for taking respite where I can," he said.

"Respite?" I spat.

"*I* kept our people intact since the worlds merged. The least they could do is thank me and serve me. Ungrateful. So many are truly ungrateful."

"Well, I'd say not so many any more," Ivas said. "Some of them are not capable of feeling much now."

"None of that," Vanir snapped. "My dear brother doesn't need the sordid details." He sneered. "There's a reason I am king and he is not."

Vanir addressed me once more. "You don't know what it takes, Eldrin. To rule, you have to do whatever needs to be done. And why would I need to force anyone to serve me, in any capacity? I'm the king."

"Let's pretend that particular rumor is a lie," I said. "You're still taxing our people within an inch of their existence. For nothing but your own wants."

"A king must look the part."

"A king is supposed to care for his people—to help them instead of burden them."

"Oh, dear brother," Vanir said, shaking his head. "This is why you'd never make a good king—too much idealistic hope." He shook Amber, jostling her head back and forth, so that it flopped like a rag doll. "Like what you had with this one."

"You were going to kill her."

"To save us."

I shook my head. Only Vanir would consider murder to be a noble pursuit. "There is always another way."

"Not this time. The barrier demands blood. Would you have demanded it from our people?"

"I would have told them the truth," I said and Vanir snorted. "They had their home taken away and will likely never see it again. They deserve that much."

Suddenly, the barrier flickered right behind Amber and Vanir, as if it knew that we were talking about it, that we were discussing providing a life to sustain it. They were so close to letting Amber be free from here—mere steps. They could have literally tossed her through the barrier, to give her a chance at life, but they wouldn't. Vanir must have followed my gaze, for he said, "Convenient that you brought her here. Looks like I'll be able to strengthen the barrier with her blood after all." His lips curled.

"You need a willing sacrifice."

"Willing has many definitions, and the barrier is thirsty."

All the blood left my face.

He would do it. He would kill Amber here, in front of me, and spill her blood for the barrier. And the worst thing was, he would come away from this a hero. He would be the one our people praised, never mind that he killed an innocent, unwilling woman to do it. The people would probably over-look his cruelty and excesses for a time, or at least pretend to, because he did this for them.

"Ivas," Vanir said, "Get rid of him."

"No!" I cried out, raising my arms, preparing both to block Ivas's attack and throw my dagger and kill Vanir, no matter what it did to me.

Then Amber moved. Her eyes opened. And right as Vanir twisted his wrist to slit her throat, she raised the skull on my robe, smashing it against Vanir's nose. Blood sprayed over her, over the skull, as Vanir howled.

I couldn't see what happened after that. Ivas attacked me, using the distraction to almost slip inside my guard. I met his blows and pushed him off, using the break in our fight to see what Amber had done to the king.

His arms were wrapped around her, the knife discarded on the ground. Amber was struggling in his grip, reaching for something, finding my robe. Somehow, my robe, the king's blood still on the skull, ended up in the air, touching the barrier—

"No!" Vanir cried out. He shrugged Amber off him, sending her rolling to the ground. "What have you done?" he screamed. Blood streamed down his face in thick rivers from his nose, splattering over his garments and Amber.

"You said the barrier needs blood," Amber said, her cut lip sending a red line down her chin. She slowly pushed herself up, struggling in the dirt. "I figured, why couldn't it use yours?"

What was happening?

My heart stopped.

"Your Majesty!" Ivas howled when Vanir began to change.

Vanir's eyes grew larger and larger like eggs, while his face started sagging. This was beyond aging—he was melting. Like the hot wax dripping off a lit candle, he collapsed and fell apart, dripping onto the ground and pooling. His bubbling flesh, a miasma of the colors that he used to be moved towards the barrier. Ivas fell to his knees, yelling for Vanir, begging for him to come back.

While the king fell apart I darted for Amber, taking her in my arms even as her head flopped against me, pulling her away from whatever was happening.

How was this happening? The barrier was consuming him, but such a thing required intent, not an accident, based on what I knew about magic. An elf or human with a cut alone wouldn't have triggered the barrier, or it would have taken someone long before this—there *had* to be the intent. Right?

But Vanir was the king—the rules were different for kings. The rules could be brutal for kings. Vanir did take an oath during his coronation...

Vanir had sworn an oath promising that he would give of himself in service to the land. To the Woods.

Apparently, the Woods decided that it was in need, and that it needed Vanir. The Woods didn't concern itself with our politics and desires—it was eternal, our lives nothing in the shadow of its sovereignty. We lived and served under the Woods' protection, and that protection came with a cost.

A cost kings had to be prepared to pay.

With her hugged tight against me, Amber and I watched, breathless, as Vanir melted and entirely disappeared. The barrier took every last bit of him until it was as if he had never existed at all.

He was gone.

CHAPTER THIRTY-TWO

AMBER

I didn't know elves could run so fast.

I mean, I knew they were fast, but Ivas was gone before we thought to look for him. Probably smart on his part. Despite winning the battle, despite my being alive, Eldrin's eyes carried a heavy weight, his hands bloodied from the fight, blood dripping from his arm from a shallow cut. He scanned the surrounding woods, hand clutching his daggers, poised to strike.

He would have killed Ivas if he stayed. Slowly.

"What now?" I asked, resting against Eldrin's chest once he gave up the search. For now. Vanir was gone, vanished like water into the soil. The wind rolled through the trees, making a familiar music, a peaceful idyll completely at odds with what we had just seen. A king had melted. Was consumed. I looked at the barrier and shivered. These Woods were alive,

I didn't doubt that, but what I had seen emphasized that the elves lived within the sphere of some ancient magic that killed as well as it preserved.

I had acted on a guess, a desperate hope. At most I thought I'd distract him enough to let Eldrin attack. I never thought my actions would unleash something so cruel and terrible.

Eldrin swallowed. "I'm the king." He shook his head, as if the reality was just occurring to him. "My brother has no other heirs, and there's no one else in the royal family in our part of the Woods. I am the king," he repeated, as if in disbelief.

"Oh," I said. "Yes, you are." If only I had the words to encourage him, even as my heart cracked.

We had shared a beautiful dream in the Woods, nights of exploring each other's bodies, and days spent with a companionship I had never known. But there was no place for me here, even with Eldrin as king. The elves wouldn't want a human as their queen, and Eldrin would need to take care of his own position—I had seen enough of elven court politics to know that Eldrin likely had a fight ahead of him. A human wouldn't fit in, and in fact, I would be a danger to him by staying. A weakness. And I had a feeling that Eldrin's struggle was only beginning. The elven court was a mess of politics, and not everyone would be happy that Eldrin was back in power.

"Do you want to go back to court with me, Amber?" Eldrin said. "Or you can go home now. For good."

"I can?"

He nodded. "The choice is yours. If you're here and speaking with me, that means the bite worked. That veinwart brought you to the brink of death, but now you are cured. There's no reason for you to stay."

I moved my arm, relieved that the familiar pain and unnatural cold was gone, other than the sting of the fresh bite. I had been so distracted by Vanir trying to kill me that I didn't realize that my shoulder no longer ached, other than the expected soreness that accompanies a wound. The bite had healed me.

Eldrin had healed me. In more ways than one.

A flock of little birds flew through the branches, hopping above us and chattering, almost as if they knew what we were saying. But did they understand the heart break that waited for me?

"What will you do?" I asked. "Now that you're king."

Eldrin took his time to answer, his gaze distant. "I need to return to Great Glen and assume my control over the throne." His jaw set. "While I *am* the king by right, a lot could change if the court realizes that Vanir is dead before I am there. I need to act quickly." And the last thing he needed was a human in the way while he did so. Our dreams while on the run quickly shattered when faced with reality. As I knew they would.

"Alright." I looked at the barrier, choking back a sob. "I think I should go home, then. We're already at the barrier. No point in dragging this out longer than we have to—and I'm guessing that it would be best if you didn't wait here longer."

He nodded slowly. "Unfortunately. Word can spread in surprising ways where the death of a king is concerned."

I lied—there was every point in my dragging this out. Because I didn't want to go. I didn't want to leave his side. I was facing the worst breakup of my life and I didn't want to say goodbye to him a moment sooner than I had to. But there was no point in staying and holding him back, in going deeper into the Woods, if I was just going to leave. It would be a distraction to him. A weakness. And who could predict what the elven court was going to do?

"Then...I think I need to go."

"Alright," he said solemnly. "If you're sure you wish to leave, you may."

"I think we both know that this is how it has to be," I said, wiping my eyes. "You know what the court would do to me."

"I know. And although I am a selfish man, I cannot ask you to stay. I cannot even ask you to come back in one year. There is no way of knowing what awaits me. But, Amber, I wish I was a more selfish man. Because there'd be no possibility I'd consider letting you go."

He ran a finger across my cheek and placed a kiss on my forehead. I relaxed, holding back tears at the thought that I would never be able to hold him like this again. Maybe I was imagining it, but it felt like he was holding on longer than necessary, too.

The moments stretched, seconds feeling like hours as we clung onto a moment that neither of us wanted to end.

And then it broke.

"Here," he said, bending down and picking up an acorn. He covered it with his closed fist for a few seconds, and when he passed it to me, it had a faint, silvery glow.

"What is this?"

"A benefit of being the king," Eldrin said with a sad smile. "You saved me, Amber. You gave me back my life, and my throne. If you ever desire to return, if it ever happens that you change your mind, this will allow you passage one time. But...I cannot promise you will be able to return to your world if you do so. And I cannot promise anything about what you will find if you come through." I would be risking finding that he was no longer king, or even dead, he meant. But I wouldn't think such things. Eldrin would manage—he'd find a way.

He had to.

Instead, I asked, "Is the barrier still going to be difficult for people to pass through? Those who have your permission, I mean."

"Probably. No magic lasts forever, and this magic is far from its home. But it will serve for a long while, if we are wise." He looked at the barrier, that shimmering thing that had caused so much trouble. "I can sense it now, like my own limb. It is strong, but not immortal. If we are lucky, it will last us until the worlds return, should that day ever come."

I tucked the acorn close against me, in a small pocket in my dress's bodice. I wouldn't use it. I couldn't use it. But I would always have that reminder of him. He had his life and destiny, and I would find mine. Somehow.

"Goodbye, Eldrin," I said, touching his cheek with my hand, and he placed his hand over mine. "Thank you. For everything."

"Goodbye, my Ember," he said with a sad smile. He gave me one last, long kiss, as if he could consume me by doing so. One that was meant to stay with me, no matter what happened. A kiss that felt like an eternity. And then it was done, his lips gone from mine forever.

It was time to go.

After one final lingering look, I faced the barrier, holding my breath as I walked through the translucent wall. The magic stuck to my skin like a wet fog, threatening to smother me. A few steps farther and the air suddenly changed, turning more humid and hotter, and full of summer once more.

I was back in the human lands.

Now on the other side, I could barely make out Eldrin's gray figure, lurking behind the wall. I waved, he slowly raised a hand and waived back, and then, alone, I began the long walk home.

CHAPTER THIRTY-THREE

ELDRIN

I stood at the barrier for a long time, far longer than I should have. It killed every part of me to watch her walk away, but it was for the best. Amber needed to be with others like her, and this realm would be chaos. Even with me being the obvious heir, there were those who would challenge me, and would contest whether the Darkening Woods had accepted me. I had to be prepared to face an attack at any moment. Far too often the Woods' throne was won with blood.

But I *was* the king.

The Woods had already accepted me, as I accepted it. It listened to me when I crafted the token to allow Amber to return, something I couldn't have done if it didn't want me as its next ruler. Maybe I should've told Amber to return in a couple months, when things were settled...

No. Even if things settled in my favor and I could protect her as queen, she had a life in her own world. Dreams. Friends and family. I couldn't ask her to give everything up. I could not ask her to bind her life to a people who were not hers, a place where she would have little that was familiar. She never asked to come to the Darkening Woods. I had taken her here unwillingly, and I had to give her the choice to return home.

If she came back to me, it would be because she chose to do so. I refused to have it any other way. Not when being here would mean overcoming a people who may not ever fully accept her, no matter what we did.

By being with me she would be giving up more than just the life she had before—she'd be giving up her place in a world that she was able to call her own. Something I had no right to ask of her.

I loved her, which meant I wanted what was best for her. Even if it wasn't with me.

I sighed, staring at the last place I saw Amber's shape walk away until it vanished. And then I turned around, striding into the Woods, my hands near my sheathed daggers.

Amber was home. Amber was safe. It was impossible for her to be harmed in the battles that were to come.

And now, I had scores to settle.

CHAPTER THIRTY-FOUR

AMBER

I f you've ever had to hitchhike in a tattered elven gown, I don't recommend it. It does nothing to protect from mosquitos or woodticks. The one thing in my favor was that the Darkening Woods had cast such a pall over the area that an old woman in a banged up SUV believed my story without many questions—that I had escaped the Woods and wanted to go home to Minneapolis.

My rescuer kept the drive lively, with a lot of commentary on how it was the overuse of antibiotics and GMOs that led to the worlds merging, but at that point I was too tired to do much other than hum in agreement. Yep, the GMOs were what put elves in our backyard. Yep. I suggested it was microplastics, just to keep the conversation spirited.

But she was a kind woman who fussed over me and fed me beef jerky. She left me at the train station in Elk River with enough money to buy a train ticket back to Minneapolis, which miraculously ran when I needed it, and then it was a hop skip and another hop to Phoebe and Emily's house via public transportation. Lucky for me, Renaissance chic was a bit of a subculture, so no one gave me a second look.

Alright, I got lots of second looks, but that was probably due to the fact that I clearly hadn't had a proper bath in weeks. And there was blood on my torn dress that I explained away as spilled chocolate milk. And my face had a few cuts. And my hair was wild and legs and arms covered in scratches. And I had that spider bite. I had obviously spent a long time in a woods, but people had seen far stranger things by this point, and thus no one bothered me, other than to offer me some acetaminophen.

I gratefully accepted.

Thus, it was roughly six hours after Eldrin and I said goodbye when I hesitatingly knocked at Phoebe and Emily's door. I needed a friend. And I needed to make sure I had a home to go back to before making that trek. The job was likely gone, and who knew what happened to my apartment. "Kidnapped by an elven prince," was the new "food poisoning" excuse for calling in sick.

"Amber?" Phoebe squeaked, opening the door to rush me inside. "What happened? Where were you?"

Within moments I was greeted by an onslaught of jackalope statues hanging on the walls, a plush rug shaped like a turkey, and a familiar scent of baking and Christmas that made me want to cry.

Shaking, I gave her a big hug, smashing my body against the shortest person I had touched in weeks. "Can I take a shower?"

CHAPTER THIRTY-FIVE

ELDRIN

Two weeks. It ended up taking only two weeks for me to consolidate my power, helped by the fact that Vanir was unpopular so that the factions I needed to assemble were ready at the first opportunity to supplant him. First, I traveled from one settlement to another, declaring that Vanir was dead, that the barrier was strong once more, and that I was now king. Most accepted me. Some didn't. Some died.

I remembered how some courtiers had treated Amber, the mockery she endured during the audience with the king. Those who whispered about her when she couldn't hear and didn't care about the fact that I could. Those who made vile jests about her. I killed no one for words alone, but if I was ever undecided, that fact was the one that often made up my mind.

The habitual doubt about my own inadequacies still plagued me, but I pushed it aside. I would do what I could for my people. Vanir wasn't the worst ruler we'd ever had, but there was much that I could do better. I *would* do better. To start, his increased taxes were stopped immediately, and I ordered an accounting to be made to restore funds to the people. Fortunately, his pleasure house was still only in the assembly stage, but it was disbanded instantly.

Managing the capital was a trickier matter. Royal succession had changed families before, and there were a few who thought perhaps this was their opportunity to place a new bloodline on the throne. Luckily, I had more friends than I thought, or, at least, those who were happy to support me.

My opponents died, their skulls added to the base of my throne. Lady Marciel, who had taunted Amber during that audience, was one. It just so happened that she tried to have me killed in my sleep in order to put her son on the throne. Some of Ivas's family members were added to my seat as well, for their part in exploiting our people. However, I only took care of those who were willing participants. I wasn't one to order death solely based on the actions of other family members. If Amber ever came back, I hoped she would be relieved that some of the most troublesome courtiers were now décor. Our court was thinned, and a lot of fresh faces filled the palace halls.

Two weeks after I said goodbye to Amber, the crown was formally placed on my head and I took my vow, swearing to serve the Woods. I made a note not to bleed near the barrier the next time it weakened, which hopefully wouldn't be for another century or two. But I would do whatever I could to make our people prosperous in our new kingdom—we needed unity, not greed.

"You're an idiot," Oristan said to me, three weeks after Amber left. The two of us were alone in my chambers, myself now secure enough in power to entertain my friendships and spend my evenings as I wished. Vanir was no longer there to hurt me every way he could, and his supporters were either dead or gone.

"I'm king now," I said, pouring myself another goblet of wine.

"Sorry. You're an idiot, *Your Majesty*."

Goblet full, I reclined in my cushioned chair, watching my friend. Oristan's arms were crossed and he had an infuriating smirk. "What now?" I asked.

"You let her go." He didn't have to specify the "her."

"She didn't want to stay here."

"Did you ask her? Did you tell her to stay?"

Did I ask her? No, not exactly. Not other than the whispered promises we had made to each other in the dark—that we would never be happy in this life without the other. That we would be together. That I was hers as long as she wanted me.

"This isn't her home," I said. "She never wanted to come here in the first place. And you know it was too dangerous here for her. The skulls at the base of my throne are still wet."

"You're doing it again," Oristan said in a sing-song voice. I waited for him to continue, because he would. "You finally found someone who made you become the Eldrin I knew you could be, and you pushed her away."

"This isn't her home," I said more firmly, though doubt ringed through me. "What would the court do to her?"

"Nothing you couldn't handle. You make all decrees now. I understand the last couple of weeks were rough, but you could have managed with her here. You never let her have the chance to stay, though, did you? A real one. You could have told her that you would hide her. Maybe there was a safer place near the barrier, and you could have made it so that she could have left if danger came too close. You know we could have figured something out."

"I was not going to risk her life." My fingers gripped my goblet's stem.

"Or were you afraid of her saying no when faced with a real choice?"

I slammed the goblet on the table. "I need to rest."

"Thought so."

As I strode out of the room, my overcoat trailing behind me, Oristan called out, "I was there, Eldrin. I saw the two of you together. And if I had to bet, I don't think the human world is her home anymore, either."

I pushed Oristan and his nagging from my mind. I was good at that. A necessary skill, if he was your friend. Besides, what did Oristan know? He didn't know Amber. He only met her a few times. How could he claim to know what she wanted better than me? Me, who loved her so much that my body ached with longing, her absence a wound that would never heal.

And what I told Amber the day she left was true—it wasn't safe for her here after Vanir died. Those who sought the throne for themselves would have used her, and harmed her, to hurt me. To control me.

It didn't matter that Vanir was gone. For Amber to be with me would mean giving up everything she knew. Once she decided to stay with me there was no going back, not if we wanted to keep the barrier intact for centuries, long enough to find a way to take us back home. Not unless we wanted to keep sacrificing ourselves to hold the barrier in place.

She would also have to make her own binding with the Woods if she wanted to fully share in my life here. There was no reason to think that it would demand a sacrifice of her flesh—I had asked the archivists after I took the throne—but she'd be tied to the Woods the same way as the rest of us.

Being with me would mean giving up everything of her world forever, and being burdened with the responsibilities of being with the king. She would have duties and obligations, her freedom gone forever.

I couldn't think about what Oristan said. I didn't have time to dwell on anything. I had a kingdom to rule.

"Your Majesty," my steward said from his place next to my throne. The man's black hair fell just below his jaw, bobbing with each word. "I have been asked to discuss with you the matter of the patrols. The former king never changed their structure from our prior home, but it may be worth considering if the routes should be altered. We are not expecting any of our old enemies—the Rulsaki are thousands of miles away now, and their numbers are much diminished. None of their large settlements came with them."

I hummed in agreement, watching the petitioners lurk in the background of the hall. I could sit on this throne for centuries without a break and there would never be an end to the people who wanted to speak to me. "Yes, have the necessary reports sent to me. It is time to assume that we will be here for the foreseeable future, and thus any threats have changed. No point in wasting our resources on something that is no longer a concern."

"Very good, Your Majesty." My steward bowed and left.

I stood, having had enough of court for the day. Our land was now smaller, which meant that the troubles that plagued it were different. I couldn't let myself think of what was happening to the Woods back at our old home—I would have to trust that my mother and brothers had kept it intact, and our family on the throne. And that throne filled by someone willing to step aside for me should the worlds ever reunite. Slowly, I stepped off the dais, preparing to leave the room. Elves moved back a respectful distance, letting me pass with a small bow.

Everyone but Lady Avalane.

Many things had changed, but her sense of timing had not.

Lady Avalane was wearing a low-cut gown, one that took a lot of restraint not to stare at out of reflex. With a boldness she never would've tried with Vanir, she moved between me and the doorway. "May I have a word, Your Majesty?" she asked.

"Of course."

"In private."

I looked around the room, at the elves who suddenly decided they had somewhere else to stand.

"Alright." I moved around her and strode out of the hall, letting her follow. Once we were in the corridor, I said, "Speak your intent."

"I wanted to congratulate you properly," Lady Avalane said, her steps keeping pace with mine. "Your reign will be one to admire for centuries."

"Thank you."

"And I noticed that you are without your family. And most of your prior...companions." Ah, there it was. I knew she wasn't here to merely give congratulations. There was an empty spot at my court, one that appealed to far too many opportunists.

"Yes, the rupture took a lot from many of us. I was not spared the loss."

"You don't have to," she said. "That is, you don't have to be alone. And we may be a smaller land than we used to be, but you will still need someone by your side that you can trust."

At that I stopped and looked at her. Really looked at her. Lady Avalane was beautiful, and well connected, and clever. And desperate to seize power, but she made no secret about it. She was the ideal elven courtier, regal and distant, one who knew her own mind and how to make anything happen.

But I couldn't help but imagine Amber's face, smirking with amusement as she encountered the courtiers. Or the way Amber carried herself through the halls, like this was an adventure she was waiting to explore.

Or the way Amber held me and took me into her, like I was the only thing she had ever wanted or would want again. She was my ember. And now, without her, I was going to stay alone in the darkness.

"I appreciate your kindness, my lady," I said, "but I think I will take solace in my own company for now." I walked away, leaving the lady stunned.

If I couldn't have Amber, I would never be content with anyone else. Because no one else could compare. And I would be damned before I betrayed my love for her in such a base manner.

Oristan was right—in letting Amber go without telling her how I felt—how I *really* felt—without fighting for a way for her to stay with me, I had made the biggest mistake of my existence. And there was nothing I could do to fix it.

CHAPTER THIRTY-SIX

AMBER

"So, you're a bartender?" Bryan asked me from across the table. The brewery was nearly empty in the early afternoon, the bare bricks and exposed piping giving the place an aura of an over-priced industrial experience. But with the place so empty, I felt like I was being interviewed in a factory. A factory with an unsettling sticky table.

"For now." I smiled sweetly, nestling my beer in my hands. My new employment as a bartender was likely to be short, but it was the only thing available. A friend of Emily's needed help on short notice, and as long as I could pour beer and mix a rum and cola, I had the skillset necessary for that establishment. Though Bryan didn't need to know that. "I'm looking for other work. What do you do?"

That was all it took. With only the gentlest prompting, Bryan was off to the races, telling me about his job that involved a lot of...I don't know, spreadsheets? A growth mindset? Money mindset? A lot of...mindsets. The entire time I nodded my head, pretending to listen, ignoring how Bryan's small eyes spent more time on my drink than on me. That was an odd thing for him to decide to stare at, but at least it wasn't my chest. And it let me notice that he was already doing some creative brushing to hide his receding hairline. Time was the cruel mistress of us all, but there was accepting it with grace, and then there was...whatever Bryan was trying to do.

How did I end up here, on a date I did not want? Phoebe. Phoebe was how I ended up here. She met this guy at the bus stop and decided that I needed to get drinks with him, something to re-acclimate me to mortal men. She must have really felt bad for me. In her words, "you dumped Adonis."

Technically I didn't dump Eldrin, and he didn't dump me. Eldrin was right. The Darkening Woods wasn't safe for me. It wasn't home.

Except it *was* my home. Because Eldrin was there.

Of course, Phoebe wouldn't understand that, and I didn't blame her. How could she? Unless one spent weeks having one's life saved multiple times by a man and then fleeing for your life through the woods with that same man, it was hard to understand. I also wasn't the best at expressing how Eldrin was more than just someone I dated—he was a part of me, one that I would never forget.

One I never wanted to.

Bryan segued into another speech about income streams and diversifying passive income and cryptocurrencies and I stopped listening. Was this going to be my life? Going on dates with uninspiring men until I found one who amused me enough to forget Eldrin?

Forget trying to find someone who surpassed him in looks. That was impossible. And that was just looks, not to mention everything else.

I huffed softly. I would be alone with cats instead, and I would be just fine. Cats were a satisfying substitute for insufficient men. Life wouldn't be too bad. I could get some plants, live ones with actual roots, too. Maybe take up weaving or something. Baking. That was something terminally single women did, right? Baking. And volunteer work.

Even though I hadn't said anything in about ten minutes, Bryan was still talking, going on about tax exemptions and the car he was buying and something about some sort of make-believe baseball game that he played through his phone. Yet Bryan was still talking at me, and not to me. Did Bryan want to be here? Did *I* even want to be here?

No, I definitely didn't. Not one bit.

What was I doing?

"Sorry, Bryan, I have to go," I said, standing and leaving the table, but not before tossing down a twenty to cover my drink.

"It's Byron."

"Yes, Byron. Sorry. Bye!" I called out, running out of the bar and leaving a very confused Byron in my wake.

I had made a mistake. Leaving Eldrin was a mistake. The greatest mistake I had ever made. I should have fought harder to stay, I should have done anything other than leave.

I did not know what waited for me in the Darkening Woods. I could end up in land where Eldrin failed at becoming king, and I could be captured and have who-knew-what done to me. I'd probably face untold dangers, and possibly even my death.

No, I wouldn't think that. As far as I was concerned, Eldrin won and would be waiting for me. That was what I was going to tell myself until shown otherwise.

Besides, what choice did I have other than this leap of faith?

One thing I knew for certain—I was not going to spend my life wondering in regret.

CHAPTER THIRTY-SEVEN

ELDRIN

Another day at court. Amber had now been gone for over a month, and ruling was mostly an unending stream of supplicants and mundane business. This was good—it gave me a chance to arrange for more celebrations, tasks that were a luxury. After everything, we deserved to celebrate. Our people were in exile, but that didn't mean we had to forget who we were. We were going to live our lives in the Darkening Woods, treasuring its constant season, and forging a place for ourselves in this new world. We were going to live, thrive, and search for a .

Vanir managed his reign with fear and control, while I was going to guide and nurture. Vanir was gone forever, and now it was my opportunity to shape my court as I saw fit.

I had finished holding court for the day and ordered the music to start and wine to be served. This was going to be an informal party, ones like my father used to host with whatever courtiers happened to be in the palace that day. We still had poets and musicians in the city, and they would be encouraged to perform once more. I would do whatever I could to establish new societies of artists, ones that rivaled what we left behind.

Orders for festivities done, I walked amongst my people. Artists from the city were gathered, sitting in a corner, heads bowed in deep debate. Young women strolled around the room, their clothing crafted from nature, delighting in this chance to be at court. The aura was relaxed, a serenity I had not felt at court since Father's reign.

"Are you pleased?" I asked Siliana, who stood by a window watching the revelry. She was wearing a dark purple gown edged with black feathers, and tiny bird skulls lined the gown's neck.

She gave me a small smile, sadness still in her gaze. A sadness I didn't think would ever leave. "I think so. But I worry for you."

"Don't. I'm not the spoiled prince I was before. I will be fine." Someday I would be. Someday I would heal.

Someday.

"You can have everything in the world," Siliana said, "but it means nothing if you don't have the one you love."

I placed a hand on Siliana's shoulder. She had left her spouse behind, and it was very likely they would never meet again in this life. "Anything you need, tell me," I said softly. "I know that is no true comfort, but I swear, I will do whatever I can."

"You have done everything that can be expected, my king," she said, giving me a little grin that I returned. "I know that I left her safe and alive—and that is enough."

Siliana was wise—I also knew that Amber was safe and alive. It was the only thing that kept me from falling into despair.

"Your Majesty," one of my guards suddenly called out. "You asked to have this guest brought to you immediately."

My heart leapt into my mouth. There were only two people for whom my guards had that order. Ivas, and—

Amber walked through the hall, a light sheen on her skin. She carried a large backpack on her shoulders and was wearing blue pants made of a rough fabric, as well as a black sleeveless shirt. Courtiers muttered, parting around her, their attention alternating between her and me. Everyone knew who she was. She eyed the other courtiers, her expression hesitant, and then when she discovered me, she stilled.

"Hello," she said with a slight grin.

"Hello," I replied. Was she real? Was I imagining her? My heart danced and I was scared to breathe or blink, lest she disappear.

Had I lost my mind? Was this a dream?

"I think Your Majesty would like time to rest, would you not?" Siliana suggested, waving her hands to give the orders before I could utter a word. Guards moved and courtiers scattered, but I paid them scant mind as Amber took cautious steps towards me.

Rest.

"Yes...yes. Rest," I said absentmindedly, not daring to look away from Amber. It would be a long time before I did so.

CHAPTER THIRTY-EIGHT

AMBER

E ldrin led me to his new rooms—the king's rooms. If I thought the rest of the palace was absurdly deca-dent, this was something beyond. The surface was lined with carved birds and leaves made of precious stones, not to mention the gold and crimson brocades that covered many surfaces. Thick green velvet drapes graced the windows, tied back with thick golden ropes accented with red crystals. Outside was the same, brilliant sun I had come to associate with the Darkening Woods, which made the sky a captivat-ing shade of blue.

"What's wrong?" Eldrin asked me, after he shut the black wooden door behind him. We were alone.

"This is all yours?" I asked, surveying a mural on the ceil-ing, an illustration of trees and elves dancing underneath the boughs.

"Yes. These are the king's chambers."

"It's...wow."

"Generations of kings' belongings are here. I suppose they are my belongings now," he added, almost as an afterthought as he stepped through the room.

Without a word, I dropped my burdensome backpack on the floor and followed him, admiring the walls and decorations. Skeletons made from onyx. Swords and daggers decorated with diamonds. Vases and sconces made of a mosaic glassware. Stained glass windows depicting autumn reds and golds. It was breathtaking. I wandered from room to room until I found a bed, a massive silk-covered monstrosity that could have held a half dozen people.

But I only wanted one. If he would have me.

"You came back," he said, standing in the doorway of his bedroom, much changed from how I saw him last. He wore a long draping black overcoat that was cut in the front to reveal matching breeches. Around his forehead rested a thick coronet of leaves, marking that he was now the king, the ultimate power in the Woods.

The king.

He stared at me, his gaze boring into me in ways I desperately missed. The crown on his head attracted my focus, his bearing regal and formal in a way that it rarely was in the Woods. It was as if he was someone strange and familiar at the same time. Yet he was still what I wanted more than anything.

"I had to." I swallowed. "I had to come back."

He approached, until he was only an arm's length away. "You're really here." A statement, not a question. His skeleton hand clenched and unclenched, the bone fingers moving in a delicate rhythm.

"...Is that alright?"

Eldrin laughed, a brilliant sound that rang through the rooms. "Alright? , so left my joy. If the king was permitted to leave this realm, I would have been searching for a way to find you. If I could have spared the barrier being weakened, I would have sent others to find you. You are the one who saved me, Amber. I love you. Letting you leave was...I shouldn't have let you leave. Without you, I was dead, my dearest heart."

"But I'm here now."

"Yes." His eyes sparkled. "Yes, you are."

Enough.

We clashed in a ravenous embrace, his lips returning to mine, dancing in a familiar cadence I had missed so desperately. His hands caressed me, as if reassuring himself that I was really there, touching my arms, my back, every inch of me that was respectable to touch, even though I was already stirring for him to place his hands on the rest of me.

But reality still had its way of reminding me that our problems were still there.

"I love you." I gave him an extra-long kiss, and then reluctantly broke away. "But, what about your court? Are you alright with me being here?" Would he want me to stay? He was the king now. Everything had changed. "I was thinking that, if it would help, maybe you could keep me somewhere else—"

"Absolutely not," he said sternly. "Most of those who resented you are now part of my throne."

"The skulls?" My eyes widened.

"Yes." He kissed me, delving into me in a way that ignited the heat in my core. "I would not tolerate anyone in my realm who would harm you or even think ill of you. I will make that very clear. To insult you is to insult me."

"I know you have other concerns. You're the king, you need to take care of your people."

"Amber" –he ran a finger down my cheek– "letting you leave was the biggest mistake I had ever made in my life, or will make. This court is yours. You are no longer a visitor, you are the queen. My queen. I refuse to think of any reign where you are not by my side. The court will adjust, and those who do not will be committing treason." He shrugged. "It is as simple as that."

"Is it?"

"Kings of the Darkening Woods are not known for their mercy, especially when it comes to those they love. I will have you by my side, Amber. You would have to cleave the worlds to tear me away from you."

What? I could really stay here? With him?

Hot tears swelled in my eyes, worry that I had been keeping inside for long weeks threatening to erupt. "And everyone will be alright with having a human queen?" I just wanted to be with him—I didn't care about ruling or power. I could have handled anything, any position, as long as it let me be with him.

"Yes," Eldrin said, patiently reassuring me again. "Because I will make it so. I don't care what happens. You are not leaving my side by any other will than your own. Ever again." He chuckled, the sound dark and sensual. "I think you will be surprised by what the elves will be able to adjust to, with time."

He kissed me harder, his hands gripping my arms with his raw strength. Slowly, he walked me backward and pushed me back on the bed, laying me down on the silk coverlet and then hovering over me. His garments draped over us, long, formal robes that had no place being here. Far too much fabric.

My heart raced, and the sweet heat in my core turned into a throbbing need.

We both sat upright and he reclined, watching as I unclasped the small skull buttons that kept on his over-robe, and then I peeled it off. He helped me with the rest, shrugging the voluminous garment to the ground. What was underneath the robe was more fitting of the Eldrin I remembered, a tunic made of fine weaving and black breeches. Only the coronet told me that there was a difference between the elf I had fallen in love with and the king he was now.

Eldrin noticed where I was looking, for he took off the coronet and tossed it in the air, catching it and flashing me a smile. Without turning his attention away from me, he set the coronet on the bed and then prowled towards me. "Do you want one?" he asked.

"I...can't say I've given it much thought." My gaze was focused on his breeches, and he noticed, for his smile turned feral.

"You're wearing far too much," he said.

"Less than you."

"My point stands."

We lunged towards each other, our movements a rushed fury to tear off our clothes and send them scattering to the ground. My bra and panties ripped in the frenzy. Who cared? The weight of our separation slammed into me, and I couldn't get my bare skin against his fast enough. Any chill I felt from the air was banished as soon as he pressed his naked body on mine, his firm muscles undulating with each movement. Desperation gathered, a painful ache and wetness that made me all-but beg him to hurry. I needed him. Now.

Both of us now bare, he laid me so that I was strewn next to him, his human-like hand propping up his head, while his skeleton one rested on my abdomen. His cock pushed against my thigh, drops of liquid spreading on my skin. I rubbed against it. It should have been someplace else, I *need-*

ed it to be somewhere else. But all Eldrin did was smile. Bastard was enjoying this.

His hand of bone traced cold lines on my skin, the sensation strange and yet now familiar. The path traced over my hips and to my thighs, where I spread my legs to welcome him. His touch lacked the warmth of his other hand, yet his movements trailed a path of fire over me, igniting me with each inch he explored.

"Eldrin," I said with a pleading gasp.

"I know." He kissed me on the forehead, his skeleton hand now moving closer to my center. "May I?" he asked, his hand perched near my entrance, toying with me. His skeleton hand moved closer, making it clear what he was asking of me.

"Yes."

That was all he needed—that one word of permission let him explore with that part of himself. The cool and solid bone plunged into me, into the wetness that waited. I shuddered and clenched around it. His hand felt so strange and yet that was part of the pleasure—the uniqueness. Nothing hurt or caused me any discomfort. Whether it was Eldrin's skill or some aspect of the hand's magic I couldn't say. All I knew was that the firm textured touch made me want more.

This hand was part of him, and I wanted everything.

"Do you like it?" he asked, and I moaned in reply. He used his skeleton thumb to flick my clit, the sharp friction perfect. Unbearably so. I arched my back, unable to stay still.

"Eldrin," I cried out. It was so much—too much.

And then I arched my back again when his thumb was replaced with his gorgeous mouth. I met his brilliant silver eyes. His mouth was wrapped around my mound, taking it fully into himself, sucking and teasing. His silver hair nestled against his angled ear, a sight that I had come to know all so well. It was enough to push me to the edge, the sensation cresting to the point I would lose all control. But right before my release came, his mouth left me, sending an unwelcome absence in his wake.

Moments later he was positioned over me, his cock hitting my inner thighs, leaving no doubt what was coming next. "When you take your pleasure..." he whispered in my ear. His length pushed against my entrance, reminding me of how much he would fill me. "...It will be because I am inside you," he finished. "With my name on your lips."

I nodded, grabbing his ass to urge him on. Whatever he wanted he'd get—anything. I'd give and do anything. I needed more. He understood, because he moistened himself on me and then worked his way in, and all feeling left except for *that*.

"Eldrin," I cried out as he pushed inside me, stretching me blissfully around him as if we had never been apart, melting into me until the first aches melted into waves of full pleasure.

"Look at you," he said, admiring how we were joined together, our bodies moving with his slow thrusts. "You fit me so perfectly. Mine." He leaned back and used his skeleton hand again, flicking my clit and grinning as I squirmed.

It was too much. Too much.

"I want—" I gasped. "I want—"

"Yes?" he asked, right as he slowly worked his way in and out of me. He knew what I wanted. Needed.

"You. More."

He kissed me in reply and thrusted harder, giving me what I yearned for. Over and over again he slammed into me, the movements blending into an unending stream of ecstasy. His mouth stifled my cries as I came, clenching harder around him. Through it all he didn't stop. He wouldn't stop. It was as if our bodies were a fire, and I couldn't tell where we began and ended.

We were together, as we always would be.

He pounded into me through my orgasm, his hips working in a jutting rhythm, extending my pleasure even further, wave after wave of glorious release. After I was done his movements became steadier, smoother, a current that tied me to him as he worked to his own climax.

"Amber. My Ember."

Several long moments later his release soon followed with a guttural cry, and then, spent, he laid next to me, holding me against him. His chest was slick with sweat, as was my back, and together we caught our breath and stared at the gilded ceiling.

"We're not leaving this bedroom, ever," he said between large breaths. "I'm the king and I command it." He pointed to his coronet that lay on the bed undisturbed, a smile curved on his lips. "That was far too short and I plan on things taking far longer. Much longer."

"We'll have to leave someday," I said, moving so that I laid against him. His arms wrapped around me, holding me as tight as he could without hurting me.

"Someday. But not today."

"No?"

"No. That was just our first coupling." He kissed my neck in a way that made my legs squirm and spread already, welcoming him to touch me wherever he wanted. "And now that that's out of the way, I can take my time."

He sighed into my hair, content, his gestures echoing the feeling in my own heart. This bed would be my home. These Woods would be my home. Because he was here.

I no longer doubted where I belonged in life, or where I was supposed to go.

Eldrin was my everything. He was my forever.

EPILOGUE

"**G**ood morning, Your Majesty," Eldrin said to me the morning after my coronation. It was now three months after I arrived in the Woods—for the second time—and I was now officially its queen. The world outside was in the throes of winter, but the Darkening Woods remained in its eternal fall.

Queen.

The gold coronet of leaves and vines sat on my night table, the only thing that I wore to the ceremony that made it through the night unscathed. Unlike my poor gown, which was now on the floor in tatters from where Eldrin tore it off me, desperate to take me when the ceremony was done and the celebration over.

I had bonded with the Woods as a part of my coronation. I said the words and made the pledge—and my heart was now sealed with it. I would share in the long years of Eldrin's life, as I was now committed to these Woods for what remained of mine.

To my eternal joy, all of my limbs still had their skin. I was willing to risk any change for Eldrin, but I was still glad I didn't have to experience that one.

I rolled over in bed from where I was laying under thick coverlets, pushing my hair out of my eyes as the sun beamed into them.

"Good morning," I said, propping up on my elbows. "You're up early."

"Maybe I like to be awake when I hold you," he said, pulling me towards him and kissing my hand. Such a chaste kiss made my breath catch and a hum of pleasure trickle through me. A familiar stiffening pressed against my thigh. I wasn't the only one thinking such things.

"Maybe I would prefer it if you—"

A knock at the door interrupted us. Eldrin frowned. "Come in," he said, while I tugged the blankets higher. It had to have been important—no one had dared bother us unexpectedly. Except for Oristan, but even he knew better than to try such a thing again.

Eldrin's servant walked in, an elf with slicked back black hair. He carried a rolled piece of paper in his hand, which bore an oddly metallic seal. Was it a metal? Or some strange wax?

"A letter, Your Majesty," the servant said with a deep bow. "It arrived this morning."

Eldrin didn't speak. But a raised eyebrow told me he understood something more about the letter than I did. After the servant was dismissed with a nod, Eldrin unrolled the letter while I snuggled against him.

"What is it?" I asked. "Is something wrong?"

"No," he said. "But it is unusual." He rolled the letter back up and offered it to me. I shook my head, trusting that he would tell me what it said himself. "The angels."

"Angels? The ones in New Jersey?"

"I'm going to assume yes since there aren't any other angels that I am aware of."

I frowned. "I didn't think things could go through the barrier."

"Objects are easier than people," Eldrin said. "When the item isn't alive the barrier isn't as...affected. Smaller animals are easier, too."

"...Now you tell me." I sighed. "I would have arranged for Phoebe and Emily to drop off supplies once in awhile." I had stocked my backpack full of spices, seeds, and books—things I absolutely refused to do without if I could help it. And pumpkin spice. Lots of pumpkin spice and things to grow and make it.

He chuckled. "I offered to try to send letters. Say the words and it can be done. We can arrange something."

I smiled. "We'll talk later." I nodded at the scroll. "Now, what is this? The angels sent us a letter?" This was starting to sound like the plot of a bad holiday movie.

He nodded. "They are requesting books from us, and gave us the exact words to look for, ones in our old language. It was addressed to Vanir, so they haven't realized there's been a change in rulership."

"Why would they want books?"

"That's just it, Amber," he said, his eyes lit with wonder. "Apparently, they think they know how to take us home."

Thank you so very much to everyone who helped me make this book a reality.

To Parker and Wilson—your dedication to what you believe in is inspiring. I couldn't have done this without your constant support, encouragement, and presence.

To Liz, my editor and literary muse—at this point I should just commission a statue or sign you up for a nice cheese subscription service or something.

To BookishAveril, my cover designer—thank you so much for the beautiful cover art!

To Emily Almanza—for reading and being awesome. Yes, that's all I've got. I'm really tired. Please don't chuck this book at me.

To my beta readers: Samantha, Taylor, Shyanne, and Beth. Thank you so much for your advice that helped me shape the story into what it is.

To my early ARC readers— you have helped me more than I can express. In particular, thank you to Kellie Lopez,

Shyanne Huff, Michelle, and Emily Almanza (again) for the extra assistance and last minute typo catching. Thank you so much.

To my husband—who went above and beyond in taking care of the house and toddler so that I have time to write. And for not asking questions when I get yet another delivery of bookmail. And for explaining that the word "delicious" cannot be used in certain contexts. And for spurring a middle-of-the-night discussion on skeletal vs. skeleton.

And, of course, to my readers—you are the reason I do this, and I am beyond honored each time someone chooses one of my books. Thank you.

AFTERWORD

Thank you so much for reading this book! With all of the amazing authors available to readers, I am so grateful each time someone chooses one of mine.

As an indie author, reviews from readers are critical, including that reviews influence how sales platforms display and recommend our books to others. Indies don't have marketing teams or corporate funding—instead, our books live because of our readers. If you're willing to leave a review for my books, or even just a rating, it means so much to me, and it helps me continue to bring more books into the world.

Thank you again for choosing to spend time with my characters, and I hope to see you again on later adventures.

-Scarlett

Scarlett D. Vine is the more romance-oriented counterpart of S.D. Vine, and is the author of *The Twice-Cursed Serpent* and *Twisted Worlds*. When she isn't reading or writing, she spends her time gardening and tending to her clowder of cats. She lives in Minnesota with her husband and son.

Made in the USA
Las Vegas, NV
17 October 2024

97010892R00204